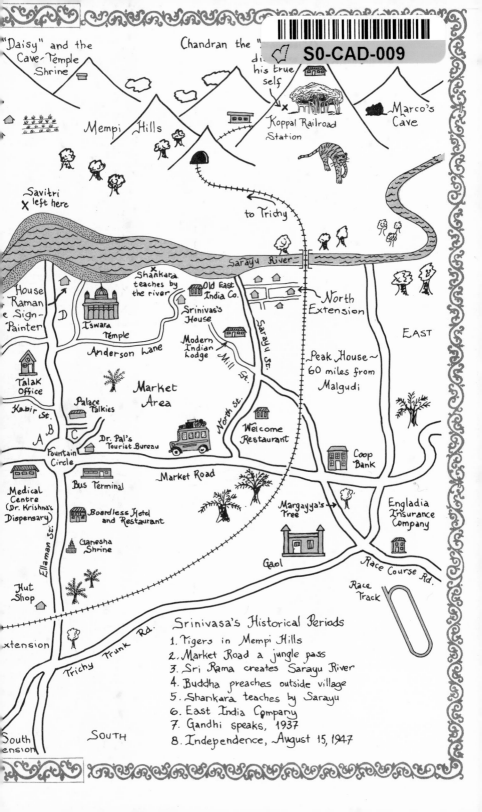

"Daisy" and the Cave-Temple Shrine

Chandran the "...di... his true self

Mempi Hills

Koppal Railroad Station

Marco's Cave

Savitri X left here

to Trichy

Sarayu River

House Raman e Sign-Painter

Shankara teaches by the river

Old East India Co.

North Extension

EAST

Iswara Temple

Srinivas's House

Anderson Lane

Modern Indian Lodge

Peak House~ 60 miles from Malgudi

Talak Office

Market Area

Mill St.

Sarayu St.

Kabir St.

Palace Talkies

North St.

Welcome Restaurant

Coop Bank

A B C

Dr. Pal's Tourist Bureau

Fountain Circle

Market Road

Margayya's Tree

Engladia Insurance Company

Medical Centre (Dr. Krishna's Dispensary)

Bus Terminal

Ellaman St.

Boardless Hotel and Restaurant

Ganesha Shrine

Gaol

Race Course Rd.

Race Track

Hut Shop

...xtension

Trichy Trunk Rd.

Srinivasa's Historical Periods
1. Tigers in Mempi Hills
2. Market Road a jungle pass
3. Sri Rama creates Sarayu River
4. Buddha preaches outside village
5. Shankara teaches by Sarayu
6. East India Company
7. Gandhi speaks, 1937
8. Independence, August 15, 1947

South ...ension

SOUTH

Malgudi Days

ALSO BY R. K. NARAYAN

Malgudí Days

R.K. Narayan

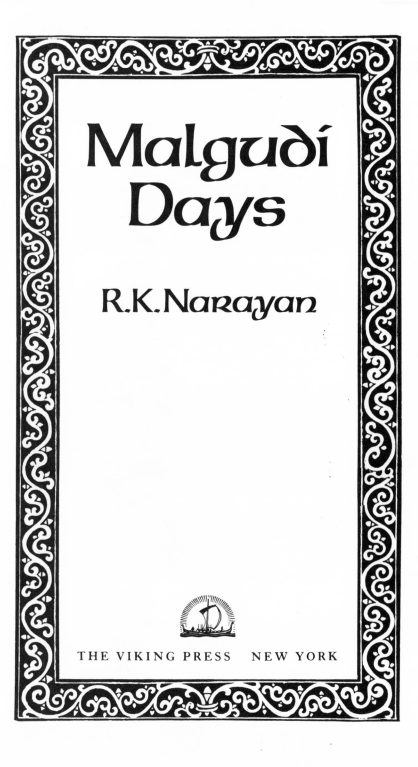

THE VIKING PRESS   NEW YORK

LIBRARY OF CONGRESS CATALOGING IN PUBLICATION DATA
Narayan, R. K., 1906–
Malgudi days.
I. Title.
PR9499.3.N3M34   1982   823   81-52204
ISBN 0-670-45178-9   AACR2

Grateful acknowledgment is made to the following publications, in which
some of these selections originally appeared: *Antaeus:* "Cat Within," "The
Edge," "The Martyr's Corner," and "Trail of the Green Blazer." *The New
Yorker:* "Naga" and "Second Opinion." *Playboy:* "God and the Cobbler."

The endpaper map has been faithfully redrawn for publication by Clarice
Borio from the original constructed by Dr. James M. Fennelly of Adelphi
University to illustrate his paper "The City of Malgudi as an Expression of
the Ordered Hindu Cosmos," delivered at the American Academy of Re-
ligion International Region Conference, 1978. It is printed in this book at
the request of R. K. Narayan. Copyright © 1982 by Viking Penguin Inc.

Printed in the United States of America
Set in Fototronic Janson
Designed by Tomoko Hanway

Second printing October 1982

CONTENTS

From *Lawley Road*

New Stories

AUTHOR'S INTRODUCTION

The short story affords a writer a welcome diversion from hard work. The novel, whether good or bad, printable or otherwise, involves considerable labour. Sheer wordage, anywhere between sixty and one hundred thousand words, looks forbidding at first, as it might well demand concentrated attention over an indefinite stretch of time. Although my novels are rather short by present-day standards, while I am at work on one I feel restless and uneasy at being shackled to a single task for months on end. At such times one's mind also becomes sentence-ridden: words last written or yet to be written keep ringing about one's ears, to the exclusion of all other sounds or sense. When the first draft has taken shape one feels lighter at heart, but the relief is short-lived. The first draft will have to be followed by a second, and possibly a third or fourth, until perfection (a chimerical pursuit) is attained. And then someday one arbitrarily decides to pack up the manuscript and mail it to one's literary agent.

At the end of every novel I have vowed never to write another one—a propitious moment to attempt a short story or two. I enjoy writing a short story. Unlike the novel, which emerges from relevant, minutely worked-out detail, the short story can be brought into existence through a mere suggestion of detail, the focus being kept on a central idea or climax.

The material available to a story writer in India is limitless. Within a broad climate of inherited culture there are endless variations: every individual differs from every other individual, not only economically, but in outlook, habits and day-to-day philosophy. It is stimulating to live in a society that is not standardized or mechanized, and is free from monotony. Under such conditions the writer has only to look out of the window to pick up a character (and thereby a story).

A short story must be short—on that point there is universal agreement, but the definition of a story is understood differently at different levels, ranging from the news reporter's use of the term to the literary pundit's profundities on the subject of plot, climax, structure and texture, with dos and don'ts for the writer. Speaking for myself, I discover a story when a personality passes through a crisis of spirit or circumstances. In the following thirty-odd tales, almost invariably the central character faces some kind of crisis and either resolves it or lives with it. But some stories may prove to be nothing more than a special or significant moment in someone's life or a pattern of existence brought to view.

I have named this volume *Malgudi Days* in order to give it a plausibly geographical status. I am often asked, "Where is Malgudi?" All I can say is that it is imaginary and not to be found on any map (although the University of Chicago Press has published a literary atlas with a map of India indicating the location of Malgudi). If I explain that Malgudi is a small town in South India I shall only be expressing a half-truth, for the characteristics of Malgudi seem to me universal.

I can detect Malgudi characters even in New York: for instance, West Twenty-third Street, where I have lived for months at a time off and on since 1959, possesses every element of Malgudi, with its landmarks and humanity remaining unchanged—the drunk lolling on the steps of the synagogue, the shop sign announcing in blazing letters *Everything in this store must go within a week. Fifty percent off on all items*, the barber, the dentist, the lawyer and the specialist in fishing hooks, tackle and rods, the five-and-ten and the delicatessen (the man greeted me with "Hi! Where have you been all this time? Where do you go for your milk and rice nowadays?" little realizing that I am not a permanent resident of Twenty-third Street or of America either)—all are there as they were, with an air of unshaken permanence and familiarity. Above all, the Chelsea Hotel, where I revisited after many years and was received with a whoop of joy by the manager, who hugged me and summoned all his staff (or those who were still alive) to meet me, including the old gentleman in a wheelchair, now one hundred and sixteen years old, a permanent resident who must have been in his early nineties when I last stayed in that hotel.

Malgudi has been only a concept but has proved good enough for my purposes. I can't make it more concrete however much I might be interrogated. When an enthusiastic television producer in London asked me recently if I would cooperate by showing him around Malgudi and introducing him to the characters in my novels for the purpose of producing an hour-long feature, I felt shaken for a moment and said out of politeness, "I am going to be busy working on a new novel. . . ."

"Another Malgudi novel?" he asked.

"Yes," I said.

"What will it be about?"

"About a tiger possessing a human soul. . . ."

"Oh, that sounds interesting! I think I will wait. It will be marvellous to include the tiger in my documentary. . . ."

R.K.N.

September 1981

from

An Astrologer's Day

AN ASTROLOGER'S DAY

Punctually at midday he opened his bag and spread out his professional equipment, which consisted of a dozen cowrie shells, a square piece of cloth with obscure mystic charts on it, a notebook and a bundle of palmyra writing. His forehead was resplendent with sacred ash and vermilion, and his eyes sparkled with a sharp abnormal gleam which was really an outcome of a continual searching look for customers, but which his simple clients took to be a prophetic light and felt comforted. The power of his eyes was considerably enhanced by their position—placed as they were between the painted forehead and the dark whiskers which streamed down his cheeks: even a half-wit's eyes would sparkle in such a setting. To crown the effect he wound a saffron-coloured turban around his head. This colour scheme never failed. People were attracted to him as bees are attracted to cosmos or dahlia stalks. He sat under the boughs of a spreading tamarind tree which flanked a path running through the Town Hall Park. It was a remarkable place in many ways: a surging crowd was always moving up and down this narrow road morning till night. A variety of trades and occupations was represented all along its way: medicine-sellers, sellers of stolen hardware and junk, magicians and, above all, an auctioneer of cheap cloth, who created enough din all day to attract the whole town. Next to him in vociferousness came a vendor of fried groundnuts, who gave his ware a fancy name each day, calling it Bombay Ice-Cream one day, and on the next Delhi Almond, and on the third Raja's Delicacy, and so on and so forth, and people flocked to him. A considerable portion of this crowd dallied before the astrologer too. The astrologer transacted his business by the light of a flare which crackled and smoked up above the groundnut heap nearby. Half the enchantment of the place was due to the fact that it did not have the benefit of municipal lighting. The place was lit up by shop lights. One or two had hissing gaslights, some had naked flares stuck on poles, some were lit up by old cycle lamps and one or two, like the astrologer's, managed without lights of their own. It was a bewildering criss-cross of light rays and moving shadows. This suited the astrologer very well, for the simple reason that he had not in the least intended to be an astrologer when he began life; and he knew no more of what was going to happen to others than he knew what was going to happen to himself next minute. He was as much a stranger to the stars as were his innocent customers. Yet he said things which pleased and astonished everyone: that was more a matter of study, practise and shrewd guesswork. All the same, it was as much an honest man's labour as any other, and he deserved the wages he carried home at the end of a day.

He had left his village without any previous thought or plan. If he had continued there he would have carried on the work of his fore-fathers—namely, tilling the land, living, marrying and ripening in his cornfield and ancestral home. But that was not to be. He had to leave home without telling anyone, and he could not rest till he left it behind a couple of hundred miles. To a villager it is a great deal, as if an ocean flowed between.

He had a working analysis of mankind's troubles: marriage, money and the tangles of human ties. Long practise had sharpened his perception. Within five minutes he understood what was wrong. He charged three pies per question and never opened his mouth till the other had spoken for at least ten minutes, which provided him enough stuff for a dozen answers and advices. When he told the person before him, gazing at his palm, "In many ways you are not getting the fullest results for your efforts," nine out of ten were disposed to agree with him. Or he questioned: "Is there any woman in your family, maybe even a distant relative, who is not well disposed towards you?" Or he gave an analysis of character: "Most of your troubles are due to your nature. How can you be otherwise with Saturn where he is? You have an impetuous nature and a rough exterior." This endeared him to their hearts immediately, for even the mildest of us loves to think that he has a forbidding exterior.

The nuts-vendor blew out his flare and rose to go home. This was a signal for the astrologer to bundle up too, since it left him in darkness except for a little shaft of green light which strayed in from somewhere and touched the ground before him. He picked up his cowrie shells and paraphernalia and was putting them back into his bag when the green shaft of light was blotted out; he looked up and saw a man standing before him. He sensed a possible client and said: "You look so careworn. It will do you good to sit down for a while and chat with me." The other grumbled some vague reply. The astrologer pressed his invitation; whereupon the other thrust his palm under his nose, saying: "You call yourself an astrologer?" The astrologer felt challenged and said, tilting the other's palm towards the green shaft of light: "Yours is a nature . . ." "Oh, stop that," the other said. "Tell me something worthwhile. . . ."

Our friend felt piqued. "I charge only three pies per question, and what you get ought to be good enough for your money. . . ." At this the other withdrew his arm, took out an anna and flung it out to him, saying, "I have some questions to ask. If I prove you are bluffing, you must return that anna to me with interest."

"If you find my answers satisfactory, will you give me five rupees?"

"No."

"Or will you give me eight annas?"

"All right, provided you give me twice as much if you are wrong," said the stranger. This pact was accepted after a little further argument. The astrologer sent up a prayer to heaven as the other lit a cheroot. The astrologer caught a glimpse of his face by the matchlight. There was a pause as cars hooted on the road, *jutka* drivers swore at their horses and the babble of the crowd agitated the semi-darkness of the park. The other sat down, sucking his cheroot, puffing out, sat there ruthlessly. The astrologer felt very uncomfortable. "Here, take your anna back. I am not used to such challenges. It is late for me today. . . ." He made preparations to bundle up. The other held his wrist and said, "You can't get out of it now. You dragged me in while I was passing." The astrologer shivered in his grip; and his voice shook and became faint. "Leave me today. I will speak to you tomorrow." The other thrust his palm in his face and said, "Challenge is challenge. Go on." The astrologer proceeded with his throat drying up. "There is a woman . . ."

"Stop," said the other. "I don't want all that. Shall I succeed in my present search or not? Answer this and go. Otherwise I will not let you go till you disgorge all your coins." The astrologer muttered a few incantations and replied, "All right. I will speak. But will you give me a rupee if what I say is convincing? Otherwise I will not open my mouth, and you may do what you like." After a good deal of haggling the other agreed. The astrologer said, "You were left for dead. Am I right?"

"Ah, tell me more."

"A knife has passed through you once?" said the astrologer.

"Good fellow!" He bared his chest to show the scar. "What else?"

"And then you were pushed into a well nearby in the field. You were left for dead."

"I should have been dead if some passer-by had not chanced to peep into the well," exclaimed the other, overwhelmed by enthusiasm. "When shall I get at him?" he asked, clenching his fist.

"In the next world," answered the astrologer. "He died four months ago in a far-off town. You will never see any more of him." The other groaned on hearing it. The astrologer proceeded.

"Guru Nayak—"

"You know my name!" the other said, taken aback.

"As I know all other things. Guru Nayak, listen carefully to what I have to say. Your village is two days' journey due north of this town. Take the next train and be gone. I see once again great danger to your life if you go from home." He took out a pinch of sacred ash and held it out to him. "Rub it on your forehead and go home. Never travel southward again, and you will live to be a hundred."

"Why should I leave home again?" the other said reflectively. "I was only going away now and then to look for him and to choke out his life if I met him." He shook his head regretfully. "He has escaped my hands. I hope at least he died as he deserved." "Yes," said the astrologer. "He was crushed under a lorry." The other looked gratified to hear it.

The place was deserted by the time the astrologer picked up his articles and put them into his bag. The green shaft was also gone, leaving the place in darkness and silence. The stranger had gone off into the night, after giving the astrologer a handful of coins.

It was nearly midnight when the astrologer reached home. His wife was waiting for him at the door and demanded an explanation. He flung the coins at her and said, "Count them. One man gave all that."

"Twelve and a half annas," she said, counting. She was overjoyed. "I can buy some *jaggery* and coconut tomorrow. The child has been asking for sweets for so many days now. I will prepare some nice stuff for her."

"The swine has cheated me! He promised me a rupee," said the astrologer. She looked up at him. "You look worried. What is wrong?"

"Nothing."

After dinner, sitting on the *pyol*, he told her, "Do you know a great load is gone from me today? I thought I had the blood of a man on my hands all these years. That was the reason why I ran away from home, settled here and married you. He is alive."

She gasped. "You tried to kill!"

"Yes, in our village, when I was a silly youngster. We drank, gambled and quarrelled badly one day—why think of it now? Time to sleep," he said, yawning, and stretched himself on the *pyol*.

THE MISSING MAIL

Though his beat covered Vinayak Mudali Street and its four parallel roads, it took him nearly six hours before he finished his round and returned to the head office in Market Road to deliver accounts. He allowed himself to get mixed up with the fortunes of the persons to whom he was carrying letters. At No. 13, Kabir Street, lived the man who had come halfway up the road to ask for a letter for so many years now. Thanappa had seen him as a youngster, and had watched him day by day greying on the *pyol*, sitting there and hoping for a big prize to come his way through solving crossword puzzles. "No prize yet," he announced to him every day. "But don't be disheartened." "Your interest has been delayed this month some-how," he said to another. "Your son at Hyderabad has written again, madam. How many children has he now?" "I did not know that you had applied for this Madras job; you haven't cared to tell me! It doesn't matter. When I bring you your appointment order you must feed me with coconut *payasam*." And at each of these places he stopped for nearly half an hour. Especially if anyone received money orders, he just settled down quite nicely, with his bags and bundles spread about him, and would not rise till he gathered an idea of how and where every rupee was going. If it was a hot day he sometimes asked for a tumbler of buttermilk and sat down to enjoy it. Every-body liked him on his beat. He was a part and parcel of their exis-tence, their hopes, aspirations and activities.

Of all his contacts, the one with which he was most intimately bound up was No. 10, Vinayak Mudali Street. Ramanujam was a senior clerk in the Revenue Division Office, and Thanappa had car-ried letters to that address for over a generation now. His earliest association with Ramanujam was years and years ago. Ramanujam's wife was away in the village. A card arrived for Ramanujam. Thanappa, as was his custom, glanced through it at the sorting table itself; and, the moment they were ready to start out, went straight to Vinayak Mudali Street, though in the ordinary course over 150 addresses preceded it. He went straight to Ramanujam's house, knocked on the door and shouted, "Postman, sir, postman." When Ramanujam opened it, he said, "Give me a handful of sugar before I give you this card. Happy father! After all these years of prayers! Don't complain that it is a daughter. Daughters are God's gift, you know. . . . Kamakshi—lovely name!"

"Kamakshi," he addressed the tall, bashful girl, years later, "get your photo ready. Ah, so shy! Here is your grandfather's card asking for your photo. Why should he want it, unless it be . . ."

"The old gentleman writes rather frequently now, doesn't he, sir?" he asked Ramanujam, as he handed him his letter and waited for him to open the envelope and go through its contents. Ramanujam looked worried after reading it. The postman asked, "I hope it's good news?" He leaned against the veranda pillar, with a stack of undelivered letters still under his arm. Ramanujam said, "My father-in-law thinks I am not sufficiently active in finding a husband for my daughter. He has tried one or two places and failed. He thinks I am very indifferent. . . ." "Elderly people have their own anxiety," the postman replied. "The trouble is," said Ramanujam, "that he has set apart five thousand rupees for this girl's marriage and is worrying me to find a husband for her immediately. But money is not everything. . . ." "No, no," echoed the postman; "unless the destined hour is at hand, nothing can help. . . ."

Day after day for months Thanappa delivered the letters and waited to be told the news. "Same old news, Thanappa. . . . Horoscopes do not agree. . . . They are demanding too much. . . . Evidently they do not approve of her appearance." "Appearance! She looks like a queen. Unless one is totally blind . . ." the postman retorted angrily. The season would be closing, with only three more auspicious dates, the last being May 20. The girl would be seventeen in a few days. The reminders from her grandfather were becoming fiercer. Ramanujam had exhausted all the possibilities and had drawn a blank everywhere. He looked helpless and miserable.

"Postman," he said, "I don't think there is a son-in-law for me anywhere. . . ."

"Oh, don't utter inauspicious words, sir," the postman said. "When God wills it . . ." He reflected for a while and said, "There is a boy in Delhi earning two hundred rupees. Makunda of Temple Street was after him. Makunda and you are of the same subcaste, I believe. . . ."

"Yes. . . ."

"They have been negotiating for months now. Over a hundred letters have passed between them already. . . . But I know they are definitely breaking off. . . . It is over some money question. . . . They have written their last message on a postcard and it has infuriated these people all the more. As if postcards were an instrument of insult! I have known most important communications being written even on picture postcards; when Rajappa went to America two years ago he used to write to his sons every week on picture post-cards. . . ." After this digression he came back to the point. "I will ask Makunda to give me the horoscope. Let us see. . . ." Next day he brought the horoscope with him. "The boy's parents are also in Delhi, so you can write to them immediately. No time to waste now."

A ray of hope touched Ramanujam's family.

"I have still a hundred letters to deliver, but I came here first because I saw this Delhi postmark. Open it and tell me what they have written," said Thanappa. He trembled with suspense. "How prompt these people are! So they approve of the photo! Who wouldn't?"

"A letter every day! I might as well apply for leave till Kamakshi's marriage is over. . . ." he said another day. "You are already talking as if it were coming off tomorrow! God knows how many hurdles we have to cross now. Liking a photo does not prove anything. . . ."

The family council was discussing an important question: whether Ramanujam should go to Madras, taking the girl with him, and meet the party, who could come down for a day from Delhi. The family was divided over the question. Ramanujam, his mother and his wife—none of them had defined views on the question, but yet they opposed each other vehemently.

"We shall be the laughingstock of the town," said Ramanujam's wife, "if we take the girl out to be shown round. . . ."

"What queer notions! If you stand on all these absurd antiquated formalities, we shall never get anywhere near a marriage. It is our duty to take the girl over even to Delhi if necessary. . . ." "It is your pleasure, then; you can do what you please; why consult me? . . ."

Tempers were at their worst, and no progress seemed possible. The postman had got into the habit of dropping in at the end of his day's work and joining in the council. "I am a third party. Listen to me," he said. "Sir, please take the train to Madras immediately. What you cannot achieve by a year's correspondence you can do in an hour's meeting."

"Here is a letter from Madras, madam. I am sure it is from your husband. What is the news?" He handed the envelope to Ramanujam's wife, and she took it in to read. He said, "I have some registered letters for those last houses. I will finish my round and come back. . . ." He returned as promised. "Have they met, madam?"

"Yes, Kamakshi's father has written that they have met the girl, and from their talk Kamakshi's father infers they are quite willing. . . ."

"Grand news! I will offer a coconut to our Vinayaka tonight."

"But," the lady added, half-overwhelmed with happiness and half-worried, "there is this difficulty. We had an idea of doing it during next *Thai* month. . . . It will be so difficult to hurry through the arrangements now. But they say that if the marriage is done it must be done on the twentieth of May. If it is postponed the boy can't marry for three years. He is being sent away for some training. . . ."

"The old gentleman is as good as his word," the postman said, delivering an insurance envelope to Ramanujam. "He has given the entire amount. You can't complain of lack of funds now. Go ahead. I'm so happy you have his approval. More than their money, we need their blessings, sir. I hope he has sent his heartiest blessings. . . ." "Oh, yes, oh, yes," replied Ramanujam. "My father-in-law seems to be very happy at this proposal."

A five-thousand-rupee marriage was a big affair for Malgudi. Ramanujam, with so short a time before him, and none to share the task of arrangements, became distraught. Thanappa placed himself at his service during all his off-hours. He cut short his eloquence, ad-

vice and exchanges in other houses. He never waited for anyone to
come up and receive the letters. He just tossed them through a
window or an open door with a stentorian "Letter, sir." If they
stopped him and asked, "What is the matter with you? In such a
hurry!" "Yes, leave me alone till the twentieth of May. I will come
and squat in your house after that"—and he was off. Ramanujam was
in great tension. He trembled with anxiety as the day approached
nearer. "It must go on smoothly. Nothing should prove a hin-
drance." "Do not worry, sir; it will go through happily, by God's
grace. You have given them everything they wanted in cash, pre-
sents and style. They are good people. . . ."

"It is not about that. It is the very last date for the year. If for
some reason some obstruction comes up, it is all finished for ever.
The boy goes away for three years. I don't think either of us would
be prepared to bind ourselves to wait for three years."

It was four hours past the *Muhurtam* on the day of the wedding.
A quiet had descended on the gathering. The young smart bridegroom from Delhi was seated in a chair under the *pandal*. Fragrance
of sandal, and flowers, and holy smoke hung about the air. People
were sitting around the bridegroom talking. Thanappa appeared at
the gate loaded with letters. Some young men ran up to him demanding, "Postman! Letters?" He held them off. "Get back. I
know to whom to deliver." He walked over to the bridegroom and
held up to him a bundle of letters very respectfully. "These are all
greetings and blessings from well-wishers, I believe, sir, and my
own go with every one of them. . . ." He seemed very proud of
performing this task, and looked very serious. The bridegroom
looked up at him with an amused smile and muttered, "Thanks."
"We are all very proud to have your distinguished self as a son-in-
law of this house. I have known that child, Kamakshi, ever since she
was a day old, and I always knew she would get a distinguished
husband," added the postman, and brought his palms together in a
salute, and moved into the house to deliver other letters and to
refresh himself in the kitchen with tiffin and coffee.

Ten days later he knocked on the door and, with a grin, handed
Kamakshi her first letter. "Ah, scented envelope! I knew it was
coming when the mail van was three stations away. I have seen
hundreds like this. Take it from me. Before he has written the tenth

letter he will command you to pack up and join him, and you will grow a couple of wings and fly away that very day, and forget for ever Thanappa and this street, isn't it so?" Kamakshi blushed, snatched the letter from his hands and ran in to read it. He said, turning away, "I don't think there is any use waiting for you to finish the letter and tell me its contents."

On a holiday, when he was sure Ramanujam would be at home, Thanappa knocked on the door and handed him a card. "Ah!" cried Ramanujam. "Bad news, Thanappa. My uncle, my father's brother, is very ill in Salem, and they want me to start immediately."

"I'm very sorry to hear it, sir," said Thanappa, and handed him a telegram. "Here's another. . . ."

Ramanujam cried, "A telegram!" He glanced at it and screamed, "Oh, he is dead!" He sat down on the *pyol*, unable to stand the shock. Thanappa looked equally miserable. Ramanujam rallied, gathered himself up and turned to go in. Thanappa said, "One moment, sir. I have a confession to make. See the date on the card."

"May the nineteenth, nearly fifteen days ago!"

"Yes, sir, and the telegram followed next day—that is, on the day of the marriage. I was unhappy to see it. . . . 'But what has happened has happened,' I said to myself, and kept it away, fearing that it might interfere with the wedding."

Ramanujam glared at the postman and said, "I would not have cared to go through the marriage when he was dying. . . ." The postman stood with bowed head and mumbled, "You can complain if you like, sir. They will dismiss me. It is a serious offence." He turned and descended the steps and went down the street on his rounds. Ramanujam watched him dully for a while and shouted, "Postman!" Thanappa turned round; Ramanujam cried, "Don't think that I intend to complain. I am only sorry you have done this. . . ."

"I understand your feelings, sir," replied the postman, disappearing around a bend.

THE DOCTOR'S WORD

People came to him when the patient was on his last legs. Dr. Raman often burst out, "Why couldn't you have come a day earlier?" The reason was obvious—visiting fee twenty-five rupees, and more than that, people liked to shirk the fact that the time had come to call in Dr. Raman; for them there was something ominous in the very association. As a result, when the big man came on the scene it was always a quick decision one way or another. There was no scope or time for any kind of wavering or whitewashing. Long years of practise of this kind had bred in the doctor a certain curt truthfulness; for that very reason his opinion was valued; he was not a mere doctor expressing an opinion but a judge pronouncing a verdict. The patient's life hung on his words. This never unduly worried Dr. Raman. He never believed that agreeable words ever saved lives. He did not think it was any of his business to provide comforting lies when as a matter of course nature would tell them the truth in a few hours. However, when he glimpsed the faintest sign of hope, he rolled up his sleeve and stepped into the arena: it might be hours or days, but he never withdrew till he wrested the prize from Yama's hands.

Today, standing over a bed, the doctor felt that he himself needed someone to tell him soothing lies. He mopped his brow with his kerchief and sat down in the chair beside the bed. On the bed lay his dearest friend in the world: Gopal. They had known each other for forty years now, starting with their kindergarten days. They could not, of course, meet as much as they wanted, each being wrapped in his own family and profession. Occasionally, on a Sunday, Gopal would walk into the consulting room and wait patiently in a corner till the doctor was free. And then they would dine together, see a picture and talk of each other's life and activities. It was a classic friendship, which endured untouched by changing times, circumstances and activities.

In his busy round of work, Dr. Raman had not noticed that Gopal had not called in for over three months now. He only remembered it when he saw Gopal's son sitting on a bench in the consulting hall one crowded morning. Dr. Raman could not talk to him for over an hour. When he got up and was about to pass on to the operating room, he called up the young man and asked, "What brings you here, sir?" The youth was nervous and shy. "Mother sent me here."

"What can I do for you?"

"Father is ill. . . ."

It was an operation day and he was not free till three in the afternoon. He rushed off straight from the clinic to his friend's house, in Lawley Extension.

Gopal lay in bed as if in sleep. The doctor stood over him and asked Gopal's wife, "How long has he been in bed?"

"A month and a half, Doctor."

"Who is attending him?"

"A doctor in the next street. He comes down once in three days and gives him medicine."

"What is his name?" He had never heard of him. "Someone I don't know, but I wish he had had the goodness to tell me about it. Why, why couldn't you have sent me word earlier?"

"We thought you would be busy and did not wish to trouble you unnecessarily." They were apologetic and miserable. There was hardly any time to be lost. He took off his coat and opened his bag. He took out an injection tube, the needle sizzled over the stove. The sick man's wife whimpered in a corner and essayed to ask questions.

"Please don't ask questions," snapped the doctor. He looked at the children, who were watching the sterilizer, and said, "Send them all away somewhere, except the eldest."

He shot in the drug, sat back in his chair and gazed at the patient's face for over an hour. The patient still remained motionless. The doctor's face gleamed with perspiration, and his eyelids drooped with fatigue. The sick man's wife stood in a corner and watched silently. She asked timidly, "Doctor, shall I make some coffee for you?"

"No," he replied, although he felt famished, having missed his midday meal. He got up and said, "I will be back in a few minutes. Don't disturb him on any account." He picked up his bag and went to his car. In a quarter of an hour he was back, followed by an assistant and a nurse. The doctor told the lady of the house, "I have to perform an operation."

"Why, why? Why?" she asked faintly.

"I will tell you all that soon. Will you leave your son here to help us, and go over to the next house and stay there till I call you?"

The lady felt giddy and sank down on the floor, unable to bear the strain. The nurse attended to her and led her out.

At about eight in the evening the patient opened his eyes and stirred slightly in bed. The assistant was overjoyed. He exclaimed enthusiastically, "Sir, he will pull through." The doctor looked at him coldly and whispered, "I would give anything to see him pull through but, but the heart . . ."

"The pulse has improved, sir."

"Well, well," replied the doctor. "Don't trust it. It is only a false flash-up, very common in these cases." He ruminated for a while and added, "If the pulse keeps up till eight in the morning, it will go on for the next forty years, but I doubt very much if we shall see anything of it at all after two tonight."

He sent away the assistant and sat beside the patient. At about eleven the patient opened his eyes and smiled at his friend. He showed a slight improvement, he was able to take in a little food. A great feeling of relief and joy went through the household. They swarmed around the doctor and poured out their gratitude. He sat in his seat beside the bed, gazing sternly at the patient's face, hardly showing any signs of hearing what they were saying to him. The sick man's wife asked, "Is he now out of danger?" Without turning his head the doctor said, "Give glucose and brandy every forty minutes; just a couple of spoons will do." The lady went away to the kitchen. She felt restless. She felt she must know the truth whatever it was. Why was the great man so evasive? The suspense was unbearable. Perhaps he could not speak so near the patient's bed. She beckoned to him from the kitchen doorway. The doctor rose and went over. She asked, "What about him now? How is he?" The doctor bit his lips and replied, looking at the floor, "Don't get excited. Unless you must know about it, don't ask now." Her eyes opened wide in terror. She clasped her hands together and implored, "Tell me the truth." The doctor replied, "I would rather not talk to you now." He turned round and went back to his chair. A terrible wailing shot through the still house; the patient stirred and looked about in bewilderment. The doctor got up again, went over to the kitchen door, drew it in securely and shut off the wail.

When the doctor resumed his seat the patient asked in the faintest whisper possible, "Is that someone crying?" The doctor advised, "Don't exert yourself. You mustn't talk." He felt the pulse. It was already agitated by the exertion. The patient asked, "Am I going? Don't hide it from me." The doctor made a deprecating noise and sat back in his chair. He had never faced a situation like this. It was not in his nature to whitewash. People attached great value to his word because of that. He stole a look at the other. The patient motioned a finger to draw him nearer and whispered, "I must know how long I am going to last. I must sign the will. It is all ready. Ask my wife for the despatch box. You must sign as a witness."

"Oh!" the doctor exclaimed. "You are exerting yourself too much. You must be quieter." He felt idiotic to be repeating it. "How fine it would be," he reflected, "to drop the whole business and run away somewhere without answering anybody any question!" The patient clutched the doctor's wrist with his weak fingers and said, "Ramu, it is my good fortune that you are here at this moment. I can trust your word. I can't leave my property unsettled. That will mean endless misery for my wife and children. You know all about Subbiah and his gang. Let me sign before it is too late. Tell me. . . ."

"Yes, presently," replied the doctor. He walked off to his car, sat in the back seat and reflected. He looked at his watch. Midnight. If the will was to be signed, it must be done within the next two hours, or never. He could not be responsible for a mess there; he knew the family affairs too well and about those wolves, Subbiah and his gang. But what could he do? If he asked him to sign the will, it would virtually mean a death sentence and destroy the thousandth part of a chance that the patient had of survival. He got down from the car and went in. He resumed his seat in the chair. The patient was staring at him appealingly. The doctor said to himself, "If my word can save his life, he shall not die. The will be damned." He called, "Gopal, listen." This was the first time he was going to do a piece of acting before a patient, simulate a feeling and conceal his judgement. He stooped over the patient and said, with deliberate emphasis, "Don't worry about the will now. You are going to live. Your heart is absolutely sound." A new glow suffused the patient's face as he heard it. He asked in a tone of relief, "Do you say so? If it comes from your lips it must be true. . . ."

The doctor said, "Quite right. You are improving every second. Sleep in peace. You must not exert yourself on any account. You must sleep very soundly. I will see you in the morning." The patient looked at him gratefully for a moment and then closed his eyes. The doctor picked up his bag and went out, shutting the door softly behind him.

On his way home he stopped for a moment at his hospital, called out his assistant and said, "That Lawley Extension case. You might expect the collapse any second now. Go there with a tube of — in hand, and give it in case the struggle is too hard at the end. Hurry up."

Next morning he was back at Lawley Extension at ten. From his car he made a dash for the sick bed. The patient was awake and looked very well. The assistant reported satisfactory pulse. The doctor put his tube to his heart, listened for a while and told the sick man's wife, "Don't look so unhappy, lady. Your husband will live to be ninety." When they were going back to the hospital, the assistant sitting beside him in the car asked, "Is he going to live, sir?"

"I will bet on it. He will live to be ninety. He has turned the corner. How he has survived this attack will be a puzzle to me all my life," replied the doctor.

GATEMAN'S GIFT

When a dozen persons question openly or slyly a man's sanity, he begins to entertain serious doubts himself. This is what happened to ex-gateman Govind Singh. And you could not blame the public either. What could you do with a man who carried about in his hand a registered postal envelope and asked, "Please tell me what there is inside"? The obvious answer was: "Open it and see. . . ." He seemed horrified at this suggestion. "Oh, no, no, can't do it," he declared, and moved off to another friend and acquaintance. Everywhere the suggestion was the same, till he thought everyone had turned mad. And then somebody said, "If you don't like to open it and yet want to know what is inside you must take it to the X-ray Institute." This was suggested by an ex-compounder who lived in the next street.

"What is it?" asked Govind Singh. It was explained to him. "Where is it?" He was directed to the City X-ray Institute.

But before saying anything further about his progress, it would be useful to go back to an earlier chapter in his history. After war service in 1914–18, he came to be recommended for a gatekeeper's post at Engladia's. He liked the job very much. He was given a khaki uniform, a resplendent band across his shoulder and a short stick. He gripped the stick and sat down on a stool at the entrance to the office. And when his chief's car pulled up at the gate he stood at attention and gave a military salute. The office consisted of a staff numbering over a hundred, and as they trooped in and out every day he kept an eye on them. At the end of the day he awaited the footsteps of the General Manager coming down the stairs, and rose stiffly and stood at attention, and after he left, the hundreds of staff poured out. The doors were shut; Singh carried his stool in, placed it

under the staircase and placed his stick across it. Then he came out
and the main door was locked and sealed. In this way he had spent
twenty-five years of service, and then he begged to be pensioned off.
He would not have thought of retirement yet, but for the fact that he
found his sight and hearing playing tricks on him; he could not catch
the Manager's footsteps on the stairs, and it was hard to recognize
him even at ten yards. He was ushered into the presence of the chief,
who looked up for a moment from his papers and muttered, "We are
very pleased with your work for us, and the company will give you a
pension of twelve rupees for life. . . ." Singh clicked his heels, saluted, turned on his heel and went out of the room, his heart brim-
ming with gratitude and pride. This was the second occasion when
the great man had spoken to him, the first being on the first day of
his service. As he had stood at his post, the chief, entering the office
just then, looked up for a moment and asked, "Who are you?"

"I'm the new gatekeeper, master," he had answered. And he
spoke again only on this day. Though so little was said, Singh felt
electrified on both occasions by the words of his master. In Singh's
eyes the chief had acquired a sort of godhood, and it would be quite
adequate if a god spoke to one only once or twice in a lifetime. In
moments of contemplation Singh's mind dwelt on the words of his
master, and on his personality.

His life moved on smoothly. The pension together with what his
wife earned by washing and sweeping in a couple of houses was
quite sufficient for him. He ate his food, went out and met a few
friends, slept and spent some evenings sitting at a cigarette shop
which his cousin owned. This tenor of life was disturbed on the first
of every month when he donned his old khaki suit, walked to his old
office and salaamed the accountant at the counter and received his
pension. Sometimes if it was closing he waited on the roadside for
the General Manager to come down, and saluted him as he got into
his car.

There was a lot of time all around him, an immense sea of leisure.
In this state he made a new discovery about himself, that he could
make fascinating models out of clay and wood dust. The discovery
came suddenly, when one day a child in the neighbourhood brought
to him its little doll for repair. He not only repaired it but made a
new thing of it. This discovery pleased him so much that he very

soon became absorbed in it. His back yard gave him a plentiful supply of pliant clay, and the carpenter's shop next to his cousin's cigarette shop sawdust. He purchased paint for a few annas. And lo! he found his hours gliding. He sat there in the front part of his home, bent over his clay, and brought into existence a miniature universe; all the colours of life were there, all the forms and creatures, but of the size of his middle finger; whole villages and towns were there, all the persons he had seen passing before his office when he was sentry there—that beggar woman coming at midday, and that cucumber vendor; he had the eye of a cartoonist for human faces. Everything went down into clay. It was a wonderful miniature reflection of the world; and he mounted them neatly on thin wooden slices, which enhanced their attractiveness. He kept these in his cousin's shop and they attracted huge crowds every day and sold very briskly. More than from the sales Singh felt an ecstasy when he saw admiring crowds clustering around his handiwork.

On his next pension day he carried to his office a street scene (which he ranked as his best), and handed it over the counter to the accountant with the request: "Give this to the Sahib, please!"

"All right," said the accountant with a smile. It created a sensation in the office and disturbed the routine of office working for nearly half an hour. On the next pension day he carried another model (children at play) and handed it over the counter.

"Did the Sahib like the last one?"

"Yes, he liked it."

"Please give this one to him—" and he passed it over the counter. He made it a convention to carry on every pension day an offering for his master, and each time his greatest reward was the accountant's stock reply to his question: "What did the Sahib say?"

"He said it was very good."

At last he made his masterpiece. A model of his office frontage with himself at his post, a car at the entrance and the chief getting down: this composite model was so realistic that while he sat looking at it, he seemed to be carried back to his office days. He passed it over the counter on his pension day and it created a very great sensation in the office. "Fellow, you have not left yourself out, either!" people cried, and looked admiringly at Singh. A sudden fear seized Singh and he asked, "The master won't be angry, I hope?"

"No, no, why should he be?" said the accountant, and Singh received his pension and went home.

A week later when he was sitting on the *pyol* kneading clay, the postman came and said, "A registered letter for you. . . ."

"For me!" Any letter would have upset Singh; he had received less than three letters in his lifetime, and each time it was a torture for him till the contents were read out. Now a registered letter! This was his first registered letter. "Only lawyers send registered letters, isn't it so?"

"Usually," said the postman.

"Please take it back. I don't want it," said Singh.

"Shall I say 'Refused'?" asked the postman. "No, no," said Singh. "Just take it back and say you have not found me. . . ."

"That I can't do. . . ." said the postman, looking serious.

Singh seemed to have no option but to scrawl his signature and receive the packet. He sat gloomily—gazing at the floor. His wife who had gone out and just returned saw him in this condition and asked, "What is it?" His voice choked as he replied, "It has come." He flung at her the registered letter. "What is it?" she asked. He said, "How should I know. Perhaps our ruin . . ." He broke down. His wife watched him for a moment, went in to attend to some domestic duty and returned, still found him in the same condition and asked, "Why not open it and see, ask someone to read it?" He threw up his arms in horror. "Woman, you don't know what you are saying. It cannot be opened. They have perhaps written that my pension is stopped, and God knows what else the Sahib has said. . . ."

"Why not go to the office and find out from them?"

"Not I! I will never show my face there again," replied Singh. "I have lived without a single remark being made against me, all my life. Now!" He shuddered at the thought of it. "I knew I was getting into trouble when I made that office model. . . ." After deeper reflection he said, "Every time I took something there, people crowded round, stopped all work for nearly an hour. . . . That must also have reached the Sahib's ears."

He wandered about saying the same thing, with the letter in his pocket. He lost his taste for food, wandered about unkempt, with his hair standing up like a halo—an unaccustomed sight, his years in military service having given him a habitual tidiness. His wife lost all peace of mind and became miserable about him. He stood at cross-roads, clutching the letter in his hand. He kept asking everyone he came across, "Tell me, what is there in this?" but he would not brook the suggestion to open it and see its contents.

So forthwith Singh found his way to the City X-ray Institute at Race Course Road. As he entered the gate he observed dozens of cars parked along the drive, and a Gurkha watchman at the gate. Some people were sitting on sofas reading books and journals. They turned and threw a brief look at him and resumed their studies. As Singh stood uncertainly at the doorway, an assistant came up and asked, "What do you want?" Singh gave a salute, held up the letter uncertainly and muttered, "Can I know what is inside this?" The assistant made the obvious suggestion. But Singh replied, "They said you could tell me what's inside without opening it—" The assistant asked, "Where do you come from?" Singh explained his life, work and outlook, and concluded, "I've lived without remark all my life. I knew trouble was coming—" There were tears on his cheeks. The assistant looked at him curiously as scores of others had done before, smiled and said, "Go home and rest. You are not all right. . . . Go, go home."

"Can't you say what is in this?" Singh asked pathetically. The assistant took it in his hand, examined it and said, "Shall I open it?" "No, no, no," Singh cried, and snatched it back. There was a look of terror in his eyes. The assembly looked up from their pages and watched him with mild amusement in their eyes. The assistant kindly put his arms on his shoulder and led him out. "You get well first, and then come back. I tell you—you are not all right."

Walking back home, he pondered over it. "Why are they all behaving like this, as if I were a madman?" When this word came to his mind, he stopped abruptly in the middle of the road and cried, "Oh! That's it, is that it?—Mad! Mad!" He shook his head gleefully as if the full truth had just dawned upon him. He now understood the looks that people threw at him. "Oh! oh!" he cried aloud. He laughed. He felt a curious relief at this realization. "I have been mad and didn't know it. . . ." He cast his mind back. Every little action of his for the last so many days seemed mad; particularly the doll-making. "What sane man would make clay dolls after twenty-five years of respectable service in an office?" He felt a tremendous freedom of limbs, and didn't feel it possible to walk at an ordinary pace. He wanted to fly. He swung his arms up and down and ran on with a whoop. He ran through the Market Road. When people stood about and watched he cried, "Hey, don't laugh at a madman, for who knows, you will also be mad when you come to make clay dolls," and charged into their midst with a war cry. When he saw children coming out of a school, he felt it would be nice to amuse their young hearts by behaving like a tiger. So he fell on his hands and knees and crawled up to them with a growl.

He went home in a terrifying condition. His wife, who was grinding chilli in the back yard, looked up and asked, "What is this?" His hair was covered with street dust; his body was splashed with mud. He could not answer because he choked with mirth as he said, "Fancy what has happened!"

"What is it?"

"I'm mad, mad." He looked at his work-basket in a corner, scooped out the clay and made a helmet of it and put it on his head. Ranged on the floor was his latest handiwork. After his last visit to the office he had been engaged in making a model village. It was a resplendent group: a dun road, red tiles, green coconut trees sway-ing, and the colour of the saris of the village women carrying water pots. He derived the inspiration for it from a memory of his own village days. It was the most enjoyable piece of work that he had so far undertaken. He lived in a kind of ecstasy while doing it. "I am going to keep this for myself. A memento of my father's village," he declared. "I will show it at an exhibition, where they will give me a medal." He guarded it like a treasure: when it was wet he never allowed his wife to walk within ten yards of it. "Keep off, we don't want your foot dust for this village. . . ."

Now, in his madness, he looked down on it. He raised his foot and stamped everything down into a multicoloured jam. They were still half-wet. He saw a donkey grazing in the street. He gathered up the jam and flung it at the donkey with the remark: "Eat this if you like. It is a nice village. . . ." And he went out on a second round. This was a quieter outing. He strode on at an even pace, breathing deeply, with the clay helmet on, out of which peeped his grey hair, his arms locked behind, his fingers clutching the fateful letter, his face tilted towards the sky. He walked down the Market Road, with

a feeling that he was the sole occupant of this globe: his madness had
given him a sense of limitless freedom, strength and buoyancy. The
remarks and jeers of the crowds gaping at him did not in the least
touch him.

While he walked thus, his eye fell on the bulb of a tall street lamp.
"Bulb of the size of a papaya fruit!" he muttered and chuckled. It had
been a long cherished desire in him to fling a stone at it; now he felt,
in his joyous and free condition, that he was free from the trammels
of convention and need not push back any inclination. He picked up
a pebble and threw it with good aim. The shattering noise of glass
was as music to his ears. A policeman put his hand on his shoulder.
"Why did you do it?" Singh looked indignant. "I like to crack glass
papaya fruit, that is all," was the reply. The constable said, "Come
to the station."

"Oh, yes, when I was in Mesopotamia they put me on half-ration
once," he said, and walked on to the station. He paused, tilted his
head to the side and remarked, "This road is not straight. . . ." A few
carriages and cycles were coming up to him. He found that everything was wrong about them. They seemed to need some advice in
the matter. He stopped in the middle of the road, stretched out his
arms and shouted, "Halt!" The carriages stopped, the cyclists jumped
off and Singh began a lecture: "When I was in Mesopotamia—I will
tell you fellows who don't know anything about anything." The
policeman dragged him away to the side and waved to the traffic to
resume. One of the cyclists who resumed jumped off the saddle
again and came towards him with, "Why! It is Singh, Singh, what
fancy dress is this? What is the matter?" Even through the haze of
his insane vision Singh could recognize the voice and the person—the
accountant at the office. Singh clicked his heels and gave a salute.
"Excuse me, sir, didn't intend to stop you. You may pass. . . ." He
pointed the way generously, and the accountant saw the letter in his
hand. He recognized it although it was mud-stained and crumpled.

"Singh, you got our letter?"

"Yes, sir— Pass. Do not speak of it. . . ."

"What is the matter?" He snatched it from his hand. "Why
haven't you opened it!" He tore open the envelope and took out of
it a letter and read aloud: "The General Manager greatly appreci-
ates the very artistic models you have sent, and he is pleased to

sanction a reward of 100 rupees and hopes it will be an encourage-
ment for you to keep up this interesting hobby."

It was translated to him word for word, and the enclosure, a
cheque for one hundred rupees, was handed to him. A big crowd
gathered to watch this scene. Singh pressed the letter to his eyes. He
beat his brow and wailed, "Tell me, sir, am I mad or not?"

"You look quite well, you aren't mad," said the accountant. Singh
fell at his feet and said with tears choking his voice, "You are a god,
sir, to say that I am not mad. I am so happy to hear it."

On the next pension day he turned up spruce as ever at the office
counter. As they handed him the envelope they asked, "What toys
are you making now?"

"Nothing, sir. Never again. It is no occupation for a sane
man. . . ." he said, received his pension and walked stiffly out of the
office.

THE BLIND DOG

It was not a very impressive or high-class dog; it was one of those commonplace dogs one sees everywhere—colour of white and dust, tail mutilated at a young age by God knows whom, born in the street, and bred on the leavings and garbage of the marketplace. He had spotty eyes and undistinguished carriage and needless pugnacity. Before he was two years old he had earned the scars of a hundred fights on his body. When he needed rest on hot afternoons he lay curled up under the culvert at the eastern gate of the market. In the evenings he set out on his daily rounds, loafed in the surrounding streets and lanes, engaged himself in skirmishes, picked up edibles on the roadside and was back at the Market Gate by nightfall.

This life went on for three years. And then a change in his life occurred. A beggar, blind in both eyes, appeared at the Market Gate. An old woman led him up there early in the morning, seated him at the gate, and came up again at midday with some food, gathered his coins and took him home at night.

The dog was sleeping nearby. He was stirred by the smell of food. He got up, came out of his shelter and stood before the blind man, wagging his tail and gazing expectantly at the bowl, as he was eating his sparse meal. The blind man swept his arms about and asked, "Who is there?" at which the dog went up and licked his hand. The blind man stroked its coat gently tail to ear and said, "What a beauty you are. Come with me—" He threw a handful of food, which the dog ate gratefully. It was perhaps an auspicious moment for starting a friendship. They met every day there, and the dog cut off much of its rambling to sit up beside the blind man and watch him receive alms morning to evening. In course of time, observing him, the dog understood that the passers-by must give a coin, and whoever went away without dropping a coin was chased by the dog; he tugged the edge of their clothes by his teeth and pulled them back to the old man at the gate and let go only after something was dropped in his bowl. Among those who frequented this place was a village urchin, who had the mischief of a devil in him. He liked to tease the blind man by calling him names and by trying to pick up the coins in his bowl. The blind man helplessly shouted and cried and whirled his staff. On Thursdays this boy appeared at the gate, carrying on his head a basket loaded with cucumber or plantain. Every Thursday afternoon it was a crisis in the blind man's life. A seller of bright-coloured but doubtful perfumes with his wares mounted on a wheeled platform, a man who spread out cheap storybooks on a gunnysack, another man who carried coloured ribbons on an elaborate frame—these were the people who usually gathered under the same arch. On a Thursday when the young man appeared at the eastern gate one of them remarked, "Blind fellow! Here comes your scourge—"

"Oh, God, is this Thursday?" he wailed. He swept his arms about and called, "Dog, dog, come here, where are you?" He made the peculiar noise which brought the dog to his side. He stroked his head and muttered, "Don't let that little rascal—" At this very moment the boy came up with a leer on his face.

"Blind man! Still pretending you have no eyes. If you are really blind, you should not know this either—" He stopped, his hand moving towards the bowl. The dog sprang on him and snapped his jaws on the boy's wrist. The boy extricated his hand and ran for his life. The dog bounded up behind him and chased him out of the market.

"See the mongrel's affection for this old fellow," marvelled the perfume-vendor.

One evening at the usual time the old woman failed to turn up, and the blind man waited at the gate, worrying as the evening grew into night. As he sat fretting there, a neighbour came up and said, "Sami, don't wait for the old woman. She will not come again. She died this afternoon—"

The blind man lost the only home he had, and the only person who cared for him in this world. The ribbon-vendor suggested, "Here, take this white tape"—he held a length of the white cord which he had been selling—"I will give this to you free of cost. Tie it to the dog and let him lead you about if he is really so fond of you—"

Life for the dog took a new turn now. He came to take the place of the old woman. He lost his freedom completely. His world came to be circumscribed by the limits of the white cord which the ribbon-vendor had spared. He had to forget wholesale all his old life—all his old haunts. He simply had to stay on for ever at the end of that string. When he saw other dogs, friends or foes, instinctively he sprang up, tugging the string, and this invariably earned him a kick from his master. "Rascal, want to tumble me down—have sense—" In a few days the dog learnt to discipline his instinct and impulse. He ceased to take notice of other dogs, even if they came up and growled at his side. He lost his own orbit of movement and contact with his fellow-creatures.

To the extent of this loss his master gained. He moved about as he had never moved in his life. All day he was on his legs, led by the dog. With the staff in one hand and the dog-lead in the other, he moved out of his home—a corner in a *choultry* veranda a few yards off the market: he had moved in there after the old woman's death. He started out early in the day. He found that he could treble his income by moving about instead of staying in one place. He moved down the *choultry* street, and wherever he heard people's voices he stopped and held out his hands for alms. Shops, schools, hospitals, hotels—he left nothing out. He gave a tug when he wanted the dog to stop, and shouted like a bullock-driver when he wanted him to move on. The dog protected his feet from going into pits, or stumping against steps or stones, and took him up inch by inch on safe ground and steps. For this sight people gave coins and helped him. Children gathered round him and gave him things to eat. A dog is essentially an active creature who punctuates his hectic rounds with well-defined periods of rest. But now this dog (henceforth to be known as Tiger) had lost all rest. He had rest only when the old man sat down somewhere. At night the old man slept with the cord turned around his finger. "I can't take chances with you—" he said. A great desire to earn more money than ever before seized his master, so that he felt any resting a waste of opportunity, and the dog had to be continuously on his feet. Sometimes his legs refused to move. But if he slowed down even slightly his master goaded him on fiercely with his staff. The dog whined and groaned under this thrust. "Don't whine, you rascal. Don't I give you your food? You want to loaf, do you?" swore the blind man. The dog lumbered up and down and round and round the marketplace with slow steps, tied down to the blind tyrant. Long after the traffic at the market ceased, you could hear the night stabbed by the far-off wail of the tired dog. It lost its original appearance. As months rolled on, bones stuck up at his haunches and ribs were reliefed through his fading coat.

The ribbon-seller, the novel-vendor and the perfumer observed it one evening when business was slack, and held a conference among themselves. "It rends my heart to see that poor dog slaving. Can't we do something?" The ribbon-seller remarked, "That rascal has started lending money for interest—I heard it from the fruit-seller—He is earning more than he needs. He has become a very devil for money—" At this point the perfumer's eyes caught the scissors dangling from the ribbon-rack. "Give it here," he said and moved on with the scissors in hand.

The blind man was passing in front of the eastern gate. The dog was straining the lead. There was a piece of bone lying on the way and the dog was straining to pick it up. The lead became taut and hurt the blind man's hand, and he tugged the string and kicked till the dog howled. It howled, but could not pass the bone lightly; it tried to make another dash for it. The blind man was heaping curses on it. The perfumer stepped up, applied the scissors and snipped the cord. The dog bounced off and picked up the bone. The blind man stopped dead where he stood, with the other half of the string dangling in his hand. "Tiger! Tiger! Where are you?" he cried. The perfumer moved away quietly, muttering, "You heartless devil! You will never get at him again! He has his freedom!" The dog went off at top speed. He nosed about the ditches happily, hurled himself on other dogs and ran round and round the fountain in the Market Square barking, his eyes sparkling with joy. He returned to his favourite haunts and hung about the butcher's shop, the tea-stall and the bakery.

The ribbon-vendor and his two friends stood at the Market Gate and enjoyed the sight immensely as the blind man struggled to find his way about. He stood rooted to the spot, waving his stick; he felt as if he were hanging in mid-air. He was wailing. "Oh, where is my dog? Where is my dog? Won't someone give him back to me? I will murder it when I get at it again!" He groped about, tried to cross the road, came near being run over by a dozen vehicles at different points, tumbled and struggled and gasped. "He'd deserve it if he was run over, this heartless blackguard—" they said, observing him. However, the old man struggled through and with the help of someone found his way back to his corner in the *choultry* veranda and sank down on his gunnysack bed, half-faint with the strain of his journey.

He was not seen for ten days, fifteen days and twenty days. Nor was the dog seen anywhere. They commented among themselves: "The dog must be loafing over the whole earth, free and happy. The beggar is perhaps gone for ever—" Hardly was this sentence uttered when they heard the familiar tap-tap of the blind man's staff. They saw him again coming up the pavement—led by the dog. "Look! Look!" they cried. "He has again got at it and tied it up—" The ribbon-seller could not contain himself. He ran up and said, "Where have you been all these days?"

"Know what happened!" cried the blind man. "This dog ran away. I should have died in a day or two, confined to my corner, no food, not an anna to earn—imprisoned in my corner. I should have perished if it continued for another day— But this thing returned—"

"When? When?"

"Last night. At midnight as I slept in bed, he came and licked my face. I felt like murdering him. I gave him a blow which he will never forget again," said the blind man. "I forgave him, after all a dog! He loafed as long as he could pick up some rubbish to eat on the road, but real hunger has driven him back to me, but he will not leave me again. See! I have got this—" and he shook the lead: it was a steel chain this time.

Once again there was the dead, despairing look in the dog's eyes. "Go on, you fool," cried the blind man, shouting like an ox-driver. He tugged the chain, poked with the stick, and the dog moved away on slow steps. They stood listening to the tap-tap going away.

"Death alone can help that dog," cried the ribbon-seller, looking after it with a sigh. "What can we do with a creature who returns to his doom with such a free heart?"

FELLOW-FEELING

The Madras–Bangalore Express was due to start in a few minutes. Trolleys and barrows piled with trunks and beds rattled their way through the bustle. Fruit-sellers and *beedi*-and-betel-sellers cried themselves hoarse. Latecomers pushed, shouted and perspired. The engine added to the general noise with the low monotonous hum of its boiler; the first bell rang, the guard looked at his watch. Mr. Rajam Iyer arrived on the platform at a terrific pace, with a small roll of bedding under one arm and an absurd yellow trunk under the other. He ran to the first third-class compartment that caught his eye, peered in and, since the door could not be opened on account of the congestion inside, flung himself in through the window.

Fifteen minutes later Madras flashed past the train in window-framed patches of sun-scorched roofs and fields. At the next halt, Mandhakam, most of the passengers got down. The compartment built to "seat 8 passengers; 4 British Troops, or 6 Indian Troops" now carried only nine. Rajam Iyer found a seat and made himself comfortable opposite a sallow, meek passenger, who suddenly removed his coat, folded it and placed it under his head and lay down, shrinking himself to the area he had occupied while he was sitting. With his knees drawn up almost to his chin, he rolled himself into a ball. Rajam Iyer threw at him an indulgent, compassionate look. He then fumbled for his glasses and pulled out of his pocket a small book, which set forth in clear Tamil the significance of the obscure *Sandhi* rites that every Brahmin worth the name performs thrice daily.

He was startled out of this pleasant languor by a series of growls coming from a passenger who had got in at Katpadi. The newcomer, looking for a seat, had been irritated by the spectacle of the meek passenger asleep and had enforced the law of the third-class. He then encroached on most of the meek passenger's legitimate space and began to deliver home-truths which passed by easy stages from impudence to impertinence and finally to ribaldry.

Rajam Iyer peered over his spectacles. There was a dangerous look in his eyes. He tried to return to the book, but could not. The bully's speech was gathering momentum.

"What is all this?" Rajam Iyer asked suddenly, in a hard tone.

"What is what?" growled back the newcomer, turning sharply on Rajam Iyer.

"Moderate your style a bit," Rajam Iyer said firmly.

"You moderate yours first," replied the other.

A pause.

"My man," Rajam Iyer began endearingly, "this sort of thing will never do."

The newcomer received this in silence. Rajam Iyer felt encouraged and drove home his moral: "Just try and be more courteous, it is your duty."

"You mind your business," replied the newcomer.

Rajam Iyer shook his head disapprovingly and drawled out a "No." The newcomer stood looking out for some time and, as if expressing a brilliant truth that had just dawned on him, said, "You are a Brahmin, I see. Learn, sir, that your days are over. Don't think you can bully us as you have been bullying us all these years."

Rajam Iyer gave a short laugh and said, "What has it to do with your beastly conduct to this gentleman?"

The newcomer assumed a tone of mock humility and said, "Shall I take the dust from your feet, O Holy Brahmin? O Brahmin, Brahmin." He continued in a singsong fashion: "Your days are over, my dear sir, learn that. I should like to see you trying a bit of bossing on us."

"Whose master is who?" asked Rajam Iyer philosophically.

The newcomer went on with no obvious relevance: "The cost of mutton has gone up out of all proportion. It is nearly double what it used to be."

"Is it?" asked Rajam Iyer.

"Yes, and why?" continued the other. "Because Brahmins have begun to eat meat and they pay high prices to get it secretly." He then turned to the other passengers and added, "And we non-Brahmins have to pay the same price, though we don't care for the secrecy."

Rajam Iyer leaned back in his seat, reminding himself of a proverb which said that if you threw a stone into a gutter it would only spurt filth in your face.

"And," said the newcomer, "the price of meat used to be five annas per pound. I remember the days quite well. It is nearly twelve annas now. Why? Because the Brahmin is prepared to pay so much, if only he can have it in secret. I have with my own eyes seen Brahmins, pukkah Brahmins with sacred threads on their bodies, carrying fish under their arms, of course all wrapped up in a towel. Ask them what it is, and they will tell you that it is plantain. Plantain that has life, I suppose! I once tickled a fellow under the arm and out came the biggest fish in the market. Hey, Brahmin," he said, turning to Rajam Iyer, "what did you have for your meal this morning?" "Who? I?" asked Rajam Iyer. "Why do you want to know?" "Look, sirs," said the newcomer to the other passengers, "why is he afraid to tell us what he ate this morning?" And turning to Rajam Iyer, "Mayn't a man ask another what he had for his morning meal?"

"Oh, by all means. I had rice, ghee, curds, *brinjal* soup, fried beans."

"Oh, is that all?" asked the newcomer, with an innocent look.

"Yes," replied Rajam Iyer.

"Is that all?"

"Yes, how many times do you want me to repeat it?"

"No offence, no offence," replied the newcomer.

"Do you mean to say I am lying?" asked Rajam Iyer.

"Yes," replied the other, "you have omitted from your list a few things. Didn't I see you this morning going home from the market with a banana, a water banana, wrapped up in a towel, under your arm? Possibly it was somebody very much like you. Possibly I mistook the person. My wife prepares excellent soup with fish. You won't be able to find the difference between *dhall* soup and fish soup. Send your wife, or the wife of the person that was exactly like you, to my wife to learn soup-making. Hundreds of Brahmins have smacked their lips over the *dhall* soup prepared in my house. I am a leper if there is a lie in anything I say."

"You are," replied Rajam Iyer, grinding his teeth. "You are a rabid leper."

"Whom do you call a leper!"

"You!"

"I? You call me a leper?"

"No. I call you a rabid leper."

"You call me rabid?" the newcomer asked, striking his chest to emphasize "me."

"You are a filthy brute," said Rajam Iyer. "You must be handed over to the police."

"Bah!" exlaimed the newcomer. "As if I didn't know what these police were."

"Yes, you must have had countless occasions to know the police. And you will see more of them yet in your miserable life, if you don't get beaten to death like the street mongrel you are," said Rajam Iyer in great passion. "With your foul mouth you are bound to come to that end."

"What do you say?" shouted the newcomer menacingly. "What do you say, you vile humbug?"

"Shut up," Rajam Iyer cried.

"You shut up."

"Do you know to whom you are talking?"

"What do I care who the son of a mongrel is?"

"I will thrash you with my slippers," said Rajam Iyer.

"I will pulp you down with an old rotten sandal," came the reply.

"I will kick you," said Rajam Iyer.

"Will you?" howled the newcomer.

"Come on, let us see."

Both rose to their feet simultaneously.

There they stood facing each other on the floor of the compartment. Rajam Iyer was seized by a sense of inferiority. The newcomer stood nine clean inches over him. He began to feel ridiculous, short and fat, wearing a loose dhoti and a green coat, while the newcomer towered above him in his grease-spotted khaki suit. Out of the corner of his eye he noted that the other passengers were waiting eagerly to see how the issue would be settled and were not in the least disposed to intervene.

"Why do you stand as if your mouth was stopped with mud?" asked the newcomer.

"Shut up," Rajam Iyer snapped, trying not to be impressed by the size of the adversary.

"Your honour said that you would kick me," said the newcomer, pretending to offer himself.

"Won't I kick you?" asked Rajam Iyer.

"Try."

"No," said Rajam Iyer, "I will do something worse."

"Do it," said the other, throwing forward his chest and pushing up the sleeves of his coat.

Rajam Iyer removed his coat and rolled up his sleeves. He rubbed his hands and commanded suddenly, "Stand still!" The newcomer was taken aback. He stood for a second baffled. Rajam Iyer gave him no time to think. With great force he swung his right arm and brought it near the other's cheek, but stopped it short without hitting him.

"Wait a minute, I think I had better give you a chance," said Rajam Iyer.

"What chance?" asked the newcomer.

"It would be unfair if I did it without giving you a chance."

"Did what?"

"You stand there and it will be over in a fraction of a second."

"Fraction of a second? What will you do?"

"Oh, nothing very complicated," replied Rajam Iyer nonchalantly, "nothing very complicated. I will slap your right cheek and at the same time tug your left ear, and your mouth, which is now under your nose, will suddenly find itself under your left ear, and, what is more, stay there. I assure you, you won't feel any pain."

"What do you say?"

"And it will all be over before you say 'Sri Rama.' "

"I don't believe it," said the newcomer.

"Well and good. Don't believe it," said Rajam Iyer carelessly. "I never do it except under extreme provocation."

"Do you think I am an infant?"

"I implore you, my man, not to believe me. Have you heard of a thing called jujitsu? Well, this is a simple trick in jujitsu perhaps known to half a dozen persons in the whole of South India."

"You said you would kick me," said the newcomer.

"Well, isn't this worse?" asked Rajam Iyer. He drew a line on the newcomer's face between his left ear and mouth, muttering, "I must admit you have a tolerably good face and round figure. But imagine yourself going about the streets with your mouth under your left ear. . . ." He chuckled at the vision. "I expect at Jalarpet station there will be a huge crowd outside our compartment to see you." The newcomer stroked his chin thoughtfully. Rajam Iyer continued, "I felt it my duty to explain the whole thing to you beforehand. I am not as hot-headed as you are. I have some consideration for your wife and children. It will take some time for the kids to recognize Papa when he returns home with his mouth under . . . How many children have you?"

"Four."

"And then think of it," said Rajam Iyer. "You will have to take your food under your left ear, and you will need the assistance of your wife to drink water. She will have to pour it in."

"I will go to a doctor," said the newcomer.

"Do go," replied Rajam Iyer, "and I will give you a thousand rupees if you find a doctor. You may try even European doctors."

The newcomer stood ruminating with knitted brow. "Now prepare," shouted Rajam Iyer, "one blow on the right cheek. I will jerk your left ear, and your mouth . . ."

The newcomer suddenly ran to the window and leaned far out of it. Rajam decided to leave the compartment at Jalarpet.

But the moment the train stopped at Jalarpet station, the newcomer grabbed his bag and jumped out. He moved away at a furious pace and almost knocked down a coconut-seller and a person carrying a trayload of coloured toys. Rajam Iyer felt it would not be necessary for him to get out now. He leaned through the window and cried, "Look here!" The newcomer turned.

"Shall I keep a seat for you?" asked Rajam Iyer.

"No, my ticket is for Jalarpet," the newcomer answered and quickened his pace.

The train had left Jalarpet at least a mile behind. The meek passenger still sat shrunk in a corner of the seat. Rajam Iyer looked over his spectacles and said, "Lie down if you like."

The meek passenger proceeded to roll himself into a ball. Rajam Iyer added, "Did you hear that bully say that his ticket was for Jalarpet?"

"Yes."

"Well," he lied, "he is in the fourth compartment from here. I saw him get into it just as the train started."

Though the meek passenger was too grateful to doubt this statement, one or two other passengers looked at Rajam Iyer sceptically.

THE TIGER'S CLAW

The man-eater's dark career was ended. The men who had laid it low were the heroes of the day. They were garlanded with chrysanthemum flowers and seated on the arch of the highest bullock cart and were paraded in the streets, immediately followed by another bullock-drawn open cart, on which their trophy lay with glazed eyes—overflowing the cart on every side, his tail trailing the dust. The village suspended all the normal activity for the day; men, women and children thronged the highways, pressing on with the procession, excitedly talking about the tiger. The tiger had held a reign of terror for nearly five years, in the villages that girt Mempi Forest.

We watched this scene, fascinated, drifting along with the crowd —till the Talkative Man patted us from behind and cried, "Lost in wonder! If you've had your eyeful of that carcass, come aside and listen to me. . . ." After the crowd surged past us, he sat us on a rock mount, under a margosa tree, and began his tale: I was once camping in Koppal, the most obscure of all the villages that lie scattered about the Mempi region. You might wonder what I was doing in that desolate corner of the earth. I'll tell you. You remember I've often spoken to you about my work as agent of a soil fertilizer company. It was the most miserable period of my life. Twenty-five days in the month, I had to be on the road, visiting nooks and corners of the country and popularizing the stuff. . . . One such journey brought me to the village Koppal. It was not really a village but just a clearing with about forty houses and two streets, hemmed in by the jungle on all sides. The place was dingy and depressing. Why our company should have sought to reach a place like this for their stuff, I can't understand. They would not have known of its existence but for the fact that it was on the railway. Yes, actually on the railway, some obscure branch-line passed through this village, though most trains did not stop there. Its centre of civilization was its railway station— presided over by a porter in blue and an old station-master, a wiz- ened man wearing a green turban, and with red and green flags always tucked under his arms. Let me tell you about the station. It was not a building but an old railway carriage, which, having served its term of life, was deprived of its wheels and planted beside the railway lines. It had one or two windows through which the station- master issued tickets, and spoke to those occasional passengers who turned up in this wilderness. A convolvulus creeper was trained over its entrance: no better use could be found for an ex-carriage.

One November morning a mixed train put me down at this sta- tion and puffed away into the forest. The station-master, with the flags under his arm, became excited on seeing me. He had seen so few travellers arriving that it gave him no end of pleasure to see a new face. He appointed himself my host immediately, and took me into the ex-compartment and seated me on a stool. He said, "Excuse me. I'll get off these papers in a minute. . . ." He scrawled over some brown sheets, put them away and rose. He locked up the station and took me to his home—a very tiny stone building consisting of just one room, a kitchen and a back yard. The station-master lived here with his wife and seven children. He fed me. I changed. He sent the porter along with me to the village, which was nearly a mile off in the interior. I gathered about me the peasants of those forty houses and lectured to them from the *pyol* of the headman's house. They listened to me patiently, received the samples and my elaborate di- rections for their use, and went away to their respective occupations, with cynical comments among themselves regarding my ideas of manuring. I packed up and started back for the station-master's house at dusk, my throat smarting and my own words ringing in my ears. Though a couple of trains were now passing, the only stopping train would be at 5:30 on the following morning. After dinner at the station-master's house, I felt the time had come for me to leave: it would be indelicate to stay on when the entire family was waiting to spread their beds in the hall. I said I would sleep on the platform till my train arrived. . . . "No, no, these are very bad parts. Not like your town. Full of tigers. . . ." the station-master said. He let me, as a special concession, sleep in the station. A heavy table, a chair and a stool occupied most of the space in the compartment. I pushed them aside and made a little space for myself in a corner. I'd at least eight hours before me. I laid myself down: all kinds of humming and rustling sounds came through the still night, and telegraph poles and night insects hummed, and bamboo bushes creaked. I got up, bolted the little station door and lay down, feeling forlorn. It became very warm, and I couldn't sleep. I got up again, opened the door slightly to let in a little air, placed the chair across the door and went back to my bed.

I fell asleep and dreamt. I was standing on the crest of a hill and watching the valley below, under a pale moonlight. Far off a line of catlike creatures was moving across the slope, half-shadows, and I stood looking at them admiringly, for they marched on with great elegance. I was so much lost in this vision that I hadn't noticed that they had moved up and come by a winding path right behind me. I turned and saw that they were not catlike in size but full-grown tigers. I made a dash to the only available shelter—the station room.

At this point the dream ended as the chair barricading the door came hurtling through and fell on me. I opened my eyes and saw at the door a tiger pushing himself in. It was a muddled moment for me: not being sure whether the dream was continuing or whether I was awake. I at first thought it was my friend the station-master who was coming in, but my dream had fully prepared my mind—I saw the thing clearly against the starlit sky, tail wagging, growling, and, above all, his terrible eyes gleaming through the dark. I understood that the fertilizer company would have to manage without my lectures from the following day. The tiger himself was rather startled by the noise of the chair and stood hesitating. He saw me quite clearly in my corner, and he seemed to be telling himself, "My dinner is there ready, but let me first know what this clattering noise is about." Somehow wild animals are less afraid of human beings than they are of pieces of furniture like chairs and tables. I have seen circus men managing a whole menagerie with nothing more than a chair. God gives us such recollections in order to save us at critical moments; and as the tiger stood observing me and watching the chair, I put out my hands and with desperate strength drew the table towards me, and also the stool. I sat with my back to the corner, the

table wedged in nicely with the corner. I sat under it, and the stool
walled up another side. While I dragged the table down, a lot of
things fell off it, a table lamp, a long knife and pins. From my shelter
I peeped at the tiger, who was also watching me with interest. Evidently he didn't like his meal to be so completely shut out of sight.
So he cautiously advanced a step or two, making a sort of rumbling
noise in his throat which seemed to shake up the little station house.
My end was nearing. I really pitied the woman whose lot it was to
have become my wife.

I held up the chair like a shield and flourished it, and the tiger
hesitated and fell back a step or two. Now once again we spent some
time watching for each other's movements. I held my breath and
waited. The tiger stood there fiercely waving its tail, which sometimes struck the side walls and sent forth a thud. He suddenly
crouched down without taking his eyes off me, and scratched the
floor with his claws. "He is sharpening them for me," I told myself.
The little shack had already acquired the smell of a zoo. It made me
sick. The tiger kept scratching the floor with his forepaws. It was the
most hideous sound you could think of.

All of a sudden he sprang up and flung his entire weight on this lot
of furniture. I thought it'd be reduced to matchwood, but fortunately
our railways have a lot of foresight and choose the heaviest timber
for their furniture. That saved me. The tiger could do nothing more
than perch himself on the roof of the table and hang down his paws:
he tried to strike me down, but I parried with the chair and stool.
The table rocked under him. I felt smothered: I could feel his breath
on me. He sat completely covering the top, and went on shooting his
paws in my direction. He would have scooped portions of me out for
his use, but fortunately I sat right in the centre, a hair's-breadth out
of his reach on any side. He made vicious sounds and wriggled over
my head. He could have knocked the chair to one side and dragged
me out if he had come down, but somehow the sight of the chair
seemed to worry him for a time. He preferred to be out of its reach.
This battle went on for a while, I cannot say how long: time had
come to a dead stop in my world. He jumped down and walked
about the table, looking for a gap; I rattled the chair a couple of
times, but very soon it lost all its terror for him; he patted the chair
and found that it was inoffensive. At this discovery he tried to hurl it

aside. But I was too quick for him. I swiftly drew it towards me and wedged it tight into the arch of the table, and the stool protected me on another side. I was more or less in a stockade made of the legs of furniture. He sat up on his haunches in front of me, wondering how best to get at me. Now the chair, table and stool had formed a solid block, with me at their heart, and they could withstand all his tricks. He scrutinized my arrangement with great interest, espied a gap and thrust his paw in. It dangled in my eyes with the curved claws opening out towards me. I felt very angry at the sight of it. Why should I allow the offensive to be developed all in his own way? I felt very indignant. The long knife from the station-master's table was lying nearby. I picked it up and drove it in. He withdrew his paw, maddened by pain. He jumped up and nearly brought down the room, and then tried to crack to bits the entire stockade. He did not succeed. He once again thrust his paw in. I employed the long knife to good purpose and cut off a digit with the claw on it. It was a fight to the finish between him and me. He returned again and again to the charge. And I cut out, let me confess, three claws, before I had done with him. I had become as bloodthirsty as he. (Those claws, mounted on gold, are hanging around the necks of my three daughters. You can come and see them if you like sometime.)

At about five in the morning the station-master and the porter arrived, and innocently walked in. The moment they stepped in the tiger left me and turned on them. They both ran at top speed. The station-master flew back to his house and shut the door. The porter on fleet foot went up a tree, with the tiger halfway up behind him. Thus they stopped, staring at each other till the goods train lumbered in after 5:30. It hissed and whistled and belched fire, till the tiger took himself down and bolted across the tracks into the jungle.

He did not visit these parts again, though one was constantly hearing of his ravages. I did not meet him again—till a few moments ago when I saw him riding in that bullock cart. I instantly recognized him by his right forepaw, where three toes and claws are missing. You seemed to be so much lost in admiration for those people who met the tiger at their own convenience, with gun and company, that I thought you might give a little credit to a fellow who has faced the same animal, alone, barehanded. Hence this narration.

When the Talkative Man left us, we moved on to the square, where they were keeping the trophy in view and hero-worshipping and feting the hunters, who were awaiting a lorry from the town. We pushed through the crowd, and begged to be shown the right forepaw of the tiger. Somebody lowered a gas lamp. Yes, three toes were missing, and a deep black scar marked the spot. The man who cut it off must have driven his knife with the power of a hammer. To a question, the hunters replied, "Can't say how it happens. We've met a few instances like this. It's said that some forest tribes, if they catch a tiger cub, cut off its claws for some talisman and let it go. They do not usually kill cubs."

ISWARAN

When the whole of the student world in Malgudi was convulsed with excitement, on a certain evening in June when the Intermediate Examination results were expected, Iswaran went about his business, looking very unconcerned and detached.

He had earned the reputation of having aged in the Intermediate Class. He entered the Intermediate Class in Albert Mission College as a youngster, with faint down on his upper lip. Now he was still there; his figure had grown brawny and athletic, and his chin had become tanned and leathery. Some people even said that you could see grey hairs on his head. The first time he failed, his parents sympathized with him, the second time also he managed to get their sympathies, but subsequently they grew more critical and unsparing, and after repeated failures they lost all interest in his examination. He was often told by his parents, "Why don't you discontinue your studies and try to do something useful?" He always pleaded, "Let me have this one last chance." He clung to university education with a ferocious devotion.

And now the whole town was agog with the expectation of the results in the evening. Boys moved about the street in groups; and on the sands of Sarayu they sat in clusters, nervously smiling and biting their fingernails. Others hung about the gates of the Senate House staring anxiously at the walls behind which a meeting was going on.

As much as the boys, if not more, the parents were agitated, except Iswaran's, who, when they heard their neighbours discussing their son's possible future results, remarked with a sigh, "No such worry for Iswaran. His results are famous and known to everyone in advance." Iswaran said facetiously, "I have perhaps passed this time, Father, who knows? I did study quite hard."

"You are the greatest optimist in India at the moment; but for this obstinate hope you would never have appeared for the same examination every year."

"I failed only in Logic, very narrowly, last year," he defended himself. At which the whole family laughed. "In any case, why don't you go and wait along with the other boys, and look up your results?" his mother asked. "Not at all necessary," Iswaran replied. "If I pass they will bring home the news. Do you think I saw my results last year? I spent my time in a cinema. I sat through two shows consecutively."

He hummed as he went in for a wash before dressing to go out. He combed his hair with deliberate care, the more so because he knew everybody looked on him as a sort of an outcast for failing so often. He knew that behind him the whole family and the town were laughing. He felt that they remarked among themselves that washing, combing his hair and putting on a well-ironed coat were luxuries too far above his state. He was a failure and had no right to such luxuries. He was treated as a sort of thick-skinned idiot. But he did not care. He answered their attitude by behaving like a desperado. He swung his arms, strode up and down, bragged and shouted, and went to a cinema. But all this was only a mask. Under it was a creature hopelessly seared by failure, desperately longing and praying for success. On the day of the results he was, inwardly, in a trembling suspense. "Mother," he said as he went out, "don't expect me for dinner tonight. I will eat something in a hotel and sit through both the shows at the Palace Talkies."

Emerging from Vinayak Street, he saw a group of boys moving up the Market Road towards the college. Someone asked: "Iswaran, coming up to see the results?"

"Yes, yes, presently. But now I have to be going on an urgent business."

"Where?"

"Palace Talkies." At this all the boys laughed. "You seem to know your results already. Do you?"

"I do. Otherwise do you think I would be celebrating it with a picture?"

"What is your number?"

"Seven-eight-five," he said, giving the first set of numbers that came to his head. The group passed on, joking, "We know you are going to get a first-class this time."

He sat in a far-off corner in the four-anna class. He looked about: not a single student in the whole theatre. All the students of the town were near the Senate House, waiting for their results. Iswaran felt very unhappy to be the only student in the whole theatre. Somehow fate seemed to have isolated him from his fellow-beings in every respect. He felt very depressed and unhappy. He felt an utter distaste for himself.

Soon the lights went out and the show started—a Tamil film with all the known gods in it. He soon lost himself in the politics and struggles of gods and goddesses; he sat rapt in the vision of a heavenly world which some film director had chosen to present. This felicity of forgetfulness lasted but half an hour. Soon the heroine of the story sat on a low branch of a tree in paradise and wouldn't move out of the place. She sat there singing a song for over half an hour. This portion tired Iswaran, and now there returned all the old pains and gloom. "Oh, lady," Iswaran appealed, "don't add to my troubles, please move on." As if she heard this appeal the lady moved off, and brighter things followed. A battle, a deluge, somebody dropping headlong from cloud-land, and somebody coming up from the bed of an ocean, a rain of fire, a rain of flowers, people dying, people rising from graves and so on. All kinds of thrills occurred on that white screen beyond the pall of tobacco smoke. The continuous babble on and off the screen, music and shouting, the cry of pedlars selling soda, the unrestrained comments of the spectators—all this din and commotion helped Iswaran to forget the Senate House and student life for a few hours.

The show ended at ten o'clock in the night. A crowd was waiting at the gate for the night show. Iswaran walked across to Ananda Bhavan—a restaurant opposite the Palace Talkies. The proprietor, a genial Bombay man, was a friend of his and cried, "Ishwar Sab, the results were announced today. What about yours?"

"I did not write any examination this year," Iswaran said.

"Why, why, I thought you paid your examination fees!"

Iswaran laughed. "You are right. I have passed my Intermediate just this evening."

"Ah, how very good. How clever you must be! If you pray to

Hanuman he will always bring you success. What are you going to do next?"

"I will go to a higher class, that is all," Iswaran said. He ordered a few tidbits and coffee and rose to go. As he paid his bill and walked out, the hotel proprietor said, "Don't leave me out when you are giving a dinner to celebrate your success."

Iswaran again purchased a ticket and went back to the picture. Once more all strifes and struggles and intrigues of gods were repeated before him. He was once again lost in it. When he saw on the screen some young men of his age singing as they sported in the waters of some distant heaven, he said, "Well might you do it, boys. I suppose you have no examination where you are. . . ." And he was seized with a longing to belong to that world.

Now the leading lady sat on the low branch of a tree and started singing, and Iswaran lost interest in the picture. He looked about for the first time. He noticed, in the semi-darkness, several groups of boys in the hall—happy groups. He knew that they must all have seen their results, and come now to celebrate their success. There were at least fifty. He knew that they must be a happy and gay lot, with their lips red from chewing betel leaves. He knew that all of them would focus their attention on him the moment the lights went up. They would all rag him about his results—all the old tedious joking over again, and all the tiresome pose of a desperado. He felt thoroughly sick of the whole business. He would not stand any more of it—the mirthful faces of these men of success and their leers. He was certain they would all look on him with the feeling that he had no business to seek the pleasure of a picture on that day.

He moved on to a more obscure corner of the hall. He looked at the screen, nothing there to cheer him: the leading lady was still there, and he knew she would certainly stay there for the next twenty minutes singing her masterpiece. . . . He was overcome with dejection. He rose, silently edged towards the exit and was out of the theatre in a moment. He felt a loathing for himself after seeing those successful boys. "I am not fit to live. A fellow who cannot pass an examination . . ." This idea developed in his mind—a glorious solution to all difficulties. Die and go to a world where there were young men free from examination who sported in lotus pools in paradise. No bothers, no disgusting Senate House wall to gaze on hopelessly, year after year. This solution suddenly brought him a feeling of relief. He felt lighter. He walked across to the hotel. The hotel man was about to rise and go to bed. "Saitji," Iswaran said, "please forgive my troubling you now. Give me a piece of paper and pencil. I have to note down something urgently." "So late as this," said the hotel man, and gave him a slip of paper and a pencil stub. Iswaran wrote down a message for his father, folded the slip and placed it carefully in the inner pocket of his coat.

He returned the pencil and stepped out of the hotel. He had only the stretch of the Race Course Road, and, turning to his right, half the Market Road to traverse, and then Ellaman Street, and then Sarayu. . . . Its dark swirling waters would close on him and end all his miseries. "I must leave this letter in my coat pocket and remember to leave my coat on the river step," he told himself.

He was soon out of Ellaman Street. His feet ploughed through the sands of the riverbank. He came to the river steps, removed his coat briskly and went down the steps. "O God," he muttered with folded hands, looking up at his stars. "If I can't pass an examination even with a tenth attempt, what is the use of my living and disgracing the world?" His feet were in water. He looked over his shoulder at the cluster of university buildings. There was a light burning on the porch of the Senate House. It was nearing midnight. It was a quarter of an hour's walk. Why not walk across and take a last look at the results board? In any case he was going to die, and why should he shirk and tremble before the board?

He came out of the water and went up the steps, leaving his coat behind, and he walked across the sand. Somewhere a time gong struck twelve, stars sparkled overhead, the river flowed on with a murmur and miscellaneous night sounds emanated from the bushes on the bank. A cold wind blew on his wet, sand-covered feet. He entered the Senate porch with a defiant heart. "I am in no fear of anything here," he muttered. The Senate House was deserted, not a sound anywhere. The whole building was in darkness, except the staircase landing, where a large bulb was burning. And noticeboards hung on the wall.

His heart palpitated as he stood tiptoe to scan the results. By the light of the bulb he scrutinized the numbers. His throat went dry. He looked through the numbers of people who had passed in third-

class. His own number was 501. The successful number before him
was 498, and after that 703. "So I have a few friends on either side,"
he said with a forced mirth. He had a wild hope as he approached the
Senate House that somehow his number would have found a place
in the list of successful candidates. He had speculated how he should
feel after that. . . . He would rush home and demand that they take
back all their comments with apologies. But now after he gazed at
the notice-board for quite a while, the grim reality of his failure
dawned on him: his number was nowhere. "The river . . ." he said.
He felt desolate, like a condemned man who had a sudden but false
promise of reprieve. "The river," Iswaran muttered. "I am going,"
he told the notice-board, and moved a few steps. "I haven't seen
how many have obtained honours." He looked at the notice-board
once again. He gazed at the top columns of the results. First-
classes—curiously enough a fellow with number one secured a first-
class, and six others. "Good fellows, wonder how they managed it!"
he said with admiration. His eyes travelled down to second-classes—
it was in two lines starting with 98. There were about fifteen. He
looked fixedly at each number before going on to the next. He came
to 350, after that 400, and after that 501 and then 600.

"Five-nought-one in second-class! Can it be true?" he shrieked.
He looked at the number again and again. Yes, there it was. He had
obtained a second-class. "If this is true I shall sit in the B.A. class
next month," he shouted. His voice rang through the silent building.
"I will flay alive anyone who calls me a fool hereafter. . . ." he
proclaimed. He felt slightly giddy. He leant against the wall. Years
of strain and suspense were suddenly relaxed; and he could hardly
bear the force of this release. Blood raced along his veins and heaved
and knocked under his skull. He steadied himself with an effort. He
softly hummed a tune to himself. He felt he was the sole occupant of
the world and its overlord. He thumped his chest and addressed the
notice-board: "Know who I am?" He stroked an imaginary moustache arrogantly, laughed to himself and asked, "Is the horse ready,
groom?" He threw a supercilious side glance at the notice-board and
strutted out like a king. He stood on the last step of the porch and
looked for his steed. He waited for a minute and commanded, "Fool,
bring the horse nearer. Do you hear?" The horse was brought
nearer. He made a movement as if mounting and whipped his horse

into a fury. His voice rang through the dark riverside, urging the horse on. He swung his arms and ran along the sands. He shouted at the top of his voice: "Keep off; the king is coming; whoever comes his way will be trampled. . . ."

"I have five hundred and one horses," he spoke to the night. The number stuck in his mind and kept coming up again and again. He ran the whole length of the riverbank up and down. Somehow this did not satisfy him. "Prime Minister," he said, "this horse is no good. Bring me the other five hundred and one horses, they are all in second-classes—" He gave a kick to the horse which he had been riding and drove it off. Very soon the Prime Minister brought him another horse. He mounted it with dignity and said, "This is better." Now he galloped about on his horse. It was a strange sight. In the dim starlight, alone at that hour, making a tap-tap with his tongue to imitate galloping hoofs. With one hand swinging and tugging the reins, and with the other stroking his moustache defiantly, he urged the horse on and on until it attained the speed of a storm. He felt like a conqueror as the air rushed about him. Soon he crossed the whole stretch of sand. He came to the water's edge, hesitated for a moment and whispered to his horse, "Are you afraid of water? You must swim across, otherwise I will never pay five-nought-one rupees for you." He felt the horse make a leap.

Next afternoon his body came up at a spot about a quarter of a mile down the course of the river. Meanwhile, some persons had already picked up the coat left on the step and discovered in the inner pocket the slip of paper with the inscription:

"My dear father: By the time you see this letter I shall be at the bottom of Sarayu. I don't want to live. Don't worry about me. You have other sons who are not such dunces as I am—"

SUCH PERFECTION

A sense of great relief filled Soma as he realized that his five years of labour were coming to an end. He had turned out scores of images in his lifetime, but he had never done any work to equal this. He often said to himself that long after the Deluge had swept the earth this Nataraja would still be standing on His pedestal.

No other human being had seen the image yet. Soma shut himself in and bolted all the doors and windows and plied his chisel by the still flame of a mud lamp, even when there was a bright sun outside. It made him perspire unbearably, but he did not mind it so long as it helped him to keep out prying eyes. He worked with a fierce concentration and never encouraged anyone to talk about it.

After all, his labours had come to an end. He sat back, wiped the perspiration off his face and surveyed his handiwork with great satisfaction. As he looked on he was overwhelmed by the majesty of this image. He fell prostrate before it, praying, "I have taken five years to make you. May you reside in our temple and bless all human beings!" The dim mud flame cast subtle shadows on the image and gave it an undertone of rippling life. The sculptor stood lost in this vision. A voice said, "My friend, never take this image out of this room. It is too perfect. . . ." Soma trembled with fear. He looked round. He saw a figure crouching in a dark corner of the room—it was a man. Soma dashed forward and clutched him by the throat. "Why did you come here?" The other writhed under the grip and replied, "Out of admiration for you. I have always loved your work. I have waited for five years. . . ."

"How did you come in?"

"With another key while you were eating inside. . . ."

Soma gnashed his teeth. "Shall I strangle you before this God and offer you as sacrifice?" "By all means," replied the other, "if it will help you in any way . . . but I doubt it. Even with a sacrifice you cannot take it out. It is too perfect. Such perfection is not for mortals." The sculptor wept. "Oh, do not say that. I worked in secrecy only for this perfection. It is for our people. It is a God coming into their midst. Don't deny them that." The other prostrated before the image and prayed aloud, "God give us the strength to bear your presence. . . ."

This man spoke to people and the great secret was out. A kind of dread seized the people of the village. On an auspicious day, Soma went to the temple priest and asked, "At the coming full moon my Nataraja must be consecrated. Have you made a place for him in the temple?" The priest answered, "Let me see the image first. . . ." He went over to the sculptor's house, gazed on the image and said, "This perfection, this God, is not for mortal eyes. He will blind us. At the first chant of prayer before him, he will dance . . . and we shall be wiped out. . . ." The sculptor looked so unhappy that the priest added, "Take your chisel and break a little toe or some other part of the image, and it will be safe. . . ." The sculptor replied that he would sooner crack the skull of his visitor. The leading citizens of the village came over and said, "Don't mistake us. We cannot give your image a place in our temple. Don't be angry with us. We have to think of the safety of all the people in the village. . . . Even now if you are prepared to break a small finger . . ."

"Get out, all of you," Soma shouted. "I don't care to bring this Nataraja to your temple. I will make a temple for him where he is. You will see that it becomes the greatest temple on earth. . . ." Next day he pulled down a portion of the wall of the room and constructed a large doorway opening on the street. He called Rama, the tom-tom beater, and said, "I will give you a silver coin for your trouble. Go and proclaim in all nearby villages that this Nataraja will be consecrated at the full moon. If a large crowd turns up, I will present you with a lace shawl."

At the full moon, men, women and children poured in from the surrounding villages. There was hardly an inch of space vacant anywhere. The streets were crammed with people. Vendors of sweets and toys and flowers shouted their wares, moving about in the crowd. Pipers and drummers, groups of persons chanting hymns,

children shouting in joy, men greeting each other—all this created a
mighty din. Fragrance of flowers and incense hung over the place.
Presiding over all this there was the brightest moon that ever shone
on earth.

The screen which had covered the image parted. A great flame of
camphor was waved in front of the image, and bronze bells rang. A
silence fell upon the crowd. Every eye was fixed upon the image. In
the flame of the circling camphor Nataraja's eyes lit up. His limbs
moved, his anklets jingled. The crowd was awe-stricken. The God
pressed one foot on earth and raised the other in dance. He destroyed the universe under his heel, and smeared the ashes over his
body, and the same God rattled the drum in his hand and by its
rhythm set life in motion again. . . . Creation, Dissolution and God
attained a meaning now; this image brought it out . . . the bells rang
louder every second. The crowd stood stunned by this vision vouchsafed to them.

At this moment a wind blew from the east. The moon's disc
gradually dimmed. The wind gathered force, clouds blotted out the
moon; people looked up and saw only pitchlike darkness above.
Lightning flashed, thunder roared and fire poured down from the
sky. It was a thunderbolt striking a haystack and setting it ablaze. Its
glare illuminated the whole village. People ran about in panic,
searching for shelter. The population of ten villages crammed in that
village. Another thunderbolt hit a house. Women and children
shrieked and wailed. The fires descended with a tremendous hiss as a
mighty rain came down. It rained as it had never rained before. The
two lakes, over which the village road ran, filled, swelled and joined
over the road. Water flowed along the streets. The wind screamed
and shook the trees and the homes. "This is the end of the world!"
wailed the people through the storm.

The whole of the next day it was still drizzling. Soma sat before
the image, with his head bowed in thought. Trays and flowers and
offerings lay scattered under the image, dampened by rain. Some of
his friends came wading in water, stood before him and asked, "Are
you satisfied?" They stood over him like executioners and repeated
the question and added, "Do you want to know how many lives have
been lost, how many homes washed out and how many were
crushed by the storm?"

"No, no, I don't want to know anything," Soma replied. "Go away. Don't stand here and talk."

"God has shown us only a slight sign of his power. Don't tempt Him again. Do something. Our lives are in your hands. Save us, the image is too perfect."

After they were gone he sat for hours in the same position, ruminating. Their words still troubled him. "Our lives are in your hands." He knew what they meant. Tears gathered in his eyes. "How can I mutilate this image? Let the whole world burn, I don't care. I can't touch this image." He lit a lamp before the God and sat watching. Far off the sky rumbled. "It is starting again. Poor human beings, they will all perish this time." He looked at the toe of the image. "Just one neat stroke with the chisel, and all troubles will end." He watched the toe, his hands trembled. "How can I?" Outside, the wind began to howl. People were gathering in front of his house and were appealing to him for help.

Soma prostrated before the God and went out. He stood looking at the road over which the two lakes had joined. Over the eastern horizon a dark mass of cloud was rolling up. "When that cloud comes over, it will wash out the world. Nataraja! I cannot mutilate your figure, but I can offer myself as a sacrifice if it will be any use. . . ." He shut his eyes and decided to jump into the lake. He checked himself. "I must take a last look at the God before I die." He battled his way through the oncoming storm. The wind shrieked. Trees shook and trembled. Men and cattle ran about in panic.

He was back just in time to see a tree crash on the roof of his house. "My home," he cried, and ran in. He picked up his Nataraja from amidst splintered tiles and rafters. The image was unhurt except for a little toe which was found a couple of yards off, severed by a falling splinter.

"God himself has done this to save us!" people cried.

The image was installed with due ceremonies at the temple on the next full moon. Wealth and honours were showered on Soma. He lived to be ninety-five, but he never touched his mallet and chisel again.

FATHER'S HELP

Lying in bed, Swami realized with a shudder that it was Monday morning. It looked as though only a moment ago it had been the last period on Friday; already Monday was here. He hoped that an earthquake would reduce the school building to dust, but that good building—Albert Mission School—had withstood similar prayers for over a hundred years now. At nine o'clock Swaminathan wailed, "I have a headache." His mother said, "Why don't you go to school in a *jutka*?"

"So that I may be completely dead at the other end? Have you any idea what it means to be jolted in a *jutka*?"

"Have you many important lessons today?"

"Important! Bah! That geography teacher has been teaching the same lesson for over a year now. And we have arithmetic, which means for a whole period we are going to be beaten by the teacher. . . . Important lessons!"

And Mother generously suggested that Swami might stay at home.

At 9:30, when he ought to have been shouting in the school prayer hall, Swami was lying on the bench in Mother's room. Father asked him, "Have you no school today?"

"Headache," Swami replied.

"Nonsense! Dress up and go."

"Headache."

"Loaf about less on Sundays and you will be without a headache on Monday."

Swami knew how stubborn his father could be and changed his tactics. "I can't go so late to the class."

"I agree, but you'll have to; it is your own fault. You should have asked me before deciding to stay away."

"What will the teacher think if I go so late?"

"Tell him you had a headache and so are late."

"He will beat me if I say so."

"Will he? Let us see. What is his name?"

"Samuel."

"Does he beat the boys?"

"He is very violent, especially with boys who come late. Some days ago a boy was made to stay on his knees for a whole period in a corner of the class because he came late, and that after getting six cuts from the cane and having his ears twisted. I wouldn't like to go late to Samuel's class."

"If he is so violent, why not tell your headmaster about it?"

"They say that even the headmaster is afraid of him. He is such a violent man."

And then Swami gave a lurid account of Samuel's violence; how when he started caning he would not stop till he saw blood on the boy's hand, which he made the boy press to his forehead like a vermilion marking. Swami hoped that with this his father would be made to see that he couldn't go to his class late. But Father's behaviour took an unexpected turn. He became excited. "What do these swine mean by beating our children? They must be driven out of service. I will see . . ."

The result was he proposed to send Swami late to his class as a kind of challenge. He was also going to send a letter with Swami to the headmaster. No amount of protest from Swami was of any avail: Swami had to go to school.

By the time he was ready Father had composed a long letter to the headmaster, put it in an envelope and sealed it.

"What have you written, Father?" Swaminathan asked apprehensively.

"Nothing for you. Give it to your headmaster and go to your class."

"Have you written anything about our teacher Samuel?"

"Plenty of things about him. When your headmaster reads it he will probably dismiss Samuel from the school and hand him over to the police."

"What has he done, Father?"

"Well, there is a full account of everything he has done in the letter. Give it to your headmaster and go to your class. You must bring an acknowledgement from him in the evening."

Swami went to school feeling that he was the worst perjurer on earth. His conscience bothered him: he wasn't at all sure if he had been accurate in his description of Samuel. He could not decide how much of what he had said was imagined and how much of it was real. He stopped for a moment on the roadside to make up his mind about Samuel: he was not such a bad man after all. Personally he was much more genial than the rest; often he cracked a joke or two centring around Swami's inactions, and Swami took it as a mark of Samuel's personal regard for him. But there was no doubt that he treated people badly. . . . His cane skinned people's hands. Swami cast his mind about for an instance of this. There was none within his knowledge. Years and years ago he was reputed to have skinned the knuckles of a boy in First Standard and made him smear the blood on his face. No one had actually seen it. But year after year the story persisted among the boys. . . . Swami's head was dizzy with confusion in regard to Samuel's character—whether he was good or bad, whether he deserved the allegations in the letter or not. . . . Swami felt an impulse to run home and beg his father to take back the letter. But Father was an obstinate man.

As he approached the yellow building he realized that he was perjuring himself and was ruining his teacher. Probably the headmaster would dismiss Samuel and then the police would chain him and put him in jail. For all this disgrace, humiliation and suffering who would be responsible? Swami shuddered. The more he thought of Samuel, the more he grieved for him—the dark face, his small red-streaked eyes, his thin line of moustache, his unshaven cheek and chin, his yellow coat; everything filled Swami with sorrow. As he felt the bulge of the letter in his pocket, he felt like an executioner. For a moment he was angry with his father and wondered why he should not fling into the gutter the letter of a man so unreasonable and stubborn.

As he entered the school gate an idea occurred to him, a sort of solution. He wouldn't deliver the letter to the headmaster immediately, but at the end of the day—to that extent he would disobey his father and exercise his independence. There was nothing wrong in it, and Father would not know it anyway. If the letter was given at the end of the day there was a chance that Samuel might do something to justify the letter.

Swami stood at the entrance to his class. Samuel was teaching arithmetic. He looked at Swami for a moment. Swami stood hoping that Samuel would fall on him and tear his skin off. But Samuel merely asked, "Are you just coming to the class?"

"Yes, sir."

"You are half an hour late."

"I know it." Swami hoped that he would be attacked now. He almost prayed: "God of Thirupathi, please make Samuel beat me."

"Why are you late?"

Swami wanted to reply, "Just to see what you can do." But he merely said, "I have a headache, sir."

"Then why did you come to the school at all?"

A most unexpected question from Samuel. "My father said that I shouldn't miss the class, sir," said Swami.

This seemed to impress Samuel. "Your father is quite right; a very sensible man. We want more parents like him."

"Oh, you poor worm!" Swami thought. "You don't know what my father has done to you." He was more puzzled than ever about Samuel's character.

"All right, go to your seat. Have you still a headache?"

"Slightly, sir."

Swami went to his seat with a bleeding heart. He had never met a man so good as Samuel. The teacher was inspecting the home lessons, which usually produced (at least, according to Swami's impression) scenes of great violence. Notebooks would be flung at faces, boys would be abused, caned and made to stand up on benches. But today Samuel appeared to have developed more tolerance and gentleness. He pushed away the bad books, just touched people with the cane, never made anyone stand up for more than a few minutes. Swami's turn came. He almost thanked God for the chance.

"Swaminathan, where is your homework?"

"I have not done any homework, sir," he said blandly.

There was a pause.

"Why—headache?" asked Samuel.

"Yes, sir."

"All right, sit down." Swami sat down, wondering what had come over Samuel. The period came to an end, and Swami felt desolate. The last period for the day was again taken by Samuel. He came this time to teach them Indian history. The period began at 3:45 and ended at 4:30. Swaminathan had sat through the previous periods thinking acutely. He could not devise any means of provoking Samuel. When the clock struck four Swami felt desperate. Half an hour more. Samuel was reading the red text, the portion describing Vasco da Gama's arrival in India. The boys listened in half-languor. Swami suddenly asked at the top of his voice, "Why did not Columbus come to India, sir?"

"He lost his way."

"I can't believe it; it is unbelievable, sir."

"Why?"

"Such a great man. Would he have not known the way?"

"Don't shout. I can hear you quite well."

"I am not shouting, sir; this is my ordinary voice, which God has given me. How can I help it?"

"Shut up and sit down."

Swaminathan sat down, feeling slightly happy at his success. The teacher threw a puzzled, suspicious glance at him and resumed his lessons.

His next chance occurred when Sankar of the first bench got up and asked, "Sir, was Vasco da Gama the very first person to come to India?"

Before the teacher could answer, Swami shouted from the back bench, "That's what they say."

The teacher and all the boys looked at Swami. The teacher was puzzled by Swami's obtrusive behaviour today. "Swaminathan, you are shouting again."

"I am not shouting, sir. How can I help my voice, given by God?" The school clock struck a quarter-hour. A quarter more. Swami felt he must do something drastic in fifteen minutes. Samuel had no doubt scowled at him and snubbed him, but it was hardly adequate. Swami felt that with a little more effort Samuel could be made to deserve dismissal and imprisonment.

The teacher came to the end of a section in the textbook and stopped. He proposed to spend the remaining few minutes putting questions to the boys. He ordered the whole class to put away their books, and asked someone in the second row, "What is the date of Vasco da Gama's arrival in India?"

Swaminathan shot up and screeched, "1648, December 20."

"You needn't shout," said the teacher. He asked, "Has your headache made you mad?"

"I have no headache now, sir," replied the thunderer brightly.

"Sit down, you idiot." Swami thrilled at being called an idiot. "If you get up again I will cane you," said the teacher. Swami sat down, feeling happy at the promise. The teacher then asked, "I am going to put a few questions on the Mughal period. Among the Mughal emperors, whom would you call the greatest, whom the strongest and whom the most religious emperor?"

Swami got up. As soon as he was seen, the teacher said emphatically, "Sit down."

"I want to answer, sir."

"Sit down."

"No, sir; I want to answer."

"What did I say I'd do if you got up again?"

"You said you would cane me and peel the skin off my knuckles and make me press it on my forehead."

"All right; come here."

Swaminathan left his seat joyfully and hopped on the platform. The teacher took out his cane from the drawer and shouted angrily, "Open your hand, you little devil." He whacked three wholesome cuts on each palm. Swami received them without blenching. After half a dozen the teacher asked, "Will these do, or do you want some more?"

Swami merely held out his hand again, and received two more; and the bell rang. Swami jumped down from the platform with a light heart, though his hands were smarting. He picked up his books, took out the letter lying in his pocket and ran to the headmaster's room. He found the door locked.

He asked the peon, "Where is the headmaster?"

"Why do you want him?"

"My father has sent a letter for him."

"He has taken the afternoon off and won't come back for a week.

You can give the letter to the assistant headmaster. He will be here now."

"Who is he?"

"Your teacher, Samuel. He will be here in a second."

Swaminathan fled from the place. As soon as Swami went home with the letter, Father remarked, "I knew you wouldn't deliver it, you coward."

"I swear our headmaster is on leave," Swaminathan began.

Father replied, "Don't lie in addition to being a coward. . . ."

Swami held up the envelope and said, "I will give this to the headmaster as soon as he is back. . . ." Father snatched it from his hand, tore it up and thrust it into the wastepaper basket under his table. He muttered, "Don't come to me for help even if Samuel throttles you. You deserve your Samuel."

THE SNAKE-SONG

We were coming out of the music hall quite pleased with the concert. We thought it a very fine performance. We thought so till we noticed the Talkative Man in our midst. He looked as though he had been in a torture chamber. We looked at him sourly and remarked, "We suppose you are one of those great men who believe that South Indian music died one hundred years ago. Or were you at any time hobnobbing with all our ancient musicians and composers, the only reason many persons like you have for thinking that all modern singing is childish and inane? Or are you one of those restless theorists who can never hear a song without splitting it into atoms?"

"None of these," answered the Talkative Man. "I am just a simple creature who knows what he is talking about. I know something of music, perhaps just a little more than anyone else here, and that is why I am horrified to see the level to which taste has sunk. . . ."

We tried to snub him by receiving his remarks in cold silence and talking among ourselves. But he followed us all the way, chatting, and we had to listen to him.

Seeing me now (said the Talkative Man), perhaps you think I am capable of doing nothing more artistic than selling chemical fertilizers to peasants. But I tell you I was at one time ambitious of becoming a musician. I came near being one. It was years and years ago. I was living at the time in Kumbum, a small village eighty miles from Malgudi. A master musician lived there. When he played on the flute, it was said, the cattle of the village followed him about. He was perhaps the greatest artist of the century, but quite content to live in obscurity, hardly known to anyone outside the village, giving concerts only in the village temple and absolutely satisfied with the small income he derived from his ancestral lands. I washed his clothes, swept his house, ran errands for him, wrote his accounts, and when he felt like it, he taught me music. His personality and presence had a value all their own, so that even if he taught only for an hour it was worth a year's tuition under anyone else. The very atmosphere around him educated one.

After three years of chipping and planing, my master felt that my music was after all taking some shape. He said, "In another year, perhaps, you may go to the town and play before a public, that is, if you care for such things." You may be sure I cared. Not for me the greatness of obscurity. I wanted wealth and renown. I dreamt of going to Madras and attending the music festival next year, and then all the districts would ring with my name. I looked on my bamboo flute as a sort of magic wand which was going to open out a new world to me.

I lived in a small cottage at the end of the street. It was my habit to sit up and practise far into the night. One night as I was just losing myself in *bhairavi raga*, there came a knock on the door. I felt irritated at the interruption.

"Who is there?" I asked.

"A *sadhu*; he wants a mouthful of food."

"At this hour! Go, go. Don't come and pester people at all hours."

"But hunger knows no time."

"Go away. I have nothing here. I myself live on my master's charity."

"But can't you give a small coin or at least a kind word to a *sadhu*? He has seen Kasi, Rameswaram . . ."

"Shut up," I cried, glared at the door and resumed my *bhairavi*.

Fifteen minutes later the knocks were repeated. I lost my temper. "Have you no sense? Why do you disturb me?"

"You play divinely. Won't you let me in? You may not give me food for my stomach, but don't deny me your music."

I didn't like anyone to be present when I practised, and this constant interruption was exasperating. "Don't stand there and argue. If you don't go at once, I will open the door and push you out."

"Ah, bad words. You needn't push me out. I am going. But remember, this is your last day of music. Tomorrow you may exchange your flute for a handful of dried dates."

I heard his wooden clogs going down the house steps. I felt relieved and played for about ten minutes. But my mind was troubled. His parting words . . . what did he mean by them? I got up, took the lantern from its nail on the wall and went out. I stood on the last step of my cottage and looked up and down the dark street, holding up the lantern. I turned in. Vaguely hoping that he might call again, I left the door half-open. I hung up the lantern and sat down. I looked at the pictures of gods on the wall and prayed to be protected from the threat of the unseen mendicant. And then I was lost in music once again.

Song after song flowed from that tiny bamboo and transformed my lonely cottage. I was no longer a petty mortal blowing through a piece of bamboo. I was among the gods. The lantern on the wall became a brilliant star illuminating a celestial hall. . . . And I came to the snake-song in *punnaga varali*. I saw the serpent in all its majesty: the very venom in its pouch had a touch of glory: now I saw its divinity as it crowned Shiva's head: Parvathi wore it as a wristlet: Subramanya played with it: and it was Vishnu's couch. . . . The whole composition imparted to the serpent a quality which inspired awe and reverence.

And now what should I see between the door and me but a black cobra! It had opened its immense hood and was swaying ecstatically. I stopped my song and rubbed my eyes to see if I was fully awake. But the moment the song ceased, the cobra turned and threw a glance at me, and moved forward. I have never seen such a black cobra and such a long one in my life. Some saving instinct told me: "Play on! Play on! Don't stop." I hurriedly took the flute to my lips and continued the song. The snake, which was now less than three yards from me, lifted a quarter of its body, with a gentle flourish reared its head, fixed its round eyes on me and listened to the music without making the slightest movement. It might have been a carven snake in black stone, so still it was.

And as I played with my eyes fixed on the snake I was so much impressed with its dignity and authority that I said to myself, "Which God would forgo the privilege of wearing this in His hair? . . ." After playing the song thrice over, I commenced a new song. The cobra sharply turned its head and looked at me as if to say,

"Now what is all this?" and let out a terrible hiss, and made a slight movement. I quickly resumed the snake-song, and it assumed once again its carven posture.

So I played he song again and again. But however great a composition might be, a dozen repetitions of it was bound to prove tiresome. I attempted to change the song once or twice, but I saw the snake stir menacingly. I vainly tried to get up and dash out, but the snake nearly stood up on its tail and promised to finish me. And so I played the same song all night. My distinguished audience showed no sign of leaving. By and by I felt exhausted. My head swam, my cheeks ached from continuous blowing and my chest seemed to be emptied of the last wisp of breath. I knew I was going to drop dead in a few seconds. It didn't seem to matter very much if the snake was going to crush me in its coils and fill me with all the venom in its sac. I flung down the flute, got up and prostrated before it, crying, "Oh, Naga Raja, you are a god; you can kill me if you like, but I can play no more. . . ."

When I opened my eyes again the snake was gone. The lantern on the wall had turned pale in the morning light. My flute lay near the doorway.

Next day I narrated my experiences to my master. He said, "Don't you know you ought not to play *punnaga varali* at night? That apart, now you can never be sure you will not get the snake in again if you play. And when he comes he won't spare you unless you sing his song over again. Are you prepared to do it?"

"No, no, a thousand times no," I cried. The memory of the song was galling. I had repeated it enough to last me a lifetime.

"If it is so, throw away your flute and forget your music. You can't play with a serpent. It is a plaything of gods. Throw away your bamboo. It is of no use to you anymore. . . ." I wept at the thought of this renunciation. My master pitied me and said, "Perhaps all will be well again if you seek your visitor of that night and beg his forgiveness. Can you find him?"

I put away my flute. I have ever since been searching for an unknown, unseen mendicant, in this world. Even today, if by God's grace I meet him, I will fall at his feet, beg his forgiveness and take up my flute again.

ENGINE TROUBLE

There came down to our town some years ago (said the Talkative Man) a showman owning an institution called the Gaiety Land. Overnight our Gymkhana Grounds became resplendent with banners and streamers and coloured lamps. From all over the district crowds poured into the show. Within a week of opening, in gate money alone they collected nearly five hundred rupees a day. Gaiety Land provided us with all sorts of fun and gambling and sideshows. For a couple of annas in each booth we could watch anything from performing parrots to crack motorcyclists looping the loop in the Dome of Death. In addition to this there were lotteries and shooting galleries where for an anna you always stood a chance of winning a hundred rupees.

There was a particular corner of the show which was in great favour. Here for a ticket costing eight annas you stood a chance of acquiring a variety of articles—pincushions, sewing machines, cameras or even a road engine. On one evening they drew ticket number 1005, and I happened to own the other half of the ticket. Glancing down the list of articles, they declared that I became the owner of the road engine! Don't ask me how a road engine came to be included among the prizes. It is more than I can tell you.

I looked stunned. People gathered round and gazed at me as if I were some curious animal. "Fancy anyone becoming the owner of a road engine!" some persons muttered, and giggled.

It was not the sort of prize one could carry home at short notice. I asked the showman if he would help me to transport it. He merely pointed at a notice which decreed that all winners should remove the prizes immediately on drawing and by their own effort. However, they had to make an exception in my case. They agreed to keep the engine on the Gymkhana Grounds till the end of their season, and then I would have to make my own arrangements to take it out. When I asked the showman if he could find me a driver he just smiled. "The fellow who brought it here had to be paid a hundred rupees for the job and five rupees a day. I sent him away and made up my mind that if no one was going to draw it, I would just leave it to its fate. I got it down just as a novelty for the show. God! What a bother it has proved!"

"Can't I sell it to some municipality?" I asked innocently. He burst into a laugh. "As a showman I have enough troubles with municipal people. I would rather keep out of their way. . . ."

My friends and well-wishers poured in to congratulate me on my latest acquisition. No one knew precisely how much a road engine would fetch; all the same they felt that there was a lot of money in it. "Even if you sell it as scrap iron you can make a few thousands," some of my friends declared. Every day I made a trip to the Gymkhana Grounds to have a look at my engine. I grew very fond of it. I loved its shining brass parts. I stood near it and patted it affectionately, hovered about it and returned home every day only at the close of the show. I was a poor man. I thought that, after all, my troubles were coming to an end. How ignorant we are! How little did I guess that my troubles had just begun.

When the showman took down his booths and packed up, I received a notice from the municipality to attend to my road engine. When I went there next day it looked forlorn with no one about. The ground was littered with torn streamers and paper decorations. The showman had moved on, leaving the engine where it stood. It was perfectly safe anywhere!

I left it alone for a few days, not knowing what to do with it. I received a notice from the municipality ordering that the engine be removed at once from the grounds, as otherwise they would charge rent for the occupation of the Gymkhana Grounds. After deep thought I consented to pay the rent, and I paid ten rupees a month for the next three months. Dear sirs, I was a poor man. Even the house which I and my wife occupied cost me only four rupees a month. And fancy my paying ten rupees a month for the road engine. It cut into my slender budget, and I had to pledge a jewel or two belonging to my wife! And every day my wife was asking me what I proposed to do with this terrible property of mine and I had no answer to give her. I went up and down the town offering it for sale to all and sundry. Someone suggested that the secretary of the local Cosmopolitan Club might be interested in it. When I approached him he laughed and asked what he could do with a road engine. "I'll dispose of it at a concession for you. You have a tennis court to be rolled every morning," I began, and even before I saw him smile I knew it was a stupid thing to say. Next someone suggested, "See the Municipal Chairman. He may buy it for the municipality." With great trepidation I went to the municipal office one day. I buttoned up my coat as I entered the chairman's room and mentioned my business. I was prepared to give away the engine at a great concession. I started a great harangue on municipal duties, the regime of this chairman and the importance of owning a road roller—but before I was done with him I knew there was greater chance of my selling it to some child on the roadside for playing with.

I was making myself a bankrupt maintaining this engine in the Gymkhana Grounds. I really hoped someday there would come my way a lump sum to make amends for all this deficit and suffering. Fresh complications arose when a cattle show came in the offing. It was to be held on the grounds. I was given twenty-four hours to get the thing out of the grounds. The show was opening in a week and the advance party was arriving and insisted upon having the engine out of the way. I became desperate; there was not a single person for fifty miles around who knew anything about a road engine. I begged every passing bus-driver to help me; but without use. I even approached the station-master to put in a word with the mail engine-driver. But the engine-driver pointed out that he had his own locomotive to mind and couldn't think of jumping off at a wayside station for anybody's sake. Meanwhile, the municipality was pressing me to clear out. I thought it over. I saw the priest of the local temple and managed to gain his sympathy. He offered me the services of his temple elephant. I also engaged fifty coolies to push the engine from behind. You may be sure this drained all my resources. The coolies wanted eight annas per head, and the temple elephant cost me seven rupees a day and I had to give it one feed. My plan was to take the engine out of the Gymkhana and then down the road to a field half a furlong off. The field was owned by a friend. He would not mind if I kept the engine there for a couple of months, when I could go to Madras and find a customer for it.

I also took into service one Joseph, a dismissed bus-driver who said that although he knew nothing of road rollers he could nevertheless steer one if it was somehow kept in motion.

It was a fine sight: the temple elephant yoked to the engine by means of stout ropes, with fifty determined men pushing it from behind, and my friend Joseph sitting in the driving seat. A huge crowd stood around and watched in great glee. The engine began to move. It seemed to me the greatest moment in my life. When it came out of the Gymkhana and reached the road, it began to behave in a strange manner. Instead of going straight down the road it showed a tendency to wobble and move zigzag. The elephant dragged it one way, Joseph turned the wheel for all he was worth without any idea of where he was going, and fifty men behind it clung to it in every possible manner and pushed it just where they liked. As a result of all this confused dragging, the engine ran straight into the opposite compound wall and reduced a good length of it to powder. At this the crowd let out a joyous yell. The elephant, disliking the behaviour of the crowd, trumpeted loudly, strained and snapped its ropes and kicked down a further length of the wall. The fifty men fled in panic, the crowd created a pandemonium. Someone slapped me in the face—it was the owner of the compound wall. The police came on the scene and marched me off.

When I was released from the lockup I found the following consequences awaiting me: (1) several yards of compound wall to be built by me; (2) wages of fifty men who ran away (they would not explain how they were entitled to the wages when they had not done their job); (3) Joseph's fee for steering the engine over the wall; (4) cost of medicine for treating the knee of the temple elephant, which had received some injuries while kicking down the wall (here again the temple authorities would not listen when I pointed out that I didn't engage an elephant to break a wall); (5) last, but not least, the demand to move the engine out of its present station.

Sirs, I was a poor man. I really could not find any means of paying these bills. When I went home my wife asked, "What is this I hear about you everywhere?" I took the opportunity to explain my difficulties. She took it as a hint that I was again asking for her jewels, and she lost her temper and cried that she would write to her father to come and take her away.

I was at my wits' end. People smiled at me when they met me in the streets. I was seriously wondering why I should not run away to my village. I decided to encourage my wife to write to her father and arrange for her exit. Not a soul was going to know what my plans were. I was going to put off my creditors and disappear one fine night.

At this point came unexpected relief in the shape of a Swamiji. One fine evening under the distinguished patronage of our Municipal Chairman a show was held in our small town hall. It was a free performance and the hall was packed with people. I sat in the gallery. Spellbound we witnessed the Swamiji's yogic feats. He bit off glass tumblers and ate them with contentment; he lay on spike boards; gargled and drank all kinds of acids; licked white-hot iron rods; chewed and swallowed sharp nails; stopped his heartbeat and buried himself underground. We sat there and watched him in stupefaction. At the end of it all he got up and delivered a speech in which he declared that he was carrying on his master's message to the people in this manner. His performance was the more remarkable because he had nothing to gain by all this extraordinary meal except the satisfaction of serving humanity, and now he said he was coming to the very masterpiece and the last act. He looked at the Municipal Chairman and asked, "Have you a road engine? I would like to have it driven over my chest." The chairman looked abashed and felt ashamed to acknowledge that he had none. The Swamiji insisted, "I *must* have a road engine."

The Municipal Chairman tried to put him off by saying, "There is no driver." The Swamiji replied, "Don't worry about it. My assistant has been trained to handle any kind of road engine." At this point I stood up in the gallery and shouted, "Don't ask him for an engine. Ask me." In a moment I was on the stage and became as important a person as the fire-eater himself. I was pleased with the recognition I now received from all quarters. The Municipal Chairman went into the background.

In return for lending him the engine he would drive it where I wanted. Though I felt inclined to ask for a money contribution I knew it would be useless to expect it from one who was doing missionary work.

Soon the whole gathering was at the compound wall opposite the Gymkhana. Swamiji's assistant was an expert in handling engines. In a short while my engine stood steaming up proudly. It was a gratifying sight. The Swamiji called for two pillows, placed one near his head and the other at his feet. He gave detailed instructions as to how the engine should be run over him. He made a chalk mark on his chest and said, "It must go exactly on this; not an inch this way or that." The engine hissed and waited. The crowd watching the show became suddenly unhappy and morose. This seemed to be a terrible thing to be doing. The Swami lay down on the pillows and said, "When I say *Om*, drive it on." He closed his eyes. The crowd watched tensely. I looked at the whole show in absolute rapture— after all, the road engine was going to get on the move.

At this point a police inspector came into the crowd with a brown envelope in his hand. He held up his hand, beckoned to the Swamiji's assistant and said, "I am sorry, I have to tell you that you can't go on with this. The magistrate has issued an order prohibiting the engine from running over him." The Swamiji picked himself up. There was a lot of commotion. The Swamiji became indignant. "I have done it in hundreds of places already and nobody questioned me about it. Nobody can stop me from doing what I like—it's my master's order to demonstrate the power of the Yoga to the people of this country, and who can question me?"

"A magistrate can," said the police inspector, and held up the order. "What business is it of yours or his to interfere in this manner?" "I don't know all that; this is his order. He permits you to do everything except swallow potassium cyanide and run this engine over your chest. You are free to do whatever you like outside our jurisdiction."

"I am leaving this cursed place this very minute," the Swamiji said in great rage, and started to go, followed by his assistant. I gripped his assistant's arm and said, "You have steamed it up. Why not take it over to that field and then go." He glared at me, shook off my hand and muttered, "With my guru so unhappy, how dare you ask me to drive?" He went away. I muttered, "You can't drive it except over his chest, I suppose?"

I made preparations to leave the town in a couple of days, leaving the engine to its fate, with all its commitments. However, nature came to my rescue in an unexpected manner. You may have heard of the earthquake of that year which destroyed whole towns in North India. There was a reverberation of it in our town, too. We were thrown out of our beds that night, and doors and windows rattled.

Next morning I went over to take a last look at my engine before leaving the town. I could hardly believe my eyes. The engine was not there. I looked about and raised a hue and cry. Search parties went round. The engine was found in a disused well nearby, with its back up. I prayed to heaven to save me from fresh complications. But the owner of the house, when he came round and saw what had happened, laughed heartily and beamed at me. "You have done me a service. It was the dirtiest water on earth in that well and the municipality was sending notice to close it, week after week. I was dreading the cost of closing, but your engine fits it like a cork. Just leave it there."

"But, but . . ."

"There are no buts. I will withdraw all complaints and charges against you, and build that broken wall myself, but only leave the thing there."

"That's hardly enough." I mentioned a few other expenses that this engine had brought on me. He agreed to pay for all that.

When I again passed that way some months later I peeped over the wall. I found the mouth of the well neatly cemented up. I heaved a sigh of great relief.

FORTY-FIVE A MONTH

Shanta could not stay in her class any longer. She had done clay-modelling, music, drill, a bit of alphabets and numbers, and was now cutting coloured paper. She would have to cut till the bell rang and the teacher said, "Now you may all go home," or "Put away the scissors and take up your alphabets—" Shanta was impatient to know the time. She asked her friend sitting next to her, "Is it five now?"

"Maybe," she replied.

"Or is it six?"

"I don't think so," her friend replied, "because night comes at six."

"Do you think it is five?"

"Yes."

"Oh, I must go. My father will be back at home now. He has asked me to be ready at five. He is taking me to the cinema this evening. I must go home." She threw down her scissors and ran up to the teacher. "Madam, I must go home."

"Why, Shanta Bai?"

"Because it is five o'clock now."

"Who told you it was five?"

"Kamala."

"It is not five now. It is—do you see the clock there? Tell me what the time is. I taught you to read the clock the other day." Shanta stood gazing at the clock in the hall, counted the figures laboriously and declared, "It is nine o'clock."

The teacher called the other girls and said, "Who will tell me the time from that clock?" Several of them concurred with Shanta and said it was nine o'clock, till the teacher said, "You are seeing only the long hand. See the short one, where is it?"

"Two and a half."

"So what is the time?"

"Two and a half."

"It is two forty-five, understand? Now you may all go to your seats—" Shanta returned to the teacher in about ten minutes and asked, "Is it five, madam, because I have to be ready at five. Otherwise my father will be very angry with me. He asked me to return home early."

"At what time?"

"Now." The teacher gave her permission to leave, and Shanta picked up her books and dashed out of the class with a cry of joy. She ran home, threw her books on the floor and shouted, "Mother, Mother," and Mother came running from the next house, where she had gone to chat with her friends.

Mother asked, "Why are you back so early?"

"Has Father come home?" Shanta asked. She would not take her coffee or tiffin but insisted on being dressed first. She opened the trunk and insisted on wearing the thinnest frock and knickers, while her mother wanted to dress her in a long skirt and thick coat for the evening. Shanta picked out a gorgeous ribbon from a cardboard soap box in which she kept pencils, ribbons and chalk bits. There was a heated argument between mother and daughter over the dress, and finally mother had to give in. Shanta put on her favourite pink frock, braided her hair and flaunted a green ribbon on her pigtail. She powdered her face and pressed a vermilion mark on her forehead. She said, "Now Father will say what a nice girl I am because I'm ready. Aren't you also coming, Mother?"

"Not today."

Shanta stood at the little gate looking down the street.

Mother said, "Father will come only after five; don't stand in the sun. It is only four o'clock."

The sun was disappearing behind the house on the opposite row, and Shanta knew that presently it would be dark. She ran in to her mother and asked, "Why hasn't Father come home yet, Mother?"

"How can I know? He is perhaps held up in the office."

Shanta made a wry face. "I don't like these people in the office. They are bad people—"

She went back to the gate and stood looking out. Her mother

shouted from inside, "Come in, Shanta. It is getting dark, don't stand there." But Shanta would not go in. She stood at the gate and a wild idea came into her head. Why should she not go to the office and call out Father and then go to the cinema? She wondered where his office might be. She had no notion. She had seen her father take the turn at the end of the street every day. If one went there, perhaps one went automatically to Father's office. She threw a glance about to see if Mother was anywhere and moved down the street.

It was twilight. Everyone going about looked gigantic, walls of houses appeared very high and cycles and carriages looked as though they would bear down on her. She walked on the very edge of the road. Soon the lamps were twinkling, and the passers-by looked like shadows. She had taken two turns and did not know where she was. She sat down on the edge of the road biting her nails. She wondered how she was to reach home. A servant employed in the next house was passing along, and she picked herself up and stood before him.

"Oh, what are you doing here all alone?" he asked. She replied, "I don't know. I came here. Will you take me to our house?" She followed him and was soon back in her house.

Venkat Rao, Shanta's father, was about to start for his office that morning when a *jutka* passed along the street distributing cinema handbills. Shanta dashed to the street and picked up a handbill. She held it up and asked, "Father, will you take me to the cinema to-day?" He felt unhappy at the question. Here was the child growing up without having any of the amenities and the simple pleasures of life. He had hardly taken her twice to the cinema. He had no time for the child. While children of her age in other houses had all the dolls, dresses and outings that they wanted, this child was growing up all alone and like a barbarian more or less. He felt furious with his office. For forty rupees a month they seemed to have purchased him outright.

He reproached himself for neglecting his wife and child—even the wife could have her own circle of friends and so on: she was after all a grown-up, but what about the child? What a drab, colourless existence was hers! Every day they kept him at the office till seven or eight in the evening, and when he came home the child was asleep.

Even on Sundays they wanted him at the office. Why did they think he had no personal life, a life of his own? They gave him hardly any time to take the child to the park or the pictures. He was going to show them that they weren't to toy with him. Yes, he was prepared even to quarrel with his manager if necessary.

He said with resolve, "I will take you to the cinema this evening. Be ready at five."

"Really! Mother!" Shanta shouted. Mother came out of the kitchen.

"Father is taking me to a cinema in the evening."

Shanta's mother smiled cynically. "Don't make false promises to the child—" Venkat Rao glared at her. "Don't talk nonsense. You think you are the only person who keeps promises—"

He told Shanta, "Be ready at five, and I will come and take you positively. If you are not ready, I will be very angry with you."

He walked to his office full of resolve. He would do his normal work and get out at five. If they started any old tricks of theirs, he was going to tell the boss, "Here is my resignation. My child's happiness is more important to me than these horrible papers of yours."

All day the usual stream of papers flowed onto his table and off it. He scrutinized, signed and drafted. He was corrected, admonished and insulted. He had a break of only five minutes in the afternoon for his coffee.

When the office clock struck five and the other clerks were leaving, he went up to the manager and said, "May I go, sir?" The manager looked up from his paper. "You!" It was unthinkable that the cash and account section should be closing at five. "How can you go?"

"I have some urgent private business, sir," he said, smothering the lines he had been rehearsing since the morning: "Herewith my resignation." He visualized Shanta standing at the door, dressed and palpitating with eagerness.

"There shouldn't be anything more urgent than the office work; go back to your seat. You know how many hours I work?" asked the manager. The manager came to the office three hours before opening time and stayed nearly three hours after closing, even on Sundays. The clerks commented among themselves, "His wife must be whipping him whenever he is seen at home; that is why the old owl seems so fond of his office."

"Did you trace the source of that ten-eight difference?" asked the manager.

"I shall have to examine two hundred vouchers. I thought we might do it tomorrow."

"No, no, this won't do. You must rectify it immediately."

Venkat Rao mumbled, "Yes, sir," and slunk back to his seat.

The clock showed 5:30. Now it meant two hours of excruciating search among vouchers. All the rest of the office had gone. Only he and another clerk in his section were working, and of course, the manager was there. Venkat Rao was furious. His mind was made up. He wasn't a slave who had sold himself for forty rupees outright. He could make that money easily; and if he couldn't, it would be more honourable to die of starvation.

He took a sheet of paper and wrote: "Herewith my resignation. If you people think you have bought me body and soul for forty rupees, you are mistaken. I think it would be far better for me and my family to die of starvation than slave for this petty forty rupees on which you have kept me for years and years. I suppose you have not the slightest notion of giving me an increment. You give yourselves heavy slices frequently, and I don't see why you shouldn't think of us occasionally. In any case it doesn't interest me now, since this is my resignation. If I and my family perish of starvation, may our ghosts come and haunt you all your life—" He folded the letter, put it in an envelope, sealed the flap and addressed it to the manager. He left his seat and stood before the manager. The manager mechanically received the letter and put it on his pad.

"Venkat Rao," said the manager, "I'm sure you will be glad to hear this news. Our officer discussed the question of increments today, and I've recommended you for an increment of five rupees. Orders are not yet passed, so keep this to yourself for the present." Venkat Rao put out his hand, snatched the envelope from the pad and hastily slipped it in his pocket.

"What is that letter?"

"I have applied for a little casual leave, sir, but I think . . ."

"You can't get any leave for at least a fortnight to come."

"Yes, sir. I realize that. That is why I am withdrawing my application, sir."

"Very well. Have you traced that mistake?"

"I'm scrutinizing the vouchers, sir. I will find it out within an hour. . . ."

It was nine o'clock when he went home. Shanta was already asleep. Her mother said, "She wouldn't even change her frock, thinking that any moment you might be coming and taking her out. She hardly ate any food; and wouldn't lie down for fear of crumpling her dress. . . ."

Venkat Rao's heart bled when he saw his child sleeping in her pink frock, hair combed and face powdered, dressed and ready to be taken out. "Why should I not take her to the night show?" He shook her gently and called, "Shanta, Shanta." Shanta kicked her legs and cried, irritated at being disturbed. Mother whispered, "Don't wake her," and patted her back to sleep.

Venkat Rao watched the child for a moment. "I don't know if it is going to be possible for me to take her out at all—you see, they are giving me an increment—" he wailed.

OUT OF BUSINESS

Little over a year ago Rama Rao went out of work when a gramophone company, of which he was the Malgudi agent, went out of existence. He had put into that agency the little money he had inherited, as security. For five years his business brought him enough money, just enough, to help him keep his wife and children in good comfort. He built a small bungalow in the Extension and was thinking of buying an old Baby car for his use.

And one day, it was a bolt from the blue, the crash came. A series of circumstances in the world of trade, commerce, banking and politics was responsible for it. The gramophone company, which had its factory somewhere in North India, automatically collapsed when a bank in Lahore crashed, which was itself the result of a Bombay financier's death. The financier was driving downhill when his car flew off sideways and came to rest three hundred feet below the road. It was thought that he had committed suicide because the previous night his wife eloped with his cashier.

Rama Rao suddenly found himself in the streets. At first he could hardly understand the full significance of this collapse. There was a little money in the bank and he had some stock on hand. But the stock moved out slowly; the prices were going down, and he could hardly realize a few hundred rupees. When he applied for the refund of his security, there was hardly anyone at the other end to receive his application.

The money in the bank was fast melting. Rama Rao's wife now tried some measures of economy. She sent away the cook and the servant; withdrew the children from a fashionable nursery school and sent them to a free primary school. And then they let out their bungalow and moved to a very small house behind the Market.

Rama Rao sent out a dozen applications a day and wore his feet out looking for employment. For a man approaching forty, looking for employment does not come very easily, especially when he has just lost an independent, lucrative business. Rama Rao was very businesslike in stating his request. He sent his card in and asked, "I wonder, sir, if you could do something for me. My business is all gone through no fault of my own. I shall be very grateful if you can give me something to do in your office. . . ."

"What a pity, Rama Rao! I am awfully sorry, there is nothing at present. If there is an opportunity I will certainly remember you."

It was the same story everywhere. He returned home in the evening; his heart sank as he turned into his street behind the Market. His wife would invariably be standing at the door with the children behind her, looking down the street. What anxious, eager faces they had! So much of trembling, hesitating hope in their faces. They seemed always to hope that he would come back home with some magic fulfilment. As he remembered the futile way in which he searched for a job, and the finality with which people dismissed him, he wished that his wife and children had less trust in him. His wife looked at his face, understood and turned in without uttering a word; the children took the cue and filed in silently. Rama Rao tried to improve matters with a forced heartiness. "Well, well. How are we all today?" To which he received mumbling, feeble responses from his wife and children. It rent his heart to see them in this condition. At the Extension how this girl would sparkle with flowers and a bright dress; she had friendly neighbours, a women's club and everything to keep her happy there. But now she hardly had the heart or the need to change in the evenings, for she spent all her time cooped up in the kitchen. And then the children. The house in the Extension had a compound and they romped about with a dozen other children; it was possible to have numerous friends in the fashionable nursery school. But here the children had no friends and could play only in the back yard of the house. Their shirts were beginning to show tears and frays. Formerly they were given new clothes once in three months. Rama Rao lay in bed and spent sleepless nights over it.

All the cash in hand was now gone. Their only source of income was the small rent they were getting for their house in the Extension. They shuddered to think what would happen to them if their tenant should suddenly leave.

It was in this condition that Rama Rao came across a journal in the Jubilee Reading Room. It was called *The Captain*. It consisted of four pages, and all of them were devoted to crossword puzzles. It offered every week a first prize of four thousand rupees.

For the next few days his head was free from family cares. He was thinking intensely of his answers: whether it should be TALLOW or FOLLOW. Whether BAD or MAD or SAD would be most apt for a clue which said, "Men who are this had better be avoided." He hardly stopped to look at his wife and children standing in the doorway when he returned home in the evenings. Week after week he invested a little money and sent his solutions, and every week he awaited the results with a palpitating heart. On the day a solution was due he hung about the newsagent's shop, worming himself into his favour in order to have a look into the latest issue of *The Captain* without paying for it. He was too impatient to wait till the journal came on the table in the Jubilee Reading Room. Sometimes the newsagent would grumble, and Rama Rao would pacify him with an awkward, affected optimism. "Please wait. When I get a prize I will give you three years' subscription in advance. . . ." His heart quailed as he opened the page announcing the prize-winners. Someone in Baluchistan, someone in Dacca and someone in Ceylon had hit upon the right set of words; not Rama Rao. It took three hours for Rama Rao to recover from this shock. The only way to exist seemed to be to plunge into the next week's puzzle; that would keep him buoyed up with hope for a few days more.

This violent alternating between hope and despair soon wrecked his nerves and balance. At home he hardly spoke to anyone. His head was always bowed in thought. He quarrelled with his wife if she refused to give him his rupee a week for the puzzles. She was of a mild disposition and was incapable of a sustained quarrel, with the result that he always got what he wanted, though it meant a slight sacrifice in household expenses.

One day the good journal announced a special offer of eight thousand rupees. It excited Rama Rao's vision of a future tenfold. He studied the puzzle. There were only four doubtful corners in it, and he might have to send in at least four entries. A larger outlay was indicated. "You must give me five rupees this time," he said to his wife, at which that good lady became speechless. He had become rather insensitive to such things these days, but even he could not help feeling the atrocious nature of his demand. Five rupees were nearly a week's food for the family. He felt disturbed for a moment; but he had only to turn his attention to speculate whether HOPE or DOPE or ROPE made most sense (for "Some people prefer this to despair") and his mind was at once at rest.

After sending away the solutions by registered post he built elaborate castles in the air. Even if it was only a share, he would get a substantial amount of money. He would send away his tenants, take his wife and children back to the bungalow in the Extension and leave all the money in his wife's hands for her to manage for a couple of years or so; he himself would take a hundred and go away to Madras and seek his fortune there. By the time the money in his wife's hands was spent, he would have found some profitable work in Madras.

On the fateful day of results Rama Rao opened *The Captain*, and the correct solution stared him in the face. His blunders were numerous. There was no chance of getting back even a few annas now. He moped about till the evening. The more he brooded over this the more intolerable life seemed. . . . All the losses, disappointments and frustrations of his life came down on him with renewed force. In the evening instead of turning homeward he moved along the Railway Station Road. He slipped in at the level crossing and walked down the line a couple of miles. It was dark. Far away the lights of the town twinkled, and the red and green light of a signal post loomed over the surroundings a couple of furlongs behind him. He had come to the conclusion that life was not worth living. If one had the misfortune to be born in the world, the best remedy was to end matters on a railway line or with a rope ("Dope? Hope?" his mind asked involuntarily). He pulled it back. "None of that," he said to it and set it rigidly to contemplate the business of dying. Wife, children . . . nothing seemed to matter. The only important thing now was total extinction. He lay across the lines. The iron was still warm.

The day had been hot. Rama Rao felt very happy as he reflected that in less than ten minutes the train from Trichinopoly would be arriving.

He lay there he did not know how long. He strained his ears to catch the sound of the train, but he heard nothing more than a vague rattling and buzzing far off. . . . Presently he grew tired of lying down there. He rose and walked back to the station. There was a good crowd on the platform. He asked someone, "What has happened to the train?"

"A goods train has derailed three stations off, and the way is blocked. They have sent up a relief. All the trains will be at least three hours late today. . . ."

"God, you have shown me mercy!" Rama Rao cried, and ran home.

His wife was waiting at the door, looking down the street. She brightened up and sighed with relief on seeing Rama Rao. She welcomed him with a warmth he had not known for over a year now. "Oh, why are you so late today?" she asked. "I was somehow feeling very restless the whole evening. Even the children were worried. Poor creatures! They have just gone to sleep."

When he sat down to eat she said, "Our tenants in the Extension bungalow came in the evening to ask if you would sell the house. They are ready to offer good cash for it immediately." She added quietly, "I think we may sell the house."

"Excellent idea," Rama Rao replied jubilantly. "This minute we can get four and a half thousand for it. Give me the half thousand and I will go away to Madras and see if I can do anything useful there. You keep the balance with you and run the house. Let us first move to a better locality. . . ."

"Are you going to employ your five hundred to get more money out of crossword puzzles?" she asked quietly. At this Rama Rao felt depressed for a moment and then swore with great emphasis, "No, no. Never again."

ATTILA

In a mood of optimism they named him "Attila." What they wanted of a dog was strength, formidableness and fight, and hence he was named after the "Scourge of Europe."

The puppy was only a couple of months old; he had square jaws, red eyes, a pug nose and a massive head, and there was every reason to hope that he would do credit to his name. The immediate reason for buying him was a series of house-breakings and thefts in the neighbourhood, and our householders decided to put more trust in a dog than in the police. They searched far and wide and met a dog fancier. He held up a month-old black-and-white puppy and said, "Come and fetch him a month hence. In six months he will be something to be feared and respected." He spread out before them a pedigree sheet which was stunning. The puppy had running in his veins the choicest and the most ferocious blood.

They were satisfied, paid an advance, returned a month later, put down seventy-five rupees and took the puppy home. The puppy, as I have already indicated, did not have a very prepossessing appearance and was none too playful, but this did not prevent his owners from sitting in a circle around him and admiring him. There was a pro-longed debate as to what he should be named. The youngest suggested, "Why not call him Tiger?"

"Every other street-mongrel is named Tiger," came the reply. "Why not Caesar?"

"Caesar! If a census was taken of dogs you would find at least fifteen thousand Caesars in South India alone. . . . Why not Fire?"

"It is fantastic."

"Why not Thunder?"

"It is too obvious."

"Grip?"

"Still obvious, and childish."

There was a deadlock. Someone suggested Attila, and a shout of joy went up to the skies. No more satisfying name was thought of for man or animal.

But as time passed our Attila exhibited a love of humanity which was sometimes disconcerting. The Scourge of Europe—could he ever have been like this? They put it down to his age. What child could help loving all creatures? In their zeal to establish this fact, they went to the extent of delving into ancient history to find out what the Scourge of Europe was like when he was a child. It was rumoured that as a child he clung to his friends and to his parents' friends so fast that often he had to be beaten and separated from them. But when he was fourteen he showed the first sign of his future: he knocked down and plunged his knife into a fellow who tried to touch his marbles. Ah, this was encouraging. Let our dog reach the parallel of fourteen years and people would get to know his real nature.

But this was a vain promise. He stood up twenty inches high, had a large frame and a forbidding appearance on the whole—but that was all. A variety of people entered the gates of the house every day: mendicants, bill-collectors, postmen, tradesmen and family friends. All of them were warmly received by Attila. The moment the gate clicked he became alert and stood up looking towards the gate. By the time anyone entered the gate Attila went blindly charging forward. But that was all. The person had only to stop and smile, and Attila would melt. He would behave as if he apologized for even giving an impression of violence. He would lower his head, curve his body, tuck his tail between his legs, roll his eyes and moan as if to say, "How sad that you should have mistaken my gesture! I only hurried down to greet you." Till he was patted on the head, stroked and told that he was forgiven, he would be in extreme misery.

Gradually he realized that his bouncing advances caused much unhappy misunderstanding. And so when he heard the gate click he hardly stirred. He merely looked in that direction and wagged his tail. The people at home did not like this attitude very much. They thought it rather a shame.

"Why not change his name to Blind Worm?" somebody asked.

"He eats like an elephant," said the mother of the family. "You can employ two watchmen for the price of the rice and meat he consumes. Somebody comes every morning and steals all the flowers in the garden and Attila won't do anything about it."

"He has better business to do than catch flower thieves," replied the youngest, always the defender of the dog.

"What is the better business?"

"Well, if somebody comes in at dawn and takes away the flowers, do you expect Attila to be looking out for him even at that hour?"

"Why not? It's what a well-fed dog ought to be doing instead of sleeping. You ought to be ashamed of your dog."

"He does not sleep all night, Mother. I have often seen him going round the house and watching all night."

"Really! Does he prowl about all night?"

"Of course he does," said the defender.

"I am quite alarmed to hear it," said the mother. "Please lock him up in a room at night, otherwise he may call in a burglar and show him round. Left alone, a burglar might after all be less successful. It wouldn't be so bad if he at least barked. He is the most noiseless dog I have ever seen in my life."

The young man was extremely irritated at this. He considered it to be the most uncharitable cynicism, but the dog justified it that very night.

Ranga lived in a hut three miles from the town. He was a "gang coolie"—often employed in road-mending. Occasionally at nights he enjoyed the thrill and profit of breaking into houses. At one o'clock that night Ranga removed the bars of a window on the eastern side of the house and slipped in. He edged along the wall, searched all the trunks and *almirahs* in the house and made a neat bundle of all the jewellery and other valuables he could pick up.

He was just starting to go out. He had just put one foot out of the gap he had made in the window when he saw Attila standing below, looking up expectantly. Ranga thought his end had come. He expected the dog to bark. But not Attila. He waited for a moment, grew tired of waiting, stood up and put his forepaws on the lap of the burglar. He put back his ears, licked Ranga's hands and rolled his eyes. Ranga whispered, "I hope you aren't going to bark. . . ."

"Don't you worry. I am not the sort," the dog tried to say.

"Just a moment. Let me get down from here," said the burglar.

The dog obligingly took away his paws and lowered himself.

"See there," said Ranga, pointing to the back yard, "there is a cat." Attila put up his ears at the mention of the cat and dashed in the direction indicated. One might easily have thought he was going to tear up a cat, but actually he didn't want to miss the pleasure of the company of a cat if there was one.

As soon as the dog left him Ranga made a dash for the gate. Given a second more he would have hopped over it. But the dog turned and saw what was about to happen and in one spring was at the gate. He looked hurt. "Is this proper?" he seemed to ask. "Do you want to shake me off?"

He hung his heavy tail down so loosely and looked so miserable that the burglar stroked his head, at which he revived. The burglar opened the gate and went out, and the dog followed him. Attila's greatest ambition in life was to wander in the streets freely. Now things seemed to be shaping up ideally.

Attila liked his new friend so much that he wouldn't leave him alone even for a moment. He lay before Ranga when he sat down to eat, sat on the edge of his mat when he slept in his hut, waited patiently on the edge of the pond when Ranga went there now and then for a wash, slept on the roadside when Ranga was at work.

This sort of companionship got on Ranga's nerves. He implored, "Oh, dog. Leave me alone for a moment, won't you?" Unmoved, Attila sat before him with his eyes glued on his friend.

Attila's disappearance created a sensation in the bungalow. "Didn't I tell you," the mother said, "to lock him up? Now some burglar has gone away with him. What a shame! We can hardly mention it to anyone."

"You are mistaken," replied the defender. "It is just a coincidence. He must have gone off on his own account. If he had been here no thief would have dared to come in. . . ."

"Whatever it is, I don't know if we should after all thank the thief for taking away that dog. He may keep the jewels as a reward for taking him away. Shall we withdraw the police complaint?"

This facetiousness ceased a week later, and Attila rose to the ranks of a hero. The eldest son of the house was going towards the market one day. He saw Attila trotting behind someone on the road.

"Hey," shouted the young man; at which Ranga turned and broke into a run. Attila, who always suspected that his new friend was waiting for the slightest chance to desert him, galloped behind Ranga.

"Hey, Attila!" shouted the young man, and he also started running. Attila wanted to answer the call after making sure of his friend; and so he turned his head for a second and galloped faster. Ranga desperately doubled his pace. Attila determined to stick to him at any cost. As a result, he ran so fast that he overtook Ranga and clumsily blocked his way, and Ranga stumbled over him and fell. As he rolled on the ground a piece of jewellery (which he was taking to a receiver of stolen property) flew from his hand. The young man recognized it as belonging to his sister and sat down on Ranga. A crowd collected and the police appeared on the scene.

Attila was the hero of the day. Even the lady of the house softened towards him. She said, "Whatever one might say of Attila, one has to admit that he is a very cunning detective. He is too deep for words."

It was as well that Attila had no powers of speech. Otherwise he would have burst into a lamentation which would have shattered the pedestal under his feet.

THE AXE

An astrologer passing through the village foretold that Velan would live in a three-storied house surrounded by many acres of garden. At this everybody gathered round young Velan and made fun of him. For Koppal did not have a more ragged and godforsaken family than Velan's. His father had mortgaged every bit of property he had, and worked, with his whole family, on other people's lands in return for a few annas a week. A three-storied house for Velan indeed! . . . But the scoffers would have congratulated the astrologer if they had seen Velan about thirty or forty years later. He became the sole occupant of Kumar Baugh—that palatial house on the outskirts of Malgudi town.

When he was eighteen Velan left home. His father slapped his face one day for coming late with the midday meal, and he did that in the presence of others in the field. Velan put down the basket, glared at his father and left the place. He just walked out of the village, and walked on and on till he came to the town. He starved for a couple of days, begged wherever he could and arrived in Malgudi, where after much knocking about, an old man took him on to assist him in laying out a garden. The garden existed only in the mind of the gardener. What they could see now was acre upon acre of weed-covered land. Velan's main business consisted in destroying all the vegetation he saw. Day after day he sat in the sun and tore up by hand the unwanted plants. And all the jungle gradually disappeared and the land stood as bare as a football field. Three sides of the land were marked off for an extensive garden, and on the rest was to be built a house. By the time the mangoes had sprouted they were laying the foundation of the house. About the time the margosa sapling had shot up a couple of yards, the walls were also coming up.

The flowers—hibiscus, chrysanthemum, jasmine, roses and canna —in the front park suddenly created a wonderland one early summer. Velan had to race with the bricklayers. He was now the chief gardener, the old man he had come to assist having suddenly fallen ill. Velan was proud of his position and responsibility. He keenly watched the progress of the bricklayers and whispered to the plants as he watered them, "Now look sharp, young fellows. The building is going up and up every day. If it is ready and we aren't, we shall be the laughingstock of the town." He heaped manure, aired the roots, trimmed the branches and watered the plants twice a day, and on the whole gave an impression of hustling nature; and nature seemed to respond. For he did present a good-sized garden to his master and his family when they came to occupy the house.

The house proudly held up a dome. Balconies with intricately carved woodwork hung down from the sides of the house; smooth, rounded pillars, deep verandas, chequered marble floors and spacious halls, ranged one behind another, gave the house such an imposing appearance that Velan asked himself, "Can any mortal live in this? I thought such mansions existed only in *Swarga Loka*." When he saw the kitchen and the dining room he said, "Why, our whole village could be accommodated in this eating place alone!" The housebuilder's assistant told him, "We have built bigger houses, things costing nearly two *lakhs*. What is this house? It has hardly cost your master a *lakh* of rupees. It is just a little more than an ordinary house, that is all. . . ." After returning to his hut Velan sat a long time trying to grasp the vision, scope and calculations of the builders of the house, but he felt dizzy. He went to the margosa plant, gripped its stem with his fingers and said, "Is this all, you scraggy one? What if you wave your head so high above mine? I can put my fingers around you and shake you up like this. Grow up, little one, grow up. Grow fat. Have a trunk which two pairs of arms can't hug, and go up and spread. Be fit to stand beside this palace; otherwise I will pull you out."

When the margosa tree came up approximately to this vision, the house had acquired a mellowness in its appearance. Successive summers and monsoons had robbed the paints on the doors and windows and woodwork of their brightness and the walls of their original colour, and had put in their place tints and shades of their own choice. And though the house had lost its resplendence, it had now a more human look. Hundreds of parrots and mynas and unnamed birds lived in the branches of the margosa, and under its shade the master's great-grandchildren and the (younger) grandchildren played and quarrelled. The master walked about leaning on a staff. The lady of the house, who had looked such a blooming creature on the inauguration day, was shrunken and grey and spent most of her time in an invalid's chair on the veranda, gazing at the garden with dull eyes. Velan himself was much changed. Now he had to depend more and more upon his assistants to keep the garden in shape. He had lost his parents, his wife and eight children out of fourteen. He had managed to reclaim his ancestral property, which was now being looked after by his sons-in-law and sons. He went to the village for *Pongal*, New Year's and *Deepavali*, and brought back with him one or the other of his grandchildren, of whom he was extremely fond.

Velan was perfectly contented and happy. He demanded nothing more of life. As far as he could see, the people in the big house too seemed to be equally at peace with life. One saw no reason why these goods things should not go on and on for ever. But Death peeped around the corner. From the servants' quarters whispers reached the gardener in his hut that the master was very ill and lay in his room downstairs (the bedroom upstairs so laboriously planned had to be abandoned with advancing age). Doctors and visitors were constantly coming and going, and Velan had to be more than ever on guard against "flower-pluckers." One midnight he was awakened and told that the master was dead. "What is to happen to the garden and to me? The sons are no good," he thought at once.

And his fears proved to be not entirely groundless. The sons were no good, really. They stayed for a year more, quarrelled among themselves and went away to live in another house. A year later some other family came in as tenants. The moment they saw Velan they said, "Old gardener? Don't be up to any tricks. We know the sort you are. We will sack you if you don't behave yourself." Velan found life intolerable. These people had no regard for a garden.

They walked on flower beds, children climbed the fruit trees and plucked unripe fruits, and they dug pits on the garden paths. Velan had no courage to protest. They ordered him about, sent him on errands, made him wash the cow and lectured to him on how to grow a garden. He detested the whole business and often thought of throwing up his work and returning to his village. But the idea was unbearable: he couldn't live away from his plants. Fortune, however, soon favoured him. The tenants left. The house was locked up for a few years. Occasionally one of the sons of the late owner came round and inspected the garden. Gradually even this ceased. They left the keys of the house with Velan. Occasionally a prospective tenant came down, had the house opened and went away after re-marking that it was in ruins—plaster was falling off in flakes, paint on doors and windows remained only in a few small patches and white ants were eating away all the cupboards and shelves. . . . A year later another tenant came, and then another, and then a third. No one remained for more than a few months. And then the house acquired the reputation of being haunted.

Even the owners dropped the practise of coming and seeing the house. Velan was very nearly the master of the house now. The keys were with him. He was also growing old. Although he did his best, grass grew on the paths, weeds and creepers strangled the flowering plants in the front garden. The fruit trees yielded their load punc-tually. The owners leased out the whole of the fruit garden for three years.

Velan was too old. His hut was leaky and he had no energy to put up new thatch. So he shifted his residence to the front veranda of the house. It was a deep veranda running on three sides, paved with chequered marble. The old man saw no reason why he should not live there. He had as good a right as the bats and the rats.

When the mood seized him (about once a year) he opened the house and had the floor swept and scrubbed. But gradually he gave up this practise. He was too old to bother about these things.

Years and years passed without any change. It came to be known as the "Ghost House," and people avoided it. Velan found nothing to grumble about in this state of affairs. It suited him excellently. Once a quarter he sent his son to the old family in the town to fetch his wages. There was no reason why this should not have gone on indefinitely. But one day a car sounded its horn angrily at the gate. Velan hobbled up with the keys.

"Have you the keys? Open the gate," commanded someone in the car.

"There is a small side-gate," said Velan meekly.

"Open the big gate for the car!"

Velan had to fetch a spade and clear the vegetation which blocked the entrance. The gates opened on rusty hinges, creaking and groaning.

They threw open all the doors and windows, went through the house keenly examining every portion and remarked, "Did you notice the crack on the dome? The walls too are cracked. . . . There is no other way. If we pull down the old ramshackle carefully we may still be able to use some of the materials, though I am not at all certain that the wooden portions are not hollow inside. . . . Heaven alone knows what madness is responsible for people building houses like this."

They went round the garden and said, "We have to clear every bit of this jungle. All this will have to go. . . ." Some mighty person looked Velan up and down and said, "You are the gardener, I suppose? We have not much use for a garden now. All the trees, except half a dozen on the very boundary of the property, will have to go. We can't afford to waste space. This flower garden . . . H'm, it is . . . old-fashioned and crude, and apart from that the front portion of the site is too valuable to be wasted. . . ."

A week later one of the sons of his old master came and told Velan, "You will have to go back to your village, old fellow. The house is sold to a company. They are not going to have a garden. They are cutting down even the fruit trees; they are offering compensation to the leaseholder; they are wiping out the garden and pulling down even the building. They are going to build small houses by the score without leaving space even for a blade of grass."

There was much bustle and activity, much coming and going, and Velan retired to his old hut. When he felt tired he lay down and slept; at other times he went round the garden and stood gazing at his plants. He was given a fortnight's notice. Every moment of it seemed to him precious, and he would have stayed till the last second with his plants but for the sound of an axe which stirred him out of his afternoon nap two days after he was given notice. The dull noise of a blade meeting a tough surface reached his ears. He got up and rushed out. He saw four men hacking the massive trunk of the old margosa tree. He let out a scream: "Stop that!" He took his staff and rushed at those who were hacking. They easily avoided the blow he aimed. "What is the matter?" they asked.

Velan wept. "This is my child. I planted it. I saw it grow. I loved it. Don't cut it down. . . ."

"But it is the company's orders. What can we do? We shall be dismissed if we don't obey, and someone else will do it."

Velan stood thinking for a while and said, "Will you at least do me this good turn? Give me a little time. I will bundle up my clothes and go away. After I am gone do what you like." They laid down their axes and waited.

Presently Velan came out of his hut with a bundle on his head. He looked at the tree-cutters and said, "You are very kind to an old man. You are very kind to wait." He looked at the margosa and wiped his eyes. "Brother, don't start cutting till I am really gone far, far away."

The tree-cutters squatted on the ground and watched the old man go. Nearly half an hour later his voice came from a distance, half-indistinctly: "Don't cut yet. I am still within hearing. Please wait till I am gone farther."

from

Lawley Road

LAWLEY ROAD

The Talkative Man said:

For years people were not aware of the existence of a Municipality in Malgudi. The town was none the worse for it. Diseases, if they started, ran their course and disappeared, for even diseases must end someday. Dust and rubbish were blown away by the wind out of sight; drains ebbed and flowed and generally looked after themselves. The Municipality kept itself in the background, and remained so till the country got its independence on the fifteenth of August 1947. History holds few records of such jubilation as was witnessed on that day from the Himalayas to Cape Comorin. Our Municipal Council caught the inspiration. They swept the streets, cleaned the drains and hoisted flags all over the place. Their hearts warmed up when a procession with flags and music passed through their streets.

The Municipal Chairman looked down benignly from his balcony, muttering, "We have done our bit for this great occasion." I believe one or two members of the Council who were with him saw tears in his eyes. He was a man who had done well for himself as a supplier of blankets to the army during the war, later spending a great deal of his gains in securing the chairmanship. That's an epic by itself and does not concern us now. My present story is different. The satisfaction the Chairman now felt was, however, short-lived. In about a week, when the bunting was torn off, he became quite dispirited. I used to visit him almost every day, trying to make a living out of news-reports to an upcountry paper which paid me two rupees for every inch of published news. Every month I could measure out about ten inches of news in that paper, which was mostly a somewhat idealized account of municipal affairs. This made me a great favourite there. I walked in and out of the Municipal Chairman's office constantly. Now he looked so unhappy that I was forced to ask, "What is wrong, Mr. Chairman?"

"I feel we have not done enough," he replied.

"Enough of what?" I asked.

"Nothing to mark off the great event." He sat brooding and then announced, "Come what may, I am going to do something great!" He called up an Extraordinary Meeting of the Council, and harangued them, and at once they decided to nationalize the names of all the streets and parks, in honour of the birth of independence. They made a start with the park at the Market Square. It used to be called the Coronation Park—whose coronation God alone knew; it might have been the coronation of Victoria or of Asoka. No one bothered about it. Now the old board was uprooted and lay on the lawn, and a brand-new sign stood in its place declaring it henceforth to be Hamara Hindustan Park.

The other transformation, however, could not be so smoothly worked out. Mahatma Gandhi Road was the most sought-after name. Eight different ward councillors were after it. There were six others who wanted to call the roads in front of their houses Nehru Road or Netaji Subash Bose Road. Tempers were rising and I feared they might come to blows. There came a point when, I believe, the Council just went mad. It decided to give the same name to four different streets. Well, sir, even in the most democratic or patriotic town it is not feasible to have two roads bearing the same name. The result was seen within a fortnight. The town became unrecognizable with new names. Gone were the Market Road, North Road, Chitra Road, Vinayak Mudali Street and so on. In their place appeared the names, repeated in four different places, of all the ministers, deputy ministers and the members of the Congress Working Committee. Of course, it created a lot of hardship—letters went where they were not wanted, people were not able to say where they lived or direct others there. The town became a wilderness with all its landmarks gone.

The Chairman was gratified with his inspired work—but not for long. He became restless again and looked for fresh fields of action.

At the corner of Lawley Extension and Market there used to be a statue. People had got so used to it that they never bothered to ask whose it was or even to look up. It was generally used by the birds as a perch. The Chairman suddenly remembered that it was the statue of Sir Frederick Lawley. The Extension had been named after him. Now it was changed to Gandhi Nagar, and it seemed impossible to keep Lawley's statue there any longer. The Council unanimously resolved to remove it. The Council with the Chairman sallied forth triumphantly next morning and circumambulated the statue. They now realized their mistake. The statue towered twenty feet above them and seemed to arise from a pedestal of molten lead. In their imagination they had thought that a vigourous resolution would be enough to topple down the statue of this satrap, but now they found that it stood with the firmness of a mountain. They realized that Britain, when she was here, had attempted to raise herself on no mean foundation. But it made them only firmer in their resolve. If it was going to mean blasting up that part of the town for the purpose, they would do it. For they unearthed a lot of history about Sir Frederick Lawley. He was a combination of Attila, the Scourge of Europe, and Nadir Shah, with the craftiness of a Machiavelli. He subjugated Indians with the sword and razed to the ground the villages from which he heard the slightest murmur of protest. He never countenanced Indians except when they approached him on their knees.

People dropped their normal occupations and loitered around the statue, wondering how they could have tolerated it for so many years. The gentleman seemed to smile derisively at the nation now, with his arms locked behind and his sword dangling from his belt. There could be no doubt that he must have been the worst tyrant imaginable: the true picture—with breeches and wig and white waistcoat and that hard, determined look—of all that has been hatefully familiar in the British period of Indian history. They shuddered when they thought of the fate of their ancestors who had to bear the tyrannies of this man.

Next the Municipality called for tenders. A dozen contractors sent in their estimates, the lowest standing at fifty thousand rupees, for removing the statue and carting it to the Muncipal Office, where they were already worried about the housing of it. The Chairman thought it over and told me, "Why don't you take it yourself? I will give you the statue free if you do not charge us anything for removing it." I had thought till then that only my municipal friends were mad, but now I found I could be just as mad as they. I began to calculate the whole affair as a pure investment. Suppose it cost me five thousand rupees to dislodge and move the statue (I knew the contractors were overestimating), and I sold it as metal for six thousand. . . . About three tons of metal might fetch anything. Or I could probably sell it to the British Museum or Westminster Abbey. I saw myself throwing up the upcountry paper job.

The Council had no difficulty in passing a resolution permitting me to take the statue away. I made elaborate arrangements for the task. . . . I borrowed money from my father-in-law, promising him a fantastic rate of interest. I recruited a team of fifty coolies to hack the pedestal. I stood over them like a slave-driver and kept shouting instructions. They put down their implements at six in the evening and returned to their attack early next day. They were specially recruited from Koppal, where the men's limbs were hardened by generations of teak-cutting in Mempi Forest.

We hacked for ten days. No doubt we succeeded in chipping the pedestal here and there, but that was all; the statue showed no sign of moving. At this rate I feared I might become bankrupt in a fortnight. I received permission from the District Magistrate to acquire a few sticks of dynamite, cordoned off the area and lighted the fuse. I brought down the knight from his pedestal without injuring any limb. Then it took me three days to reach the house with my booty. It was stretched out on a specially designed carriage drawn by several bullocks. The confusion brought about by my passage along Market Road, the crowd that followed uttering jokes, the incessant shouting and instructions I had to be giving, the blinding heat of the day, Sir F.'s carriage coming to a halt at every inconvenient spot and angle, moving neither forwards nor backwards, holding up the traffic on all sides, and darkness coming on suddenly with the statue nowhere near my home—all this was a nightmare I wish to pass over. I mounted guard over him on the roadside at night. As he lay on his back staring at the stars, I felt sorry for him and said, "Well, this is what you get for being such a haughty imperialist. It never pays." In due course, he was safely lodged in my small house. His head and shoulders were in my front hall, and the rest of him stretched out into the street through the doorway. It was an obliging community there at Kabir Lane and nobody minded this obstruction.

The Municipal Council passed a resolution thanking me for my services. I wired this news to my paper, tacking onto it a ten-inch story about the statue. A week later the Chairman came to my house in a state of agitation. I seated him on the chest of the tyrant. He said, "I have bad news for you. I wish you had not sent up that news item about the statue. See these . . ." He held out a sheaf of telegrams. They were from every kind of historical society in India, all protesting against the removal of the statue. We had all been misled about Sir F. All the present history pertained to a different Lawley of the time of Warren Hastings. This Frederick Lawley (of the statue) was a military governor who had settled down here after the Mutiny. He cleared the jungles and almost built the town of Malgudi. He established here the first cooperative society for the whole of India, and the first canal system by which thousands of acres of land were irrigated from the Sarayu, which had been dissipating itself till then. He established this, he established that, and he died in the great Sarayu floods while attempting to save the lives of villagers living on its banks. He was the first Englishman to advise the British Parliament to involve more and more Indians in all Indian affairs. In one of his despatches he was said to have declared, "Britain must quit India someday for her own good."

The Chairman said, "The government have ordered us to reinstate the statue." "Impossible!" I cried. "This is my statue and I will keep it. I like to collect statues of national heroes." This heroic sentiment impressed no one. Within a week all the newspapers in the country were full of Sir Frederick Lawley. The public caught the enthusiasm. They paraded in front of my house, shouting slogans. They demanded the statue back. I offered to abandon it if the Municipality at least paid my expenses in bringing it here. The public viewed me as their enemy. "This man is trying to black-market even a statue," they remarked. Stung by it, I wrote a placard and hung it on my door: *Statue for sale. Two and a half tons of excellent metal. Ideal gift for a patriotic friend. Offers above ten thousand will be considered.* It infuriated them and made them want to kick me, but they had been brought up in a tradition of non-violence and so they picketed my house; they lay across my door in relays holding a flag and shouting slogans. I had sent away my wife and children to the village in order to make room for the statue in my house, and so this picketing did not bother me—only I had to use the back door a great deal. The Municipality sent me a notice of prosecution under the Ancient Monuments Act which I repudiated in suitable terms. We were getting into bewildering legalities—a battle of wits between me and the municipal lawyer. The only nuisance about it was that an abnormal quantity of correspondence developed and choked up an already congested household.

I clung to my statue, secretly despairing how the matter was ever going to end. I longed to be able to stretch myself fully in my own house.

Six months later relief came. The government demanded a report from the Municipality on the question of the statue, and this together with other lapses on the part of the Municipality made them want to know why the existing Council should not be dissolved and re-elections ordered. I called on the Chairman and said, "You will have to do something grand now. Why not acquire my house as a National Trust?"

"Why should I?" he asked.

"Because," I said, "Sir F. is there. You will never be able to cart him to his old place. It'll be a waste of public money. Why not put him up where he is now? He has stayed in the other place too long. I'm prepared to give you my house for a reasonable price."

"But our funds don't permit it," he wailed.

"I'm sure you have enough funds of your own. Why should you depend on the municipal funds? It'll indeed be a grand gesture on your part, unique in India. . . ." I suggested he ought to relieve himself of some of his old blanket gains. "After all . . . how much more you will have to spend if you have to fight another election!" It appealed to him. We arrived at a figure. He was very happy when he saw in the papers a few days later: "The Chairman of Malgudi Municipality has been able to buy back as a present for the nation the statue of Sir Frederick Lawley. He proposed to install it in a newly acquired property which is shortly to be converted into a park. The Municipal Council have resolved that Kabir Lane shall be changed to Lawley Road."

TRAIL OF THE GREEN BLAZER

The Green Blazer stood out prominently under the bright sun and blue sky. In all that jostling crowd one could not help noticing it. Villagers in shirts and turbans, townsmen in coats and caps, beggars bare-bodied and women in multicoloured saris were thronging the narrow passage between the stalls and moving in great confused masses, but still the Green Blazer could not be missed. The jabber and babble of the marketplace was there, as people harangued, disputed prices, haggled or greeted each other; over it all boomed the voice of a Bible-preacher, and when he paused for breath, from another corner the loudspeaker of a health van amplified on malaria and tuberculosis. Over and above it all the Green Blazer seemed to cry out an invitation. Raju could not ignore it. It was not in his nature to ignore such a persistent invitation. He kept himself half-aloof from the crowd; he could not afford to remain completely aloof or keep himself in it too conspicuously. Wherever he might be, he was harrowed by the fear of being spotted by a policeman; today he wore a loincloth and was bare-bodied, and had wound an enormous turban over his head, which overshadowed his face completely, and he hoped that he would be taken for a peasant from a village.

He sat on a stack of cast-off banana stalks beside a shop awning and watched the crowd. When he watched a crowd he did it with concentration. It was his professional occupation. Constitutionally he was an idler and had just the amount of energy to watch in a crowd and put his hand into another person's pocket. It was a gamble, of course. Sometimes he got nothing out of a venture, counting himself lucky if he came out with his fingers intact. Sometimes he picked up a fountain pen, and the "receiver" behind the Municipal Office would not offer even four annas for it, and there was always the

danger of being traced through it. Raju promised himself that someday he would leave fountain pens alone; he wouldn't touch one even
if it were presented to him on a plate; they were too much bother—
inky, leaky and next to worthless if one could believe what the
receiver said about them. Watches were in the same category, too.

What Raju loved most was a nice, bulging purse. If he saw one he
picked it up with the greatest deftness. He took the cash in it, flung
it far away and went home with the satisfaction that he had done his
day's job well. He splashed a little water over his face and hair and
tidied himself up before walking down the street again as a normal
citizen. He bought sweets, books and slates for his children, and
occasionally a jacket-piece for his wife, too. He was not always easy
in mind about his wife. When he went home with too much cash, he
had always to take care to hide it in an envelope and shove it under a
roof tile. Otherwise she asked too many questions and made herself
miserable. She liked to believe that he was reformed and earned the
cash he showed her as commission; she never bothered to ask what
the commissions were for: a commission seemed to her something
absolute.

Raju jumped down from the banana stack and followed the Green
Blazer, always keeping himself three steps behind. It was a nicely
calculated distance, acquired by intuition and practise. The distance
must not be so much as to obscure the movement of the other's hand
to and from his purse, nor so close as to become a nuisance and
create suspicion. It had to be finely balanced and calculated—the
same sort of calculations as carry a *shikari* through his tracking of
game and see him safely home again. Only this hunter's task was
more complicated. The hunter in the forest could count his day a
success if he laid his quarry flat; but here one had to extract the heart
out of the quarry without injuring it.

Raju waited patiently, pretending to be examining some rolls of
rush mat, while the Green Blazer spent a considerable length of time
drinking a coconut at a nearby booth. It looked as though he would
not move again at all. After sucking all the milk in the coconut, he
seemed to wait interminably for the nut to be split and the soft white
kernel scooped out with a knife. The sight of the white kernel
scooped and disappearing into the other's mouth made Raju, too,

crave for it. But he suppressed the thought: it would be inept to be spending one's time drinking and eating while one was professionally occupied; the other might slip away and be lost forever. . . . Raju saw the other take out his black purse and start a debate with the coconut-seller over the price of coconuts. He had a thick, sawing voice which disconcerted Raju. It sounded like the growl of a tiger, but what jungle-hardened hunter ever took a step back because a tiger's growl sent his heart racing involuntarily! The way the other haggled didn't appeal to Raju either; it showed a mean and petty temperament . . . too much fondness for money. Those were the narrow-minded troublemakers who made endless fuss when a purse was lost. . . . The Green Blazer moved after all. He stopped before a stall flying coloured balloons. He bought a balloon after an endless argument with the shopman—a further demonstration of his meanness. He said, "This is for a motherless boy. I have promised it him. If it bursts or gets lost before I go home, he will cry all night, and I wouldn't like it at all."

Raju got his chance when the other passed through a narrow stile, where people were passing four-thick in order to see a wax model of Mahatma Gandhi reading a newspaper.

Fifteen minutes later Raju was examining the contents of the purse. He went away to a secluded spot, behind a disused well. Its crumbling parapet seemed to offer an ideal screen for his activities. The purse contained ten rupees in coins and twenty in currency notes and a few annas in nickel. Raju tucked the annas at his waist in his loincloth. "Must give them to some beggars," he reflected generously. There was a blind fellow yelling his life out at the entrance to the fair and nobody seemed to care. People seemed to have lost all sense of sympathy these days. The thirty rupees he bundled into a knot at the end of his turban and wrapped this again round his head. It would see him through the rest of the month. He could lead a clean life for at least a fortnight and take his wife and children to a picture.

Now the purse lay limp within the hollow of his hand. It was only left for him to fling it into the well and dust off his hand and then he might walk among princes with equal pride at heart. He peeped into the well. It had a little shallow water at the bottom. The purse might float, and a floating purse could cause the worst troubles on earth. He opened the flap of the purse in order to fill it up with pebbles before drowning it. Now, through the slit at its side, he saw a balloon folded and tucked away. "Oh, this he bought. . . ." He remembered the other's talk about the motherless child. "What a fool to keep this in the purse," Raju reflected. "It is the carelessness of parents that makes young ones suffer," he ruminated angrily. For a moment he paused over a picture of the growling father returning home and the motherless one waiting at the door for the promised balloon, and this growling man feeling for his purse . . . and, oh! it was too painful!

Raju almost sobbed at the thought of the disappointed child—the motherless boy. There was no one to comfort him. Perhaps this ruffian would beat him if he cried too long. The Green Blazer did not look like one who knew the language of children. Raju was filled with pity at the thought of the young child—perhaps of the same age as his second son. Suppose his wife were dead . . . (personally it might make things easier for him, he need not conceal his cash under the roof); he overcame this thought as an unworthy side issue. If his wife should die it would make him very sad indeed and tax all his ingenuity to keep his young ones quiet. . . . That motherless boy must have his balloon at any cost, Raju decided. But how? He peeped over the parapet across the intervening space at the far-off crowd. The balloon could not be handed back. The thing to do would be to put it back into the empty purse and slip it into the other's pocket.

The Green Blazer was watching the heckling that was going on as the Bible-preacher warmed up to his subject. A semicircle was asking, "Where is your God?" There was a hubbub. Raju sidled up to the Green Blazer. The purse with the balloon (only) tucked into it was in his palm. He'd slip it back into the other's pocket.

Raju realized his mistake in a moment. The Green Blazer caught hold of his arm and cried, "Pickpocket!" The hecklers lost interest in the Bible and turned their attention to Raju, who tried to look appropriately outraged. He cried, "Let me go." The other, without giving a clue to what he proposed, shot out his arm and hit him on the cheek. It almost blinded him. For a fraction of a second Raju lost his awareness of where and even who he was. When the dark mist lifted and he was able to regain his vision, the first figure he noticed in the foreground was the Green Blazer, looming, as it seemed, over the whole landscape. His arms were raised ready to strike again. Raju cowered at the sight. He said, "I . . . I was trying to put back your purse." The other gritted his teeth in fiendish merriment and crushed the bones of his arm. The crowd roared with laughter and badgered him. Somebody hit him again on the head.

Even before the Magistrate Raju kept saying, "I was only trying to put back the purse." And everyone laughed. It became a stock joke in the police world. Raju's wife came to see him in jail and said, "You have brought shame on us," and wept.

Raju replied indignantly, "Why? I was only trying to put it back."

He served his term of eighteen months and came back into the world—not quite decided what he should do with himself. He told himself, "If ever I pick up something again, I shall make sure I don't have to put it back." For now he believed God had gifted the likes of him with only one-way deftness. Those fingers were not meant to put anything back.

THE MARTYR'S CORNER

Just at that turning between Market Road and the lane leading to the chemist's shop he had his establishment. If anyone doesn't like the word "establishment," he is welcome to say so, because it was actually something of a vision spun out of air. At eight you would not see him, and again at ten you would see nothing, but between eight and ten he arrived, sold his goods and departed.

Those who saw him remarked thus, "Lucky fellow! He has hardly an hour's work a day and he pockets ten rupees—what graduates are unable to earn! Three hundred rupees a month!" He felt irritated when he heard such glib remarks and said, "What these folk do not see is that I sit before the oven practically all day frying all this stuff. . . ."

He got up when the cock in the next house crowed; sometimes it had a habit of waking up at three in the morning and letting out a shriek. "Why has the cock lost its normal sleep?" Rama wondered as he awoke, but it was a signal he could not miss. Whether it was three o'clock or four, it was all the same to him. He had to get up and start his day.

At about 8:15 in the evening he arrived with a load of stuff. He looked as if he had four arms, so many things he carried about him. His equipment was the big tray balanced on his head, with its assortment of edibles, a stool stuck in the crook of his arm, a lamp in another hand, a couple of portable legs for mounting his tray. He lit the lamp, a lantern which consumed six pies' worth of kerosene every day, and kept it near at hand, since he did not like to depend only upon electricity, having to guard a lot of loose cash and a variety of miscellaneous articles.

When he set up his tray with the little lamp illuminating his display, even a confirmed dyspeptic could not pass by without throwing a look at it. A heap of *bondas*, which seemed puffed and big but melted in one's mouth; *dosais*, white, round and limp, looking like layers of muslin; *chappatis* so thin that you could lift fifty of them on a little finger; duck's eggs, hard-boiled, resembling a heap of ivory balls; and perpetually boiling coffee on a stove. He had a separate aluminum pot in which he kept chutney, which went gratis with almost every item.

He always arrived in time to catch the cinema crowd coming out after the evening show. A pretender to the throne, a young scraggy fellow, sat on his spot until he arrived and did business, but our friend did not let that bother him unduly. In fact, he felt generous enough to say, "Let the poor rat do his business when I am not there." This sentiment was amply respected, and the pretender moved off a minute before the arrival of the prince among caterers.

His customers liked him. They said in admiration, "Is there another place where you can get coffee for six pies and four *chappatis* for an anna?" They sat around his tray, taking what they wanted. A dozen hands hovered about it every minute, because his customers were entitled to pick up, examine and accept their stuff after proper scrutiny.

Though so many hands were probing the lot, he knew exactly who was taking what: he knew by an extraordinary sense which of the *jutka*-drivers was picking up *chappatis* at a given moment; he could even mention his licence number; he knew that the stained hand nervously coming up was that of the youngster who polished the shoes of passers-by; and he knew exactly at what hour he would see the wrestler's arm searching for the perfect duck's egg, which would be knocked against the tray corner before consumption.

His custom was drawn from the population swarming the pavement: the boot-polish boys, for instance, who wandered to and fro with brush and polish in a bag, endlessly soliciting, "Polish, sir, polish!" Rama had a soft corner in his heart for the waifs. When he saw some fat customer haggling over the payment to one of these youngsters he felt like shouting, "Give the poor fellow a little more. Don't grudge it. If you pay an anna more he can have a *dosai* and a *chap-pati*. As it is, the poor fellow is on half-rations and remains half-starved all day."

It rent his heart to see their hungry, hollow eyes; it pained him to note the rags they wore; and it made him very unhappy to see the tremendous eagerness with which they came to him, laying aside their brown bags. But what could he do? He could not run a charity show; that was impossible. He measured out their half-glass of coffee correct to the fraction of an inch, but they could cling to the glass as long as they liked.

The blind beggar, who whined for alms all day in front of the big hotel, brought him part of his collection at the end of the day and demanded refreshment . . . and the grass-selling women. He disliked serving women; their shrill, loud voices got on his nerves. These came to him after disposing of head-loads of grass satisfactorily. And that sly fellow with a limp who bought a packet of mixed fare every evening and carried it to a prostitute-like creature standing under a tree on the pavement opposite.

All the coppers that men and women of this part of the universe earned through their miscellaneous jobs ultimately came to him at the end of the day. He put all this money into a little cloth bag dangling from his neck under his shirt, and carried it home, soon after the night show had started at the theatre.

He lived in the second lane behind the market. His wife opened the door, throwing into the night air the scent of burnt oil which perpetually hung about their home. She snatched from his hands all his encumbrances, put her hand under his shirt to pull out his cloth bag and counted the cash immediately. They gloated over it. "Five rupees invested in the morning has brought us another five. . . ." They ruminated on the exquisite mystery of this multiplication. She put back into his cloth bag the capital for further investment on the morrow, and carefully separated the gains and put them away in a little wooden box that she had brought from her parents' house years before.

After dinner, he tucked a betel leaf and tobacco in his cheek and slept on the *pyol* of his house, and had dreams of traffic constables bullying him to move on and health inspectors saying that he was spreading all kinds of disease and depopulating the city. But fortunately in actual life no one bothered him very seriously. He gave an occasional packet of his stuff to the traffic constable going off duty or to the health-department menial who might pass that way.

The health officer no doubt came and said, "You must put all this under a glass lid, otherwise I shall destroy it all someday. . . . Take care!" But he was a kindly man who did not pursue any matter but wondered in private, "How his customers survive his food, I can't understand! I suppose people build up a sort of immunity to such poisons, with all that dust blowing on it and the gutter behind. . . ." Rama no doubt violated all the well-accepted canons of cleanliness and sanitation, but still his customers not only survived his fare but seemed actually to flourish on it, having consumed it for years without showing signs of being any the worse for it.

Rama's life could probably be considered a most satisfactory one, without agitation or heartburn of any kind. Why could it not go on forever, endlessly, till the universe itself cooled off and perished, when by any standard he could be proved to have led a life of pure effort? No one was hurt by his activity and money-making, and not many people could be said to have died of taking his stuff; there were no more casualties through his catering than, say, through the indifferent municipal administration.

But such security is unattainable in human existence. The gods grow jealous of too much contentment anywhere, and they show their displeasure all of a sudden. One night, when he arrived as usual at his spot, he found a babbling crowd at the corner where he normally sat. He said authoritatively. "Leave way, please." But no one cared. It was the young shop-boy of the stationer's that plucked his sleeve and said, "They have been fighting over something since the evening. . . ."

"Over what?" asked Rama.

"Over something. . . ." the boy said. "People say someone was stabbed near the Sales Tax Office when he was distributing notices about some votes or something. It may be a private quarrel. But who cares? Let them fight who want a fight."

Someone said, "How dare you speak like that about us?"

Everyone turned to look at this man sourly. Someone in that crowd remarked, "Can't a man speak . . . ?"

His neighbour slapped him for it. Rama stood there with his load about him, looking on helplessly. This one slap was enough to set off a fuse. Another man hit another man, and then another hit another, and someone started a cry, "Down with . . ."

"Ah, it is as we suspected, preplanned and organized to crush us," another section cried.

People shouted, soda-water bottles were used as missiles. Everyone hit everyone else. A set of persons suddenly entered all the shops and demanded that these be closed. "Why?" asked the shopmen.

"How can you have the heart to do business when . . . ?"

The restraints of civilized existence were suddenly abandoned. Everyone seemed to be angry with everyone else. Within an hour the whole scene looked like a battlefield. Of course the police came to the spot presently, but this made matters worse, since it provided another side to the fight. The police had a threefold task: of maintaining law and order and also maintaining themselves intact and protecting some party whom they believed to be injured. Shops that were not closed were looted.

The cinema house suddenly emptied itself of its crowd, which rushed out to enter the fray at various points. People with knives ran about, people with bloodstains groaned and shouted, ambulance vans moved here and there. The police used *lathis* and tear gas, and finally opened fire. Many people died. The public said that the casualties were three thousand, but the official communiqué maintained that only five were injured and four and a quarter killed in the police firing. At midnight Rama emerged from his hiding place under a culvert and went home.

The next day Rama told his wife, "I won't take out the usual quantity. I doubt if there will be anyone there. God knows what devil has seized all those folk! They are ready to kill each other for some votes. . . ." His instinct was right. There were more policemen than public on Market Road and his corner was strongly guarded. He had to set up his shop on a farther spot indicated by a police officer.

Matters returned to normal in about ten days, when all the papers clamoured for a full public inquiry into this or that: whether the firing was justified and what precautions were taken by the police to prevent this flare-up and so on. Rama watched the unfolding of contemporary history through the shouts of newsboys, and in due course tried to return to his corner. The moment he set up his tray and took his seat, a couple of young men wearing badges came to him and said, "You can't have your shop here."

"Why not, sir?"

"This is a holy spot on which our leader fell that day. The police aimed their guns at his heart. We are erecting a monument here. This is our place; the Municipality have handed this corner to us."

Very soon this spot was cordoned off, with some congregation or the other always there. Money-boxes jingled for collections and people dropped coins. Rama knew better than anyone else how good the place was for attracting money. They collected enough to set up a memorial stone and, with an ornamental fencing and flower pots, entirely transformed the spot.

Austere, serious-looking persons arrived there and spoke among themselves. Rama had to move nearly two hundred yards away, far into the lane. It meant that he went out of the range of vision of his customers. He fell on their blind spot. The cinema crowd emerging from the theatre poured away from him; the *jutka*-drivers who generally left their vehicles on the roadside for a moment while the traffic constable showed indulgence and snatched a mouthful found it inconvenient to come so far; the boot-boys patronized a fellow on the opposite footpath, the scraggy pretender, whose fortunes seemed to be rising.

Nowadays Rama prepared a limited quantity of snacks for sale, but even then he had to carry back remnants; he consumed some of it himself, and the rest, on his wife's advice, he warmed up and brought out for sale again next day. One or two who tasted the stuff reacted badly and spread the rumour that Rama's quality was not what it used to be. One night, when he went home with just two annas in his bag, he sat up on the *pyol* and announced to his wife, "I believe our business is finished. Let us not think of it anymore."

He put away his pans and trays and his lamp, and prepared himself for a life of retirement. When all his savings were exhausted he went to one Restaurant Kohinoor, from which loudspeakers shrieked all day, and queued up for a job. For twenty rupees a month he waited eight hours a day on the tables. People came and went, the radio music frayed his nerves, but he stuck on; he had to. When some customer ordered him about too rudely, he said, "Gently, brother. I was once a hotel-owner myself." And with that piece of reminiscence he attained great satisfaction.

WIFE'S HOLIDAY

Kannan sat at the door of his hut and watched the village go its way. Sami the oil-monger was coming up the street driving his ox before him. He remarked while passing, "This is your idling day, is it? Why don't you come to the Mantapam this afternoon?" Some more people passed, but Kannan hardly noticed anyone. The oil-monger's words had thrown him into a dream. The Mantapam was an ancient pillared structure, with all its masonry cracking and crumbling down on the tank bund. It served as a clubhouse for Kannan and his friends, who gathered there on an afternoon and pursued the game of dice with considerable intensity and fury. Kannan loved not only the game but also the muddy smell of the place, the sky seen through the cracking arches and the far-off hillocks. He hummed a little tune to himself at the thought of the Mantapam.

He knew people would call him an idler for sitting there at his door and sunning himself. But he didn't care. He would not go to work; there was no one to goad him out of the house—his wife being still away. It was with a quiet joy that he put her into a bullock cart and saw her off a few days ago. He hoped her parents would insist on her staying on at least ten days more, though it meant a wrench for him to be parted from his little son. But Kannan accepted it as an inevitable price to pay for his wife's absence. He reflected, "If she were here, would she let me rest like this?" He would have to be climbing coconut trees, clearing their tops of beetles and other pests, plucking down coconuts, haggling with miserly tree-owners, and earning his rupee a day.

Now he celebrated his wife's absence by staying at home most of the day. But the worst of it was that he had not a quarter of an anna anywhere about him and he wouldn't see a coin unless he climbed some trees for it today. He stretched his legs and arms and brooded how it would feel to go up a tree now. Of course the ten trees in the back yard of that big house needed attention: that work awaited him anytime he cared to go there. But it was impossible. His limbs felt stiff and unwieldy and seemed good only for the visit to the Mantapam. But what was the use of going there empty-handed? If only he had four annas on hand, he could probably return home with a rupee in the evening. But that woman! He felt indignant at the thought of his wife, who did not seem to think that he deserved to keep an anna of his hard-earned cash about him. Without four annas to call one's own! He had been drudging and earning for years now, ever since . . . He gave up the attempt to think it out, since it took him into the realm of numbers, and numbers were complex and elusive except when one rolled the dice and counted cash.

An idea struck him and he suddenly rose to his feet and turned in. In a corner there was a large tin trunk, painted black years ago—the most substantial possession of that household. It was his wife's. He sat down before it and stared at the lock hopelessly. It was a cast-iron lock with sharp edges. He took hold of it and tugged at it, and, much to his surprise, it came off. "God is kind to me," he told himself, and threw open the lid. He beheld his wife's prized possessions there: a few jackets and two or three saris, one of which he had bought her as a young bridegroom. He was surprised that she should still preserve it though it was . . . it was . . . he checked himself at the threshold of numbers once again. "She can preserve it because she is too nig-gardly to wear it, I suppose!" he remarked and laughed, pleased at this malicious conclusion. He threw aside the clothes impatiently and searched for a little wooden box in which she usually kept her cash. He found it empty but for a smooth worn-out copper just left there for luck. "Where is all the cash gone?" he asked angrily. He brooded, "She must have taken every anna for her brother or some-one there. Here I slave all the day, only to benefit her brother, is it? . . . Next time I see her brother, I will wring his neck," he said to himself with considerable satisfaction. Rummaging further he caught sight of a cigarette tin in a corner of the box. He shook it. It jingled satisfactorily with coins. He felt tender at the sight of it. It was his little son's, a red cigarette tin. He remembered how the little fellow had picked it from the rubbish dump behind the travellers' bungalow

and come running, clutching it to his bosom. The boy had played
with the red tin a whole day in the street, filling it with dust and
emptying it. And then Kannan had suggested he make a money-box
of it, the young fellow protesting against it vigourously. But Kannan
argued with him elaborately; and became so persuasive that his son
presently accepted the proposition with enthusiasm. "When the box
is full I will buy a motorcar like that boy in the big house. I must also
have a mouth-harmonium and a green pencil." Kannan laughed up-
roariously on hearing his son's plans. He took the tin to the blacksmith, sealed its lid with lead and had a slit cut on it—just wide
enough to admit a coin. It became a treasure for the young fellow,
and he often held it aloft to his father for him to drop a copper in.
The boy quite often asked with a puckered brow, "Father, is it full?
When can I open it?" He always kept it in his mother's trunk, safely
tucked away amidst the folds of her saris, and would not rest till he
saw the trunk properly locked up again. Watching him, Kannan
often remarked proudly, "Very careful boy. He will do big things.
We must send him to a school in the town."

Now Kannan shook the box, held the slit up to light and tried to
find out how much it contained. A dull resentment that he felt at the
thought of his wife made him prey to a wicked idea. He held the box
upside down and shook it violently till he felt deaf with the clanging
of coins. But not one came out of it. The blacksmith had made a
good job of it—the slit was exactly the thickness of a coin, which
could go one way through it. No power on earth could shake a coin
out of it again. After a while Kannan paused to ask himself, "Am I
right in taking my youngster's money?" "Why not?" whispered a
voice within seductively. "Son and father are the same. Moreover,
you are going to double or treble the amount, and then you can put
it all back into the box. That way it is really a benefit you are
conferring on the son by opening this little box." That settled it. He
looked about for something with which to widen the slit. He got up
and ransacked an odd assortment of useless things—strings, bottle-
corks, cast-off ox-shoe, and so on. Not a single sharp instrument
anywhere. What had happened to that knife? He felt annoyed at the
thought of his wife, that woman's habit of secreting away everything
on earth, or perhaps she had carried it away to her brother. He
clutched the box and kept banging it against the floor for a while. It

only lost shape and looked battered, but it would not yield its treasure. He looked about. There was a framed picture of a god hanging by a nail on the wall. He took down the picture and plucked out the nail. He threw a look at the god on the floor, felt uneasy and briefly pressed his eyes to its feet. He brought in a piece of stone, poised the nail over the box with one hand and brought the stone down on it with the other. The nail slipped sideways and the stone hit his thumb and crushed it to a blue. He yelled with pain and flung away the box. It lay in a corner and seemed to look back at him viciously. "You dog!" he hissed at it. He sat nursing his thumb for a while, looked again at the red tin and said, "I will deal with you now." He went to the kitchen-corner and came out bearing a large stone pestle with both hands over his head. He held the pestle high above the box and dropped it vertically. It proved too much even for that box, which flattened and split sideways. He put his fingers in, scooped out the coins hungrily and counted: six annas in three-pie copper coins. He tucked up the coins at his waist in his dhoti, locked the door and started out.

At Mantapam luck deserted him, or rather never came near him. Within a short time he lost all his money. He continued on credit for a while till someone suggested he should give up his place to someone else more solvent. He rose abruptly and started homeward while the sun was still bright.

As he turned into his lane, he saw at the other end his wife coming up with a bundle in one hand and the youngster clinging to the other. Kannan stood stunned. "May it be a dream!" he muttered to himself. She came nearer and said, "A bus came this way and I returned home." She was going towards the door. He watched her in a sort of dull panic. Her box with all its contents scattered, the god's picture on the floor, the battered red tin—she would see them all at once the moment she stepped in. The situation was hopeless. He opened the door mechanically. "Why do you look like that?" she asked, going in. His son held a couple of coins up to him. "Uncle gave me these. Put them into the box." A groan of misery escaped Kannan. "Why do you do that, Father?" the boy asked. Kannan held up his thumb and mumbled, "Nothing. I have crushed my thumb." He followed them in, resigning himself to face an oncoming storm.

A SHADOW

Sambu demanded, "You must give me four annas to see the film tomorrow." His mother was horrified. How could this boy! She had been dreading for six months past the arrival of the film. How could people bear to see him on the screen when they knew he was no more? She had had a vague hope that the producers might not release the picture out of consideration for her feelings. And when a procession appeared in the street with tom-tom and band, and with young boys carrying placards and huge coloured portraits of her husband, she resolved to go out of town for a while; but it was a desperate and unpractical resolve. Now the picture had arrived. Her husband was going to speak, move and sing, for at least six hours a day in that theatre three streets off.

Sambu was as delighted as if his father had come back to life. "Mother, won't you also come and see the picture?"

"No."

"Please, please. You must come."

She had to explain to him how utterly impossible it would be for her to see the picture. The boy had a sort of ruthless logic: "Why should it be impossible? Aren't you seeing his photos, even that big photo on the wall, every day?"

"But these photos do not talk, move or sing."

"And yet you prefer them to the picture which has life!"

The whole of the next day Sambu was in great excitement. In his classroom whenever his master took his eyes off him for a moment he leant over and whispered to his neighbour, "My father was paid ten thousand rupees to act in that film. I am seeing it this evening. Aren't you also coming?"

"To see *Kumari!*" sneered his friend. He hated Tamil pictures. "I won't even pass that way."

"This is not like other Tamil films. My father used to read the story to us every night. It is a very interesting story. He wrote the whole story himself. He was paid ten thousand rupees for writing and acting. I will take you to the picture if you are also coming."

"I won't see a Tamil picture."

"This is not an ordinary Tamil picture. It is as good as an English picture."

But Sambu's friend was adamant. Sambu had to go alone and see the picture. It was an attempt at a new style in Tamil films—a modern story with a minimum of music. It was the story of Kumari, a young girl who refused to marry at fourteen but wanted to study in a university and earn an independent living, and was cast away by her stern father (Sambu's father) and forgiven in the end.

Sambu, sitting in the four-anna class, was eagerly waiting for the picture to begin. It was six months since he had seen his father, and he missed him badly at home.

The hall darkened. Sambu sat through the trailers and slide advertisements without enthusiasm. Finally, his father came on the screen. He was wearing just the dhoti and shirt he used to wear at home; he was sitting at his table just as he used to sit at home. And then a little girl came up, and he patted her on the head and spoke to her exactly as he used to speak to Sambu. And then Father taught the girl arithmetic. She had a slate on her knee and he dictated to her: "A cartman wants two annas per mile. Rama has three annas on hand. How far will the cartman carry him?" The girl chewed her slate pencil and blinked. Father was showing signs of impatience. "Go on, Kumari," Sambu muttered. "Say something, otherwise you will receive a slap presently. I know him better than you do." Kumari, however, was a better arithmetician than Sambu. She gave the right answer. Father was delighted. How he would jump about in sheer delight whenever Sambu solved a sum correctly! Sambu was reminded of a particular occasion when by sheer fluke he blundered through a puzzle about a cistern with a leak and a tap above it. How father jumped out of his chair when he heard Sambu declare that it would take three hours for the cistern to fill again.

When the film ended and the lights were switched on, Sambu turned about and gazed at the aperture in the projection room as if his father had vanished into it. The world now seemed to be a poorer place without Father. He ran home. His mother was waiting for him at the door. "It is nine o'clock. You are very late."

"I would have loved it if the picture had lasted even longer. You are perverse, Mother. Why won't you see it?"

Throughout the dinner he kept talking. "Exactly as Father used to sing, exactly as he used to walk, exactly . . ." His mother listened to him in grim silence.

"Why don't you say something, Mother?"

"I have nothing to say."

"Don't you like the picture?"

She didn't answer the question. She asked, "Would you like to go and see the picture again tomorrow?"

"Yes, Mother. If possible every day as long as the picture is shown. Will you give me four annas every day?"

"Yes."

"Will you let me see both the shows every day?"

"Oh, no. You can't do that. What is to happen to your lessons?"

"Won't you come and see the picture, Mother?"

"No, impossible."

For a week more, three hours in the day, Sambu lived in his father's company, and felt depressed at the end of every show. Every day it was a parting for him. He longed to see the night show too, but Mother bothered too much about school lessons. Time was precious, but Mother did not seem to understand it; lessons could wait, but not Father. He envied those who were seeing the picture at night.

Unable to withstand his persuasions anymore, his mother agreed to see the picture on the last day. They went to the night show. She sat in the women's class. She had to muster all her courage to sit down for the picture. She had a feeling of great relief as long as the slide advertisements and trailer pieces lasted. When the picture began, her heart beat fast. Her husband talking to his wife on the screen, playing with his child, singing, walking, dressing; same clothes, same voice, same anger, same joy—she felt that the whole thing was a piece of cruelty inflicted on her. She shut her eyes several times, but the picture fascinated her: it had the fascination of a thing which is painful. And then came a scene in which he reclined in a chair reading a newspaper. How he would sit absorbed in a newspaper! In their years of married life, how often had she quarrelled with him for it! Even on the last day he had sat thus after dinner, in his canvas chair, with the newspaper before him; she had lost her temper at the sight of it and said, "You and your newspaper! I could as well go and sleep off the rest of the day," and left his company. When she saw him later he had fallen back in his chair with the sheets of newspaper over his face. . . .

This was an unbearable scene. A sob burst from her.

Sambu, sitting in his seat on the men's side, liked to see his father in the newspaper scene because the girl would presently come and ask him what he was reading, annoy him with questions and get what she deserved: Father would shout, "Kumari! Will you go out or shall I throw you out?" That girl didn't know how to behave with Father, and Sambu disliked her intensely. . . .

While awaiting eagerly the snubbing of the girl, Sambu heard a burst of sobbing in the women's class; presently there was a scramble of feet and a cry: "Put the lights on! Accident to someone!" The show was stopped. People went hither and thither. Sambu, cursing this interruption, stood up on a bench to see what the matter was. He saw his mother being lifted from the floor. "That is my mother! Is she also dead?" screamed Sambu, and jumped over the barrier. He wailed and cried. Someone told him, "She has only fainted. Nothing has happened to her. Don't make a fuss." They carried her out and laid her in the passage. The lights were put out again, people returned to their seats and the show continued. Mother opened her eyes, sat up and said, "Let us go away."

"Yes, Mother." He fetched a *jutka* and helped her into it. As he was climbing into it himself, from the darkened hall a familiar voice said, "Kumari! Will you go out or shall I throw you out?" Sambu's heart became heavy and he burst into tears: he was affected both by his mother's breakdown and by the feeling that this was the final parting from his father. They were changing the picture next day.

A WILLING SLAVE

No one in the house knew her name; no one for a moment thought that she had any other than Ayah. None of the children ever knew when she had first come into the family, the eldest being just six months old when she entered service; now he was seventeen and studied in a college. There were five children after him, and the last was four years old.

The Ayah repeatedly renewed her infancy with each one of them, kept pace with them till they left her behind and marched forward. And then she slipped back to the youngest and grew up with him or her. It might be said that the limit to which she could go in years was six; if she stepped beyond that boundary she proved herself a blundering nuisance. For instance, how hard it was for her to conduct herself in the servant world, which consisted of the cook, two men servants, a maid servant, a gardener and his unpaid assistant. Their jokes fell flat on her, their discussions did not interest her and she reported to her mistress everything that she heard. The gardener very nearly lost his job once for his opinion of his master, which was duly conveyed by the Ayah. She was fairly unpopular in the servants' quarters. She constituted herself a time-keeper, and those who came late for work could not escape her notice. The moment a latecomer was sighted, the old woman would let out such a scream demanding an explanation that the mistress of the house would come out and levy a fine.

This was an entirely self-imposed task, just as she also kept an eye on the home-tutor who came in the mornings and taught children arithmetic and English. The Ayah hovered about all the time the teacher was present, for she had a suspicion that he would torture the children. She viewed all teachers as her enemies and all schools as

prison houses. She thought it was a cruel perversity that made people
send children to school. She remembered how her two children
(now grandfathers) used to come home and demand three pies for
buying some herb, a paste of which was indispensable for preparing
their skins for the next day's pinching and caning. They said that the
school inspector himself had ordered the purchase of the herb. It was
a part of their education.

She had asked once or twice, "Why do you stand there and allow
yourselves to be beaten?"

"We have got to do it," the boys answered. "It is a part of our
studies. It seems that our teachers won't get their wages unless they
cane us a certain number of times every day."

The old woman had no occasion to know more about teachers.
And so she kept a watch over the home-tutor. If he so much as raised
his voice, she checked him with, "Don't you try any of your tricks
on these angels. These are no ordinary children. If you do anything,
my master will lock you up in jail. Be careful." Her other self-
imposed tasks were to see that the baker's boy didn't cycle on the
lawn, that the newspaper man didn't drop the paper into the nursery
and that the servant didn't doze off in the afternoon; she also attended on guests, took charge of their clothes and acted as an inter-
mediary between them and washing boy; and above all, when
everyone in the house was out, she shut and bolted all the doors, sat
down on the front porch and acted as the watchman. These were all
her secondary duties. Her main job, for which she received two
meals a day, fifteen rupees a month and three saris a year, kept her
active for over twelve hours in the day.

At six in the morning, Radha, the last child of the house, shouted
from her bed upstairs, "Ayah!" And the Ayah would run up the
stairs as fast as her size permitted, because Radha would not give
more than a quarter of an hour's interval between shouts. And now
when the Ayah stood near the cot and parted the mosquito net,
Radha would ask, "Where were you, Ayah?"

"Here all the time, my darling."

"Were you here all night?"

"Of course I was."

"Were you sleeping or sitting up?"

"Oh, would I lie down when my Radha was sleeping? I was

sitting up with a knife in my hand. If any bad men had tried to come near you, I would have chopped off their heads."

"Where is the knife?"

"I just went down and put it away."

"Won't you let me have a look at the knife, Ayah?"

"Oh, no. Children must never see it. When you grow up into a big girl, when you are tall enough to touch the lock of that *almirah*, I will show you the knife. Would you like to be very tall?"

"Yes, I can then open the *almirah* and take the biscuits myself, isn't it so, Ayah?"

"Yes, yes. But you will never be tall if you stay in bed in the mornings. You must get up, wash and drink milk, and you will see how very fast you grow. Three days ago you were so high because you got up without giving me any trouble."

After drinking her glass of milk Radha would run into the garden and suggest that they play trains. The Ayah now had to take out a tricycle and a doll. Radha sat on the tricycle clasping the doll to her bosom, and the Ayah bent nearly double and pushed the tricycle. The tricycle was the train, the flower pots were stations and the circular fernhouse was Bangalore. Ayah was the engine driver, the doll was Radha and Radha was her mother sometimes and sometimes the man who commanded the train to stop or go. Now and then the Ayah stopped to take out her pouch and put a piece of tobacco into her mouth. "Why has the train stopped?" demanded Radha.

"The screw is loose, I am fitting it up."

"You are chewing?"

"Yes, but it is not tobacco. It is a medicine for headache. I bought it from the medicine-seller at this station."

"Is there a medicine-seller here?"

"Yes, yes," said the Ayah and pointed at the jasmine bush.

Radha looked at the bush and said, "Oh, Seller, give some good medicine for my poor Ayah. She has such a bad headache, Doctor."

At Bangalore the train stopped for a long time. There the Ayah was asked to lie down and sleep on a patch of sand and Radha went round the town with the child. . . . The game went on till Radha's mother called her in for a bath, and after that the Ayah was free for an hour or more.

At midday she squatted amidst toys in the nursery, her immense figure contrasting grotesquely with the tiny elephants and horses, cooking vessels and dolls around her. She and Radha sat a yard apart, but each was in her own house. They cooked, performed *puja* and called on each other. It was easy for Radha to spring up and pay Ayah a visit, but it would be an extreme torture for the Ayah to return the call in the same manner, and so if the Ayah stooped forward it was accepted as a visit. After playing this game for an hour the Ayah felt drowsy and said, "Radha, night has come. Let us go to bed so that we may get up early in the morning."

"Is it already night?"

"It is. I lit the lamp hours ago," replied the Ayah, indicating some knickknack which stood for the lamp.

"Good night, Ayah. . . . You must also lie down." The Ayah cleared a space for herself and lay down.

"Are you asleep, Ayah?"

"Yes, just 'play' sleep, not real. . . ." the Ayah said every five minutes, and very soon Radha fell asleep.

The Ayah's duties commenced again at four o'clock. Radha kept her running continuously till eight, when she had to be carried off to her bed. In bed she had to have her stories. The Ayah squatted below the cot and narrated the story of the black monkey which rolled in a sack of chalk powder, became white and married a princess; at the wedding somebody sprinkled water on him and he came out in his true color; he was chased out; presently a *dhobi* took pity on him and washed, bleached and ironed him, in which state he regained the affection of the princess. When the story was over, Radha said, "I don't like to sleep. Let us play something." Ayah asked, "Do you want the Old Fellow in?" The mention of the Old Fellow worked wonders, and child after child was kept in terror of him. He was supposed to be locked up in a disused dog kennel in the compound. He was always shouting for the Ayah. He was ever ready to break the door open and carry her away. The Ayah always referred to him in scathing language: "I have beaten that scoundrel into pulp. Very bad fellow, disgusting monkey. He won't leave me in peace even for a moment. If you don't sleep, how can I find the time to go and kick him back into his house?"

Once in three months the Ayah oiled and combed her hair, put on a bright sari, bade everyone in the house an elaborate goodbye and started for Saidapet. There she had her home. The only evidence others had of her far-off home was the presence of a couple of rowdy-looking men in the back yard of the bungalow at the beginning of every month. The Ayah spoke of them as "those Saidapet robbers."

"Why do you encourage them?" asked her mistress sometimes.

"What can I do? It is the price I pay for having borne them for nine months." And she received her month's pay and divided most of it between them.

So old, clumsy and so very unwieldy, it was often a wonder to others how she was going to get in and out of buses, reach Saidapet and return. But she would be back by the evening, bringing a secret gift of peppermints for Radha, secret because she had often been warned not to give unclean sweets to the children.

Once she went to Saidapet and did not return in the evening. Radha stood on the porch gazing at the gate. Even the next day there was no sign of her. Radha wept. Her mother and others were furious. "She has perhaps been run over and killed," they said. "Such a blundering, blind fool. I am surprised it didn't happen before. She must have taken it into her head to give herself a holiday suddenly. I will dismiss her for this. No one is indispensable. These old servants take too much for granted, they must be taught a lesson."

Three days later the Ayah stood before the lady of the house and saluted her. The lady was half-glad to see her and half-angry. "You will never get leave again or you may go away once and for all. Why didn't you return in time? . . ." The Ayah laughed uncontrollably; even her dark face was flushed, and her eyes were bright.

"Why do you laugh, you idiot? What is the matter?" The Ayah covered her face with her sari and mumbled, "He has come . . ." And she giggled.

"Who?"

"The Old Fellow . . ." At the mention of the Old Fellow, Radha, who had all the time been tightly hugging the Ayah, freed herself, ran into the kitchen and shut the door.

"Who is the Old Fellow?" asked the lady.

"I can't tell his name," the Ayah said shyly.

"Your husband?"

"Yes," said Ayah and writhed awkwardly. "He wants me to cook for him and look after him. . . . The man was there when I went home. He sat as if he had never gone out of the house. He gave me a fright, madam. He is out there in the garden. Please, won't you look at him?" The lady went out and saw a wizened old man standing in the drive.

"Salute our lady, don't stand there and blink," the Ayah said. The old man raised his arm stiffly and salaamed. He said, "I want Thayi." It seemed odd to hear the Ayah being called by her name. "I want Thayi. She is to cook for me. She must go with me," he said sullenly.

"You want to go, Ayah?"

The Ayah averted her face and shook with laughter. "He went away years ago. He was in Ceylon tea gardens. How could anyone know he was coming? The *circar* sent him back. Who will take care of him now?"

Half an hour later she walked out of the house, led by a husband proud of his slave. She took leave, in a most touching and ceremonious manner, of everyone except Radha, who refused to come out of the kitchen. When the Ayah stood outside the kitchen door and begged her to come out, Radha asked, "Is the Old Fellow carrying you off?"

"Yes, dear, bad fellow."

"Who left the door of the dog house open?"

"No one. He broke it open."

"What does he want?"

"He wants to carry me off," said the Ayah.

"I won't come out till he is gone. All right. Go, go before he comes here for you." The Ayah acted on this advice after waiting at the kitchen door for nearly half an hour.

LEELA'S FRIEND

Sidda was hanging about the gate at a moment when Mr. Sivasanker was standing in the front veranda of his house, brooding over the servant problem.

"Sir, do you want a servant?" Sidda asked.

"Come in," said Mr. Sivasanker. As Sidda opened the gate and came in, Mr. Sivasanker subjected him to a scrutiny and said to himself, "Doesn't seem to be a bad sort. . . . At any rate, the fellow looks tidy."

"Where were you before?" he asked.

Sidda said, "In a bungalow there," and indicated a vague somewhere, "in the doctor's house."

"What is his name?"

"I don't know, master," Sidda said. "He lives near the market."

"Why did they send you away?"

"They left the town, master," Sidda said, giving the stock reply.

Mr. Sivasanker was unable to make up his mind. He called his wife. She looked at Sidda and said, "He doesn't seem to me worse than the others we have had." Leela, their five-year-old daughter, came out, looked at Sidda and gave a cry of joy. "Oh, Father!" she said, "I like him. Don't send him away. Let us keep him in our house." And that decided it.

Sidda was given two meals a day and four rupees a month, in return for which he washed clothes, tended the garden, ran errands, chopped wood and looked after Leela.

"Sidda, come and play!" Leela would cry, and Sidda had to drop any work he might be doing and run to her, as she stood in the front garden with a red ball in her hand. His company made her supremely happy. She flung the ball at him and he flung it back. And then she said, "Now throw the ball into the sky." Sidda clutched the ball, closed his eyes for a second and threw the ball up. When the ball came down again, he said, "Now this has touched the moon and come. You see here a little bit of the moon sticking." Leela keenly examined the ball for traces of the moon and said, "I don't see it."

"You must be very quick about it," said Sidda, "because it will all evaporate and go back to the moon. Now hurry up. . . ." He covered the ball tightly with his fingers and allowed her to peep through a little gap.

"Ah, yes," said Leela. "I see the moon, but is the moon very wet?"

"Certainly, it is," Sidda said.

"What is in the sky, Sidda?"

"God," he said.

"If we stand on the roof and stretch our arm, can we touch the sky?"

"Not if we stand on the roof here," he said. "But if you stand on a coconut tree you can touch the sky."

"Have you done it?" asked Leela.

"Yes, many times" said Sidda. "Whenever there is a big moon, I climb a coconut tree and touch it."

"Does the moon know you?"

"Yes, very well. Now come with me. I will show you something nice." They were standing near the rose plant. He said, pointing, "You see the moon there, don't you?"

"Yes."

"Now come with me," he said, and took her to the back yard. He stopped near the well and pointed up. The moon was there, too. Leela clapped her hands and screamed in wonder, "The moon here! It was there! How is it?"

"I have asked it to follow us about."

Leela ran in and told her mother, "Sidda knows the moon." At dusk he carried her in and she held a class for him. She had a box filled with catalogues, illustrated books and stumps of pencils. It gave her great joy to play the teacher to Sidda. She made him squat on the floor with a pencil between his fingers and a catalogue in front of him. She had another pencil and a catalogue and commanded, "Now write." And he had to try and copy whatever she wrote in the pages of her catalogue. She knew two or three letters of the alphabet and could draw a kind of cat and crow. But none of these could Sidda copy even remotely. She said, examining his effort, "Is this how I have drawn the crow? Is this how I have drawn the *B*?" She pitied him and redoubled her efforts to teach him. But that good fellow, though an adept at controlling the moon, was utterly incapable of plying the pencil. Consequently, it looked as though Leela would keep him there pinned to his seat till his stiff, inflexible wrist cracked. He sought relief by saying, "I think your mother is calling you in to dinner." Leela would drop the pencil and run out of the room, and the school hour would end.

After dinner Leela ran to her bed. Sidda had to be ready with a story. He sat down on the floor near the bed and told incomparable stories: of animals in the jungle, of gods in heaven, of magicians who could conjure up golden castles and fill them with little princesses and their pets. . . .

Day by day she clung closer to him. She insisted upon having his company all her waking hours. She was at his side when he was working in the garden or chopping wood, and accompanied him when he was sent on errands.

One evening he went out to buy sugar and Leela went with him. When they came home, Leela's mother noticed that a gold chain Leela had been wearing was missing. "Where is your chain?" Leela looked into her shirt, searched and said, "I don't know." Her mother gave her a slap and said, "How many times have I told you to take it off and put it in the box?"

"Sidda, Sidda!" she shouted a moment later. As Sidda came in, Leela's mother threw a glance at him and thought the fellow already looked queer. She asked him about the chain. His throat went dry. He blinked and answered that he did not know. She mentioned the police and shouted at him. She had to go back into the kitchen for a moment because she had left something in the oven. Leela followed her, whining, "Give me some sugar, Mother, I am hungry." When they came out again and called, "Sidda, Sidda!" there was no answer. Sidda had vanished into the night.

Mr. Sivasanker came home an hour later, grew very excited over all this, went to the police station and lodged a complaint.

After her meal Leela refused to go to bed. "I won't sleep unless Sidda comes and tells me stories. . . . I don't like you, Mother. You are always abusing and worrying Sidda. Why are you so rough?"

"But he has taken away your chain. . . ."

"Let him. It doesn't matter. Tell me a story."

"Sleep, sleep," said Mother, attempting to make her lie down on her lap.

"Tell me a story, Mother," Leela said. It was utterly impossible for her mother to think of a story now. Her mind was disturbed. The thought of Sidda made her panicky. The fellow, with his knowledge of the household, might come in at night and loot. She shuddered to think what a villain she had been harboring all these days. It was God's mercy that he hadn't killed the child for the chain. . . . "Sleep, Leela, sleep," she cajoled.

"Can't you tell the story of the elephant?" Leela asked.

"No."

Leela made a noise of deprecation and asked, "Why should not Sidda sit in our chair, Mother?" Mother didn't answer the question. Leela said a moment later, "Sidda is gone because he wouldn't be allowed to sleep inside the house just as we do. Why should he always be made to sleep outside the house, Mother? I think he is angry with us, Mother."

By the time Sivasanker returned, Leela had fallen asleep. He said, "What a risk we took in engaging that fellow. It seems he is an old criminal. He has been in jail half a dozen times for stealing jewellery from children. From the description I gave, the inspector was able to identify him in a moment."

"Where is he now?" asked the wife.

"The police know his haunts. They will pick him up very soon, don't worry. The inspector was furious that I didn't consult him before employing him. . . ."

Four days later, just as Father was coming home from the office, a police inspector and a constable brought in Sidda. Sidda stood with bowed head. Leela was overjoyed. "Sidda! Sidda!" she cried, and ran down the steps to meet him.

"Don't go near him," the inspector said, stopping her.

"Why not?"

"He is a thief. He has taken away your gold chain."

"Let him. I will have a new chain," Leela said, and all of them laughed. And then Mr. Sivasanker spoke to Sidda; and then his wife addressed him with a few words on his treachery. They then asked him where he had put the chain.

"I have not taken it," Sidda said feebly, looking at the ground.

"Why did you run away without telling us?" asked Leela's mother. There was no answer.

Leela's face became red. "Oh, policemen, leave him alone. I want to play with him."

"My dear child," said the police inspector, "he is a thief."

"Let him be," Leela replied haughtily.

"What a devil you must be to steal a thing from such an innocent child!" remarked the inspector. "Even now it is not too late. Return it. I will let you off, provided you promise not to do such a thing again." Leela's father and mother, too, joined in this appeal. Leela felt disgusted with the whole business and said, "Leave him alone, he hasn't taken the chain."

"You are not at all a reliable prosecution witness, my child," observed the inspector humorously.

"No, he hasn't taken it!" Leela screamed.

Her father said, "Baby, if you don't behave, I will be very angry with you."

Half an hour later the inspector said to the constable, "Take him to the station. I think I shall have to sit with him tonight." The constable took Sidda by the hand and turned to go. Leela ran behind them crying, "Don't take him. Leave him here, leave him here." She clung to Sidda's hand. He looked at her mutely, like an animal. Mr. Sivasanker carried Leela back into the house. Leela was in tears.

Every day when Mr. Sivasanker came home he was asked by his wife, "Any news of the jewel?" and by his daughter, "Where is Sidda?"

"They still have him in the lockup, though he is very stubborn and won't say anything about the jewel," said Mr. Sivasanker.

"Bah! What a rough fellow he must be!" said his wife with a shiver.

"Oh, these fellows who have been in jail once or twice lose all fear. Nothing can make them confess."

A few days later, putting her hand into the tamarind pot in the kitchen, Leela's mother picked up the chain. She took it to the tap and washed off the coating of tamarind on it. It was unmistakably Leela's chain. When it was shown to her, Leela said, "Give it here. I want to wear the chain."

"How did it get into the tamarind pot?" Mother asked.

"Somehow," replied Leela.

"Did you put it in?" asked Mother.

"Yes."

"When?"

"Long ago, the other day."

"Why didn't you say so before?"

"I don't know," said Leela.

When Father came home and was told, he said, "The child must not have any chain hereafter. Didn't I tell you that I saw her carrying it in her hand once or twice? She must have dropped it into the pot sometime. . . . And all this bother on acount of her."

"What about Sidda?" asked Mother.

"I will tell the inspector tomorrow . . . in any case, we couldn't have kept a criminal like him in the house."

MOTHER AND SON

Ramu's mother waited till he was halfway through dinner and then introduced the subject of marriage. Ramu merely replied, "So you are at it again!" He appeared more amused than angry, and so she brought out her favourite points one by one: her brother's daughter was getting on to fourteen, the girl was good-looking and her brother was prepared to give a handsome dowry; she (Ramu's mother) was getting old and wanted a holiday from housekeeping: she might die any moment and then who would cook Ramu's food and look after him? And the most indisputable argument: a man's luck changed with marriage. "The harvest depends not on the hand that holds the plough but on the hand which holds the pot." Earlier in the evening Ramu's mother had decided that if he refused again or exhibited the usual sullenness at the mention of marriage, she would leave him to his fate; she would leave him absolutely alone even if she saw him falling down before a coming train. She would never more interfere in his affairs. She realized what a resolute mind she possessed, and felt proud of the fact. That was the kind of person one ought to be. It was all very well having a mother's heart and so on, but even a mother could have a limit to her feelings. If Ramu thought he could do what he pleased just because she was only a mother, she would show him he was mistaken. If he was going to slight her judgement and feelings, she was going to show how indifferent she herself could be. . . .

With so much preparation she broached the subject of marriage and presented a formidable array of reasons. But Ramu just brushed them aside and spoke slightingly of the appearance of her brother's daughter. And then she announced, "This is the last time I am speaking about this. Hereafter I will leave you alone. Even if I see you drowning I will never ask why you are drowning. Do you understand?"

"Yes." Ramu brooded. He could not get through his Intermediate even at the fourth attempt; he could not get a job, even at twenty rupees a month. And here was Mother worrying him to marry. Of all girls, his uncle's! That protruding tooth alone would put off any man. It was incredible that he should be expected to marry that girl. He had always felt that when he married he would marry a girl like Rezia, whom he had seen in two or three Hindi films. Life was rusty and sterile, and Ramu lived in a stage of perpetual melancholia and depression; he loafed away his time, or slept, or read old newspapers in a free reading room. . . .

He now sat before his dining leaf and brooded. His mother watched him for a moment and said, "I hate your face. I hate anyone who sits before his leaf with that face. A woman only ten days old in widowhood would put on a more cheerful look."

"You are saying all sorts of things because I refuse to marry your brother's daughter," he replied.

"What do I care? She is a fortunate girl and will get a really decent husband." Ramu's mother hated him for his sullenness. It was this gloomy look that she hated in people. It was unbearable. She spoke for a few minutes, and he asked, "When are you going to shut up?"

"My life is nearly over," said the mother. "You will see me shutting up once and for all very soon. Don't be impatient. You ask me to shut up! Has it come to this?"

"Well, I only asked you to give me some time to eat."

"Oh, yes. You will have it soon, my boy. When I am gone you will have plenty of time, my boy."

Ramu did not reply. He ate his food in silence. "I only want you to look a little more human when you eat," she said.

"How is it possible with this food?" asked Ramu.

"What do you say?" screamed the mother. "If you are so fastidious, work and earn like all men. Throw down the money and demand what you want. Don't command when you are a pauper."

When the meal was over, Ramu was seen putting on his sandals. "Where are you going?" asked the mother.

"Going out," he curtly replied, and walked out, leaving the street door ajar.

Her duties for the day were over. She had scrubbed the floor of the kitchen, washed the vessels and put them in a shining row on the wooden shelf, returned the short scrubbing broom to its corner and closed the kitchen window.

Taking the lantern and closing the kitchen door, she came to the front room. The street door stood ajar. She became indignant at her son's carelessness. The boy was indifferent and irresponsible and didn't feel bound even to shut the street door. Here she was wearing out her palm scrubbing the floor night after night. Why should she slave if he was indifferent? He was old enough to realize his responsibilities in life.

She took out her small wooden box and put into her mouth a clove, a cardamom and a piece of areca nut. Chewing these, she felt more at peace with life. She shut the door without bolting it and lay down to sleep.

Where could Ramu have gone? She began to feel uneasy. She rolled her mat, went out, spread it on the *pyol* and lay down. She muttered to herself the holy name of Sri Rama in order to keep out disturbing thoughts. She went on whispering, "Sita Rama Rama . . ." But she ceased unconsciously. Her thoughts returned to Ramu. What did he say before going out? "I am just going out for a stroll, Mother. Don't worry. I shall be back soon." No, it was not that. Not he. Why was the boy so secretive about his movements? That was impudent and exasperating. But, she told herself, she deserved no better treatment with that terrible temper and cutting tongue of hers. There was no doubt that she had conducted herself abominably during the meal. All her life this had been her worst failing: this tendency, while in a temper, to talk without restraint. She even felt that her husband would have lived for a few more years if she had spoken to him less. . . . Ramu had said something about the food. She would include more vegetables and cook better from tomorrow. Poor boy . . .

She fell asleep. Somewhere a gong sounded one, and she woke up. One o'clock? She called, "Ramu, Ramu."

She did not dare to contemplate what he might have done with himself. Gradually she came to believe that her words during the meal had driven him to suicide. She sat up and wept. She was working herself up to a hysterical pitch. When she closed her eyes to press out the gathering tears, the vision of her son's body floating in Kukanahalli Tank came before her. His striped shirt and mill dhoti were sodden and clung close to his body. His sandals were left on one of the tank steps. His face was bloated beyond all recognition.

She screamed aloud and jumped down from the *pyol*. She ran along the whole length of Old Agrahar Street. It was deserted. Electric lights twinkled here and there. Far away a *tonga* was rattling on, the *tonga*-driver's song faintly disturbing the silence; the blast of a night constable's whistle came to her ears, and she stopped running. She realized that after all it might be only her imagination. He might have gone away to the drama, which didn't usually close before three in the morning. She rapidly uttered the holy name of Sri Rama in order to prevent the picture of Kukanahalli Tank coming before her mind.

She had a restless night. Unknown to herself, she slept in snatches and woke up with a start every time the gong boomed. The gong struck six through the chill morning.

Tears streaming down her face, she started for Kukanahalli Tank. Mysore was just waking to fresh life. Milkmen with slow cows passed along. Municipal sweepers were busy with their long brooms. One or two cycles passed her.

She reached the tank, not daring even once to look at the water. She found him sleeping on one of the benches that lined the bund. For just a second she wondered if it might be his corpse. She shook him vigourously, crying "Ramu!" She heaved a tremendous sigh of relief when he stirred.

He sat up, rubbing his eyes. "Why are you here, Mother?"

"What a place to sleep in!"

"Oh, I just fell asleep," he said.

"Come home," she said. She walked on and he followed her. She saw him going down the tank steps. "Where are you going?"

"Just for a wash," Ramu explained.

She clung to his arm and said vehemently, "No, don't go near the water."

He obeyed her, though he was slightly baffled by her vehemence.

New Stories

NAGA

The boy took off the lid of the circular wicker basket and stood looking at the cobra coiled inside, and then said, "Naga, I hope you are dead, so that I may sell your skin to the pursemakers; at least that way you may become useful." He poked it with a finger. Naga raised its head and looked about with a dull wonder. "You have become too lazy even to open your hood. You are no cobra. You are an earthworm. I am a snake charmer attempting to show you off and make a living. No wonder so often I have to stand at the bus stop pretending to be blind and beg. The trouble is, no one wants to see you, no one has any respect for you and no one is afraid of you, and do you know what that means? I starve, that is all."

Whenever the boy appeared at the street door, householders shooed him away. He had seen his father operate under similar conditions. His father would climb the steps of the house unmindful of the discouragement, settle down with his basket and go through his act heedless of what anyone said. He would pull out his gourd pipe from the bag and play the snake tune over and over, until its shrill, ear-piercing note induced a torpor and made people listen to his preamble: "In my dream, God Shiva appeared and said, 'Go forth and thrust your hand into that crevice in the floor of my sanctum.' As you all know, Shiva is the Lord of Cobras, which he ties his braid with, and its hood canopies his head; the great God Vishnu rests in the coils of Adi-Shesha, the mightiest serpent, who also bears on his thousand heads this Universe. Think of the armlets on goddess Parvathi! Again, elegant little snakes. How can we think that we are wiser than our gods? Snake is a part of a god's ornament, and not an ordinary creature. I obeyed Shiva's command—at midnight walked out and put my arm into the snake hole."

At this point his audience would shudder and someone would ask, "Were you bitten?"

"Of course I was bitten, but still you see me here, because the same god commanded, 'Find that weed growing on the old fort wall.' No, I am not going to mention its name, even if I am offered a handful of sovereigns."

"What did you do with the weed?"

"I chewed it; thereafter no venom could enter my system. And the terrible fellow inside this basket plunged his fangs into my arms like a baby biting his mother's nipple, but I laughed and pulled him out, and knocked off with a piece of stone the fangs that made him so arrogant; and then he understood that I was only a friend and well-wisher, and no trouble after that. After all, what is a serpent? A great soul in a state of penance waiting to go back to its heavenly world. That is all, sirs."

After this speech, his father would flick open the basket lid and play the pipe again, whereupon the snake would dart up like spring-work, look about and sway a little; people would be terrified and repelled, but still enthralled. At the end of the performance, they gave him coins and rice, and sometimes an old shirt, too, and occa-sionally he wangled an egg if he observed a hen around; seizing Naga by the throat, he let the egg slide down its gullet, to the delight of the onlookers. He then packed up and repeated the performance at the next street or at the bazaar, and when he had collected suffi-cient food and cash he returned to his hut beside the park wall, in the shade of a big tamarind tree. He cooked the rice and fed his son, and they slept outside the hut, under the stars.

The boy had followed his father ever since he could walk, and when he attained the age of ten his father let him handle Naga and harangue his audience in his own style. His father often said, "We must not fail to give Naga two eggs a week. When he grows old, he will grow shorter each day; someday he will grow wings and fly off, and do you know that at that time he will spit out the poison in his fangs in the form of a brilliant jewel, and if you possessed it you could become a king?"

————

One day when the boy had stayed beside the hut out of laziness, he noticed a tiny monkey gambolling amidst the branches of the tamarind tree and watched it with open-mouthed wonder, not even noticing his father arrive home.

"Boy, what are you looking at? Here, eat this," said the father, handing him a packet of sweets. "They gave it to me at that big house, where some festival is going on. Naga danced to the pipe wonderfully today. He now understands all our speech. At the end of his dance, he stood six feet high on the tip of his tail, spread out his hood, hissed and sent a whole crowd scampering. Those people enjoyed it, though, and gave me money and sweets." His father looked happy as he opened the lid of the basket. The cobra raised its head. His father held it up by the neck, and forced a bit of a sweet between its jaws, and watched it work its way down. "He is now one of our family and should learn to eat what we eat," he said. After struggling through the sweet, Naga coiled itself down, and the man clapped the lid back.

The boy munched the sweet with his eyes still fixed on the monkey. "Father, I wish I were a monkey. I'd never come down from the tree. See how he is nibbling all that tamarind fruit. . . . Hey, monkey, get me a fruit!" he cried.

The man was amused, and said, "This is no way to befriend him. You should give him something to eat, not ask him to feed you."

At which the boy spat out his sweet, wiped it clean with his shirt, held it up and cried, "Come on, monkey! Here!"

His father said, "If you call him 'monkey,' he will never like you. You must give him a nice name."

"What shall we call him?"

"Rama, name of the master of Hanuman, the Divine Monkey. Monkeys adore that name."

The boy at once called, "Rama, here, take this." He flourished his arms, holding up the sweet, and the monkey did pause in its endless antics and notice him. The boy hugged the tree trunk, and heaved himself up, and carefully placed the sweet on the flat surface of a forking branch, and the monkey watched with round-eyed wonder. The boy slid back to the ground and eagerly waited for the monkey to come down and accept the gift. While he watched and the monkey was debating within himself, a crow appeared from somewhere and took away the sweet. The boy shrieked out a curse.

His father cried, "Hey, what? Where did you learn this foul word? No monkey will respect you if you utter bad words." Ultimately, when the little monkey was tempted down with another piece of sweet, his father caught him deftly by the wrist, holding him off firmly by the scruff to prevent his biting.

Fifteen days of starvation, bullying, cajoling and dangling of fruit before the monkey's eyes taught him what he was expected to do. First of all, he ceased trying to bite or scratch. And then he realized that his mission in life was to please his master by performing. At a command from his master, he could demonstrate how Hanuman, the Divine Monkey of the *Ramayana*, strode up and down with tail ablaze and set Ravana's capital on fire; how an oppressed village daughter-in-law would walk home carrying a pitcher of water on her head; how a newlywed would address his beloved (chatter, blink, raise the brow and grin); and, finally, what was natural to him— tumbling and acrobatics on top of a bamboo pole. When Rama was ready to appear in public, his master took him to a roadside-tailor friend of his and had him measured out for a frilled jacket, leaving the tail out, and a fool's cap held in position with a band under his small chin. Rama constantly tried to push his cap back and rip it off, but whenever he attempted it he was whacked with a switch, and he soon resigned himself to wearing his uniform until the end of the day. When his master stripped off Rama's clothes, the monkey performed spontaneous somersaults in sheer relief.

Rama became popular. Schoolchildren screamed with joy at the sight of him. Householders beckoned to him to step in and divert a crying child. He performed competently, earned money for his master and peanuts for himself. Discarded baby clothes were offered to him as gifts. The father-son team started out each day, the boy with the monkey riding on his shoulder and the cobra basket carried by his father at some distance away—for the monkey chattered and shrank, his face disfigured with fright, whenever the cobra hissed and reared itself up. While the young fellow managed to display the tricks of the monkey to a group, he could hear his father's pipe farther off. At the weekly market fairs in the villages around, they were a familiar pair, and they became prosperous enough to take a bus home at the end of the day. Sometimes as they started to get on, a timid passenger would ask, "What's to happen if the cobra gets out?"

"No danger. The lid is secured with a rope," the father replied.

There would always be someone among the passengers to remark, "A snake minds its business until you step on its tail."

"But this monkey?" another passenger said. "God knows what he will be up to!"

"He is gentle and wise," said the father, and offered a small tip to win the conductor's favor.

They travelled widely, performing at all market fairs, and earned enough money to indulge in an occasional tiffin at a restaurant. The boy's father would part company from him in the evening, saying, "Stay. I've a stomach ache; I'll get some medicine for it and come back," and return tottering late at night. The boy felt frightened of his father at such moments, and, lying on his mat, with the monkey tethered to a stake nearby, pretended to be asleep. Father kicked him and said, "Get up, lazy swine. Sleeping when your father slaving for you all day comes home for speech with you. You are not my son but a bastard." But the boy would not stir.

One night the boy really fell asleep, and woke up in the morning to find his father gone. The monkey was also missing. "They must have gone off together!" he cried. He paced up and down and called, "Father!" several times. He then peered into the hut and found the round basket intact in its corner. He noticed on the lid of the basket some coins, and felt rather pleased when he counted them and found eighty paise in small change. "It must all be for me," he said to himself. He felt promoted to adulthood, handling so much cash. He felt rich but also puzzled at his father's tactics. Ever since he could remember, he had never woken up without finding his father at his side. He had a foreboding that he was not going to see his father anymore. Father would never at any time go out without announcing his purpose—for a bath at the street tap, or to seek medicine for a "stomach ache," or to do a little shopping.

The boy lifted the lid of the basket to make sure that the snake at least was there. It popped up the moment the lid was taken off. He looked at it, and it looked at him for a moment. "I'm your master now. Take care." As if understanding the changed circumstances, the snake darted its forked tongue and half-opened its hood. He tapped it down with his finger, saying, "Get back. Not yet." Would it be any use waiting for his father to turn up? He felt hungry. Wondered if it'd be proper to buy his breakfast with the coins left on the basket lid. If his father should suddenly come back, he would slap him for taking the money. He put the lid back on the snake, put the coins back on the lid as he had found them and sat at the mouth of the hut, vacantly looking at the tamarind tree and sighing for his monkey, which would have displayed so many fresh and unexpected pranks early in the morning. He reached for a little cloth bag in which was stored a variety of nuts and fried pulses to feed the monkey. He opened the bag, examined the contents and put a handful into his mouth and chewed: "Tastes so good. Too good for a monkey, but Father will . . ." His father always clouted his head when he caught him eating nuts meant for the monkey. Today he felt free to munch the nuts, although worried at the back of his mind lest his father should suddenly remember and come back for the monkey food. He found the gourd pipe in its usual place, stuck in the thatch. He snatched it up and blew through its reeds, feeling satisfied that he could play as well as his father and that the public would not know the difference; only it made him cough a little and gasp for breath. The shrill notes attracted the attention of people passing by the hut, mostly day labourers carrying spades and pickaxes and women carrying baskets, who nodded their heads approvingly and remarked, "True son of the father." Everyone had a word with him. All knew him in that colony of huts, which had cropped up around the water fountain. All the efforts of the municipality to dislodge these citizens had proved futile; the huts sprang up as often as they were destroyed, and when the municipal councillors realized the concentration of voting power in this colony, they let the squatters alone, except when some V.I.P. from Delhi passed that way, and then they were asked to stay out of sight, behind the park wall, till the eminent man had flashed past in his car.

"Why are you not out yet?" asked a woman.

"My father is not here," the boy said pathetically. "I do not know where he is gone." He sobbed a little.

The woman put down her basket, sat by his side and asked, "Are you hungry?"

"I have money," he said.

She gently patted his head and said, "Ah, poor child! I knew your mother. She was a good girl. That she should have left you adrift like this and gone heavenward!" Although he had no memory of his mother, at the mention of her, tears rolled down his cheeks, and he licked them off with relish at the corner of his mouth. The woman suddenly said, "What are you going to do now?"

"I don't know," he said. "Wait till my father comes."

"Foolish and unfortunate child. Your father is gone."

"Where?" asked the boy.

"Don't ask me," the woman said. "I talked to a man who saw him go. He saw him get into the early-morning bus, which goes up the mountains, and that strumpet in the blue sari was with him."

"What about the monkey?" the boy asked. "Won't it come back?"

She had no answer to this question. Meanwhile, a man hawking rice cakes on a wooden tray was crying his wares at the end of the lane. The woman hailed him in a shrill voice and ordered, "Sell this poor child two *idlies*. Give him freshly made ones, not yesterday's."

"Yesterday's stuff not available even for a gold piece," said the man.

"Give him the money," she told the boy. The boy ran in and fetched some money. The woman pleaded with the hawker, "Give him something extra for the money."

"What extra?" he snarled.

"This is an unfortunate child."

"So are others. What can I do? Why don't you sell your earrings and help him? I shall go bankrupt if I listen to people like you and start giving more for less money." He took the cash and went on. Before he reached the third hut, the boy had polished off the *idlies*—so soft and pungent, with green chutney spread on top.

The boy felt more at peace with the world now, and able to face his problems. After satisfying herself that he had eaten well, the woman rose to go, muttering, "Awful strumpet, to seduce a man from his child." The boy sat and brooded over her words. Though he gave no outward sign of it, he knew who the strumpet in the blue sari was. She lived in one of those houses beyond the park wall and was always to be found standing at the door, and seemed to be a fixture there. At the sight of her, his father would slow down his pace and tell the boy, "You keep going. I'll join you." The first time it happened, after waiting at the street corner, the boy tied the monkey to a lamppost and went back to the house. He did not find either his father or the woman where he had left them. The door of the house was shut. He raised his hand to pound on it, but restrained himself and sat down on the step, wondering. Presently the door opened and his father emerged, with the basket slung over his shoulder as usual; he appeared displeased at the sight of the boy and raised his hand to strike him, muttering, "Didn't I say, 'Keep going'?" The boy ducked and ran down the street, and heard the blue-sari woman remark, "Bad, mischievous devil, full of evil curiosity!" Later, his father said, "When I say go, you must obey."

"What did you do there?" asked the boy, trying to look and sound innocent, and the man said severely, "You must not ask questions."

"Who is she? What is her name?"

"Oh, she is a relative," the man said. To further probing questions he said, "I went in to drink tea. You'll be thrashed if you ask more questions, little devil."

The boy said, as an afterthought, "I only came back thinking that you might want me to take the basket," whereupon his father said sternly, "No more talk. You must know, she is a good and lovely person." The boy did not accept this description of her. She had called him names. He wanted to shout from rooftops, "Bad, bad, and bad woman and not at all lovely!" but kept it to himself. Whenever they passed that way again, the boy quickened his pace, without looking left or right, and waited patiently for his father to join him at the street corner. Occasionally his father followed his example and passed on without glancing at the house if he noticed, in place of the woman, a hairy-chested man standing at the door, massaging his potbelly.

The boy found that he could play the pipe, handle the snake and feed it also—all in the same manner as his father used to. Also, he could knock off the fangs whenever they started to grow. He earned enough each day, and as the weeks and months passed he grew taller, and the snake became progressively tardy and flabby and hardly stirred its coils. The boy never ceased to sigh for the monkey. The worst blow his father had dealt him was the kidnapping of his monkey.

When a number of days passed without any earnings, he decided to rid himself of the snake, throw away the gourd pipe and do something else for a living. Perhaps catch another monkey and train it. He had watched his father and knew how to go about this. A monkey on his shoulder would gain him admission anywhere, even into a palace. Later on, he would just keep it as a pet and look for some other profession. Start as a porter at the railway station—so many trains to watch every hour—and maybe get into one someday and out into the wide world. But the first step would be to get rid of Naga. He couldn't afford to find eggs and milk for him.

He carried the snake basket along to a lonely spot down the river course, away from human habitation, where a snake could move about in peace without getting killed at sight. In that lonely part of Nallappa's grove, there were many mounds, crevasses and anthills. "You could make your home anywhere there, and your cousins will be happy to receive you back into their fold," he said to the snake. "You should learn to be happy in your own home. You must forget me. You have become useless, and we must part. I don't know where my father is gone. He'd have kept you until you grew wings and all that, but I don't care." He opened the lid of the basket, lifted the snake and set it free. It lay inert for a while, then raised its head, looked at the outside world without interest, and started to move along tardily, without any aim. After a few yards of slow motion, it turned about, looking for its basket home. At once the boy snatched up the basket and flung it far out of the snake's range. "You will not go anywhere else as long as I am nearby." He turned the snake round, to face an anthill, prodded it on and then began to run at full speed in the opposite direction. He stopped at a distance, hid himself behind a tree and watched. The snake was approaching the slope of the anthill. The boy had no doubt now that Naga would find the hole on its top, slip itself in and vanish from his life forever. The snake crawled halfway up the hill, hesitated and then turned round and came along in his direction again. The boy swore, "Oh, damned snake! Why don't you go back to your world and stay there? You won't find me again." He ran through Nallappa's grove and stopped to regain his breath. From where he stood, he saw his Naga glide along majestically across the ground, shining like a silver ribbon under the bright sun. The boy paused to say "Goodbye" before making his exit. But looking up he noticed a white-necked Brahmany kite sailing in the blue sky. "Garuda," he said in awe. As was the custom, he made obeisance to it by touching his eyes with his fingertips. Garuda was the vehicle of God Vishnu and was sacred. He shut his eyes in a brief prayer to the bird. "You are a god, but I know you eat snakes. Please leave Naga alone." He opened his eyes and saw the kite skimming along a little nearer, its shadow almost trailing the course of the lethargic snake. "Oh!" he screamed. "I know your purpose." Garuda would make a swoop and dive at the right moment and stab his claws into that foolish Naga, who had refused the shelter of the anthill, and carry him off for his dinner. The boy dashed back to the snake, retrieving his basket on the way. When he saw the basket, Naga slithered back into it, as if coming home after a strenuous public performance.

Naga was eventually reinstated in his corner at the hut beside the park wall. The boy said to the snake, "If you don't grow wings soon enough, I hope you will be hit on the head with a bamboo staff, as it normally happens to any cobra. Know this: I will not be guarding you forever. I'll be away at the railway station, and if you come out of the basket and adventure about, it will be your end. No one can blame me afterward."

SELVI

At the end of every concert, she was mobbed by autograph hunters. They would hem her in and not allow her to leave the dais. At that moment Mohan, slowly progressing towards the exit, would turn round and call across the hall, "Selvi, hurry up. You want to miss the train?" "Still a lot of time," she could have said, but she was not in the habit of ever contradicting him; for Mohan this was a golden chance not to be missed, to order her in public and demonstrate his authority. He would then turn to a group of admirers waiting to escort him and Selvi, particularly Selvi, to the car, and remark in apparent jest, "Left to herself, she'll sit there and fill all the autograph books in the world till doomsday, she has no sense of time."

The public viewed her as a rare, ethereal entity; but he alone knew her private face. "Not bad-looking," he commented within himself when he first saw her, "but needs touching up." Her eyebrows, which flourished wildly, were trimmed and arched. For her complexion, by no means fair, but just on the borderline, he discovered the correct skin cream and talcum which imparted to her brow and cheeks a shade confounding classification. Mohan did not want anyone to suspect that he encouraged the use of cosmetics. He had been a follower of Mahatma Gandhi and spent several years in prison, wore only cloth spun by hand and shunned all luxury; there could be no question of his seeking modern, artificial aids to enhance the personality of his wife. But he had discovered at some stage certain subtle cosmetics through a contact in Singapore, an adoring fan of Selvi's, who felt only too honoured to be asked to supply them regularly, and to keep it a secret.

When Selvi came on the stage, she looked radiant, rather than dark, brown or fair, and it left the public guessing and debating, whenever the question came up, as to what colour her skin was. There was a tremendous amount of speculation on all aspects of her life and person wherever her admirers gathered, especially at a place like the Boardless where much town-talk was exchanged over coffee at the tables reserved for the habitués. Varma, the proprietor, loved to overhear such conversation from his pedestal at the cash counter, especially when the subject was Selvi. He was one of her worshippers, but from a distance, often feeling, "Goddess Lakshmi has favoured me; I have nothing more to pray for in the line of wealth or prosperity, but I crave for the favour of the other goddess, that is Saraswathi, who is in our midst today as Selvi the divine singer; if only she will condescend to accept a cup of coffee or sweets from my hand, how grand it would be! But alas, whenever I bring a gift for her, *he* takes it and turns me back from the porch with a formal word of thanks." Varma was only one among the thousands who had a longing to meet Selvi. But she was kept in a fortress of invisible walls. It was as if she was fated to spend her life either in solitary confinement or fettered to her gaoler in company. She was never left alone, even for a moment, with anyone. She had been wedded to Mohan for over two decades and had never spoken to anyone except in his presence.

Visitors kept coming all day long for a *darshan* from Selvi, but few ever reached her presence. Some were received on the ground floor, some were received on the lawns, some were encouraged to go up the staircase—but none could get a glimpse of her, only of Mohan's secretary or of the secretary's secretary. Select personalities, however, were received ceremoniously in the main hall upstairs and seated on sofas. Ordinary visitors would not be offered seats, but they could occupy any bench or chair found scattered here and there and wait as long as they pleased—and go back wherever they came from.

Their home was a huge building of East India Company days, displaying arches, columns and gables, once the residence of Sir Frederick Lawley (whose statue stood in the town-square), who had kept a retinue of forty servants to sweep and dust the six oversized halls built on two floors, with tall doors and gothic windows and Venetian shutters, set on several acres of ground five miles away from the city on the road to Mempi Hills. The place was wooded with enormous trees; particularly important was an elm (or oak or beech, no one could say) at the gate, planted by Sir Frederick, who had brought the seedling from England, said to be the only one of its kind in India. No one would tenant the house, since Sir Frederick's spirit was said to hover about the place, and many weird tales were current in Malgudi at that time. The building had been abandoned since 1947, when Britain quit India. Mohan, who at some point made a bid for it, said, "Let me try. Gandhiji's non-violence rid the country of the British rule. I was a humble disciple of Mahatmaji and I should be able to rid the place of a British ghost by the same technique!" He found money to buy the house when Selvi received a fee for lending her voice to a film-star, who just moved her lips, synchronizing with Selvi's singing, and attained much glory for her performance in a film. But thereafter Mohan definitely shut out all film offers. "I'll establish Selvi as a unique phenomenon on her own, not as a voice for some fat cosmetic-dummy."

Bit by bit, by assiduous publicity and word-of-mouth recommendation, winning the favour of every journalist and music critic available, he had built up her image to its present stature. Hard work it was over the years. At the end, when it bore fruit, her name acquired a unique charm, her photograph began to appear in one publication or another every week. She was in demand everywhere. Mohan's office was besieged by the organizers of musical events from all over the country. "Leave your proposal with my secretary, and we will inform you after finalizing our calendar for the quarter," he would tell one. To another, he would say, "My schedule is tight till 1982—if there is any cancellation we'll see what can be done. Remind me in October of 1981, I'll give you a final answer." He rejected several offers for no other reason than to preserve a rarity value for Selvi. When Mohan accepted an engagement, the applicant (more a supplicant) felt grateful, notwithstanding the exorbitant fee, of which half was to be paid immediately in cash without a receipt. He varied his tactics occasionally. He would specify that all the earnings of a certain concert should go to some fashionable social-service organization carrying well-known names on its list of patrons. He would accept no remuneration for the performance itself, but ask for expenses in cash, which would approximate his normal fee. He was a financial expert who knew how to conjure up money and at the same time keep Income Tax at arm's length. Pacing his lawns and corridors restlessly, his mind was always busy, planning how to organize and manoeuvre men and money. Suddenly he would pause, summon his stenographer and dictate, or pick up the phone and talk at length into it.

In addition to the actual professional matters, he kept an eye on public relations, too; he attended select, exclusive parties, invited eminent men and women to dinner at Lawley Terrace; among the guests would often be found a sprinkling of international figures, too; on his walls hung group photographs of himself and Selvi in the company of the strangest assortment of personalities—Tito, Bulganin, Yehudi Menuhin, John Kennedy, the Nehru family, the Pope, Charlie Chaplin, yogis and sportsmen and political figures, taken under various circumstances and settings.

At the Boardless there was constant speculation about Selvi's early life. Varma heard at the gossip table that Selvi had been brought up by her mother in a back row of Vinayak Mudali Street, in a small house with tiles falling off, with not enough cash at home to put the tiles back on the roof, and had learnt music from her, practising with her brother and sister accompanying her on their instruments.

At this time Mohan had a photo studio on Market Road. Once Selvi's mother brought the girl to be photographed for a school magazine after she had won the first prize in a music competition. Thereafter Mohan visited them casually now and then, as a sort of well-wisher of the family, sat in the single chair their home provided, drank coffee and generally behaved as a benign god to that family by his advice and guidance. Sometimes he would request Selvi to sing, and then dramatically leave the chair and sit down on the floor crosslegged with his eyes shut, in an attitude of total absorption in her melody, to indicate that in the presence of such an inspired artist it would be blasphemous to sit high in a chair.

Day after day, he performed little services for the family, and then gradually took over the management of their affairs. At the Boardless, no one could relate with certainty at what point exactly he began to refer to Selvi as his wife or where, when or how they were married. No one would dare investigate it too closely now.

Mohan had lost no time in investing the money earned from the film in buying Lawley Terrace. After freshening up its walls with lime wash and paints, on an auspicious day he engaged Gaffur's taxi, and took Selvi and the family to the Terrace.

While her mother, brother and sister grew excited at the dimension of the house as they passed through the six halls, looked up at the high ceilings and clicked their tongues, Selvi herself showed no reaction; she went through the house as if through the corridors of a museum. Mohan was a little disappointed and asked, "How do you like this place?" At that all she could say in answer was, "It looks big." At the end of the guided tour, he launched on a description and history (avoiding the hauntings) of the house. She listened, without any show of interest. Her mind seemed to be elsewhere. They were all seated on the gigantic settees of the Company days, which had come with the property, left behind because they could not be moved. She didn't seem to notice even the immensity of the furniture on which she was seated. As a matter of fact, as he came to realize later, in the course of their hundreds of concert tours she was habitually oblivious of her surroundings. In any setting—mansion or Five Star Hotel with luxurious guest rooms and attendants, or a small-town or village home with no special facilities or privacy—she looked equally indifferent or contented; washed, dressed and was ready for the concert at the appointed time in the evening. Most days she never knew or questioned where she was to sing or what fee they were getting. Whenever he said, "Pack and get ready," she filled a trunk with her clothes, toiletry and tonic pills, and was ready, not even questioning where they were going. She sat in a reserved seat in the train when she was asked to do so, and was ready to leave when Mohan warned her they would have to get off at the next stop. She was undemanding, unenquiring, uncomplaining. She seemed to exist without noticing anything or anyone, rapt in some secret melody or thought of her own.

In the course of a quarter-century, she had become a national figure; travelled widely in and out of the country. They named her the Goddess of Melody. When her name was announced, the hall, any hall, filled up to capacity and people fought for seats. When she appeared on the dais, the audience was thrilled as if vouchsafed a vision, and she was accorded a thundering ovation. When she settled down, gently cleared her throat and hummed softly to help the accompanists tune their instruments, a silence fell among the audience.

Her voice possessed a versatility and reach which never failed to transport her audience. Her appeal was alike to the common, unsophisticated listener as to pandits, theorists and musicologists, and even those who didn't care for any sort of music liked to be seen at her concerts for prestige's sake.

During a concert, wherever it might be—Madras, Delhi, London, New York or Singapore—Mohan occupied as a rule the centre seat in the first row of the auditorium and rivetted his gaze on the singer, leaving people to wonder whether he was lost in her spell or whether he was inspiring her by thought-transference. Though his eyes were on her, his mind would be busy doing complicated arithmetic with reference to monetary problems, and he would also watch unobtrusively for any tape-recorder that might be smuggled into the hall (he never permitted recording), and note slyly the reactions of the V.I.P.s flanking him.

He planned every concert in detail. He would sit up in the afternoon with Selvi and suggest gently but firmly, "Wouldn't you like to start with the 'Kalyani Varnam'—the minor one?" And she would say, "Yes," never having been able to utter any other word in her life. He would continue, "The second item had better be Thiagaraja's composition in Begada, it'll be good to have a contrasting raga," and then his list would go on to fill up about four hours. "Don't bother to elaborate any *Pallavi* for this audience, but work out briefly a little detail in the Thodi composition. Afterwards you may add any item you like, light *Bhajans, Javalis* or folk-songs," offering her a freedom which was worthless since the programme as devised would be tight-fitting for the duration of the concert, which, according to his rule, should never exceed four hours. "But for my planning and guidance, she'd make a mess, which none realizes," he often reflected.

Everyone curried Mohan's favour and goodwill in the hope that it would lead him to the proximity of the star. Mohan did encourage a particular class to call on him and received them in the Central Hall of Lawley Terrace; he would call aloud to Selvi when such a person arrived, "Here is So-and-so come." It would be no ordinary name— only a minister or an inspector general of police or the managing director of a textile mill, or a newspaper editor, who in his turn would always be eager to do some favour for Mohan, hoping thereby to be recognized eventually by Selvi as a special friend of the family. Selvi would come out of her chamber ten minutes after being summoned and act her part with precision: a wonderful smile, and *namaste*, with her palms gently pressed together, which would send a thrill down the spine of the distinguished visitor, who would generally refer to her last concert and confess how deeply moving it had been, and how a particular raga kept ringing in his ears all that evening, long after the performance. Selvi had appropriate lines in reply to such praise: "Of course, I feel honoured that my little effort has pleased a person of your calibre," while Mohan would interpose with a joke or a personal remark. He didn't want any visitor, however important, to hold her attention, but would draw it to himself at the right moment. At the end Mohan would feel gratified that his tutored lines, gestures and expressions were perfectly delivered by Selvi. He would congratulate himself on shaping her so successfully into a celebrity. "But for my effort, she'd still be another version of her mother and brother, typical Vinayak Mudali Street products, and nothing beyond that. I am glad I've been able to train her so well."

In order that she might quickly get out of the contamination of Vinayak Mudali Street, he gently, unobtrusively, began to isolate her from her mother, brother and sister. As time went on, she saw less and less of them. At the beginning a car would be sent to fetch them, once a week; but as Selvi's public engagements increased, her mother and others were gradually allowed to fade out of her life. Selvi tried once or twice to speak to Mohan about her mother, but he looked annoyed and said, "They must be all right. I'll arrange to get them—but where is the time for it? When we are able to spend at least three days at home, we will get them here." Such a break was rare—generally they came home by train or car and left again within twenty-four hours. On occasions when they did have the time, and if she timidly mentioned her mother, he would almost snap, "I know, I know, I'll send Mani to Vinayak Street—but some other time. We have asked the Governor to lunch tomorrow and they will expect you to sing, informally of course, for just thirty minutes." "The day after that?" Selvi would put in hesitantly, and he would ignore her and move off to make a telephone call. Selvi understood, and resigned herself to it, and never again mentioned her mother. "If my own mother can't see me!" she thought again and again, in secret anguish, having none to whom she could speak her feelings.

Mohan, noticing that she didn't bother him about her mother anymore, felt happy that she had got over the obsession. "That's the right way. Only a baby would bother about its mother." He congratulated himself again on the way he was handling her.

Months and years passed thus. Selvi did not keep any reckoning of it, but went through her career like an automaton, switching on and off her music as ordered.

They were in Calcutta for a series of concerts when news of her mother's death reached her. When she heard it, she refused to come out of her room in the hotel, and wanted all her engagements cancelled. Mohan, who went into her room to coax her, swiftly withdrew when he noticed her tear-drenched face and dishevelled hair. All through the train journey back, she kept looking out of the window and never spoke a word, although Mohan did his best to engage her in talk. He was puzzled by her mood. Although she was generally not talkative, she would at least listen to whatever was said to her and intersperse an occasional monosyllabic comment. Now for a stretch of a thirty-six-hour journey she never spoke a word or looked in his direction. When they reached home, he immediately arranged to take her down to Vinayak Mudali Street, and accompanied her himself to honour the dead officially, feeling certain that his gesture would be appreciated by Selvi. Both the big car and Mohan in his whitest handspun clothes seemed ill-fitting in those surroundings. His car blocked half the street in which Selvi's mother had lived. Selvi's sister, who had married and had children in Singapore, could not come, and her brother's whereabouts were unknown. A neighbour dropped in to explain the circumstances of the old lady's death and how they had to take charge of the body and so forth. Mohan tried to cut short his narration and send him away, since it was unusual to let a nondescript talk to Selvi directly. But she said to Mohan, "You may go back to the Terrace if you like. I'm staying here." Mohan had not expected her to talk to him in that manner. He felt confused and muttered, "By all means . . . I'll send back the car. . . . When do you want it?"

"Never. I'm staying here as I did before. . . ."

"How can you? In this street!" She ignored his objection and said,

"My mother was my guru; here she taught me music, lived and died. . . . I'll also live and die here; what was good for her is good for me too. . . ."

He had never known her to be so truculent or voluble. She had been for years so mild and complaisant that he never thought she could act or speak beyond what she was taught. He lingered, waited for a while hoping for a change of mood. Meanwhile, the neighbour was going on with his narration, omitting no detail of the old lady's last moments and the problems that arose in connection with the performance of the final obsequies. "I did not know where to reach you, but finally we carried her across the river and I lit the pyre with my own hands and dissolved the ashes in the Sarayu. After all, I'd known her as a boy, and you remember how I used to call her Auntie and sit up and listen when you were practising. . . . Oh! not these days of course, I can't afford to buy a ticket, or get anywhere near the hall where you sing."

Mohan watched in consternation. He had never known her to go beyond the script written by him. She had never spoken to anyone or stayed in a company after receiving his signal to terminate the interview and withdraw. Today it didn't work. She ignored his signal, and the man from Vinayak neighbourhood went on in a frenzy of reliving the funeral; he felt triumphant to have been of help on a unique occasion.

After waiting impatiently, Mohan rose to go. "Anything you want to be sent down?"

"Nothing," she replied. He saw that she had worn an old sari, and had no makeup or jewellery, having left it all behind at the Terrace.

"You mean to say, you'll need nothing?"

"I need nothing. . . ."

"How will you manage?" She didn't answer. He asked weakly, "You have the series at Bhopal, shall I tell them to change the dates?" For the first time he was consulting her on such problems.

She simply said, "Do what you like."

"What do you mean by that?" No answer.

He stepped out and drove away; the car had attracted a crowd, which now turned its attention to Selvi. They came forward to stare at her—a rare luxury for most, the citadel having been impregnable all these years; she had been only a hearsay and a myth to most people. Someone said, "Why did you not come to your mother's help? She was asking for you!" Selvi broke down and was convulsed with sobs.

Three days later Mohan came again to announce, "On the thirtieth you have to receive an honorary degree at the Delhi University. . . ." She just shook her head negatively. "The Prime Minister will be presiding over the function."

When pressed, she just said, "Please leave me out of all this, leave me alone, I want to be alone hereafter. I can't bear the sight of anyone. . . ."

"Just this one engagement. Do what you like after that. Otherwise it will be most compromising. Only one day at Delhi, we will get back immediately—also you signed the gramophone contract for recording next month. . . ." She didn't reply. Her look suggested that it was not her concern. "You'll be landing me in trouble; at least, the present commitments . . ." It was difficult to carry on negotiations with a crowd watching and following every word of their talk. He wished he could have some privacy with her, but this was a one-room house, where everybody came and stood about or sat down anywhere. If he could get her alone, he would either coax her or wring her neck. He felt helpless and desperate, and suddenly turned round and left.

He came again a week later. But it proved no better. She neither welcomed him nor asked him to leave. He suggested to her to come to the car; this time he had brought his small car. She declined his invitation. "After all, that woman was old enough to die," he reflected. "This fool is ruining her life. . . ."

He allowed four more weeks for the mourning period and visited her again, but found a big gathering in her house, overflowing into the street. She sat at the back of the little hall, holding up her *thambura*, and was singing to the audience as if it were an auditorium. A violinist and a drummer had volunteered to play the accompaniments. "She is frittering away her art," he thought. She said, "Come, sit down." He sat in a corner, listened for a while and slipped away unobtrusively. Again and again, he visited her and found, at all hours of the day, people around her, waiting for her music. News about her free music sessions spread, people thronged there in cars, bicycles and on foot. Varma of the Boardless brought a box of sweets wrapped in gilt paper, and handed it to Selvi silently and went away, having realized his ambition to approach his goddess with an offering. Selvi never spoke unnecessarily. She remained brooding and withdrawn all day, not noticing or minding anyone coming in or going out.

Mohan thought he might be able to find her alone at least at night. At eleven o'clock one night he left his car in Market Road and walked to Vinayak Mudali Street. He called in softly through the door of Selvi's house, "My dear, it's me, I have to talk to you urgently. Please open the door, please," appealing desperately through the darkened house. Selvi opened a window shutter just a crack and said firmly, "Go away, it's not proper to come here at this hour. . . ." Mohan turned back with a lump in his throat, swearing half-aloud, "Ungrateful wretch. . . ."

SECOND OPINION

I stole in like a cat, unlocked my door, struck a match and lit a
kerosene lantern. I had to make sure that I did not wake up my
mother. Like a hunter stalking in a jungle, who is careful not to
crackle the dry leaves underfoot, I took stealthy steps along the front
passage to my room at the other end past a window in the hall. The
moment I shut the door of my cubicle, I was lord of my own universe—which seemed to me boundless, although enclosing a space of
only eight feet by ten. The sloping roof tiles harboured vermin of
every type, cobwebs hung down like festoons, lizards ensconced
behind ancient calendars on the walls darted up and down ambush-
ing little creatures that crawled about, urging them on their evolu-
tionary path. Every gnat at death was reborn a better creature, and
ultimately, after a series of lives, became an ape and a human being,
who merged ultimately in a supreme indivisible godhood. With such
an outlook, a result of miscellaneous, half-understood reading, there
could be no place for a spray or duster! I never allowed anyone to
clean my room.

I never touched the brass vessel left outside my door, containing
my supper, unless I felt hungry. How could I ever feel hunger while
all day I had been sipping coffee at the Boardless—although I didn't
have to spend a paisa on it. It just flowed my way. Varma generally
ordered a cup for himself every two hours to make sure that his
restaurant's reputation was not being unmade in the kitchen. Invariably, he ordered for me, too, not only as an act of hospitality, but as a
means of obtaining a "second opinion," to quote my doctor. I'll
deviate a little to describe Dr. Kishen of the M.M.C. (Malgudi Medical Centre). Those days when I believed in being useful at home, I
used to take my mother, off and on, to see the doctor. Whatever

disadvantage we might have had in inheriting that rambling old
house, its location was certainly an asset. Kabir Street, running parallel to Market Road, had numerous connecting lanes; and one could
always step across to reach the doctor or the vegetable market.
M.M.C. was centrally situated, as Dr. Kishen never failed to mention while examining your tongue or chest, when you couldn't enter
into an argument. "Do you see why there is greater rush here than
at other places?—it's because if you measure, you will find this is
equidistant from anywhere in this city. . . ."

After his equidistant observation, he'd invariably conclude an examination with, ". . . such is my diagnosis, go for a second opinion if
you like. . . ." Varma was also like-minded, I suppose. He seemed to
be very unsure of the quality of his own coffee even after tasting it,
and always wanted my confirmation. And then in the course of the
day others dropped in, the six o'clock group, which occupied a corner in the hall and over coffee exchanged all the town gossip, and
always insisted that I join them, with the result that when I came
home at night, I had no appetite for the contents of the brass tiffin-
box.

Early morning a young servant came to take away the vessel for
washing. She was about ten years old, with sparkling eyes set in tan-
coloured rotund cheeks, with whitest teeth, and a pigtail terminating
in a red ribbon. I was fond of her, and wished I were a painter and
could execute a world's masterpiece on canvas. She knew that she
was my favourite and could approach my room with impunity. She
would lift the vessel and cry out, "Oh, untouched?"

"Hush," I'd say, "not so loudly. . . ." She would smile mis-
chievously and say, "Oh, oh!" and I knew the next minute it would
become world news. In a short while my mother would appear at
my door to demand an explanation, and to say, "If this sort of thing
goes on, I don't know where it is going to take us. . . . I sliced
cucumber specially for you, and you don't hesitate to throw it
away. . . . At least mention your likes and dislikes. You won't do
even that, but just reject." I didn't mind what she said as long as she
remained on the threshold and did not step into my room. I sat on
my mat, leaning back on the wall and listened impassively to whatever she said, reflecting how difficult it was to practise one's philosophy of detachment; Siddhartha did wisely in slipping away at

midnight when others were asleep, to seek illumination. In my own way I, too, was seeking illumination, but continued to remain in bondage. The common roof, the married state (ultimately, of course), every kind of inheritance and every bit of possession acted as a deadly tentacle. Following this realization, the first thing I abandoned was furniture and, in a manner of speaking, also the common roof of the main house, since my cubicle was detached. It was not at all easy.

Our father's house had many mansions and apparently was designed for a milling crowd. Our front door opened on Kabir Street and our back door on the river Sarayu, which flowed down rather tamely at some distance from our house although you could hear it roaring along wildly in spate when it rained on Mempi Hills. It was all right as a vision to open the little door at our back yard, and sit at the edge of the flowing river to listen to its music; but now the back door had practically sealed itself firmly along the grooves with the dust and rust of decades, and the river had become inaccessible, owing to thorns and wild vegetation choking the path. I have heard my mother describe how in her younger days they had treated the river as a part of the home, every house in Kabir Street having access to it through a back door, how they bathed and washed and took water in pots, and how the men sat on its sandbank at dusk and dawn for their prayers. That was before wells were dug in every house. "The river used to be much nearer to us in those days," she would assert; "it's somehow moved away so far out. When wells were dug people became lazy and neglected the river; and no wonder she has drawn herself away; though in those days you could touch the water if you stretched your arm through the back door. But have you noticed how at Ellaman Street, even today, the river nestles closer to the houses, since they care for it and cherish it. They have built steps and treat her with respect. They never fail to light and float the lamps in *Karthik* month. . . . Whereas in our street people are lazy and indifferent. In those days, I begged your father not to dig a well, which encouraged others also. . . ." She could never forgive the well-diggers.

"But, Mother, it's the same water of the river that we are getting in the well. . . ."

"What does that mean? How?" And then I had to explain to her the concept of the underground water table; carried away by its poetry and philosophy, I would conclude, "You see, under the earth it's all one big sheet of water, perhaps hundreds or even thousands of cubic feet, all connected; a big connected water sheet, just as you say Brahman is all-pervading in this form and that in the universe—" She would cut me short with, "I don't know what has come over you, I talk of a simple matter like water and you go on talking like a prophet. . . ."

In those days I spent a great deal of my time sitting in the back portion of our home, which had an open courtyard with a corridor running along the kitchen, store and dining room, where my mother spent most of her time. In those days I had nothing much to do except sit down, leaning on the pillar, and attempt to enlighten my mother's mind on modern ways. But she was impervious to my theories. We were poles apart. Not only on the river, but on every question, she held a view which, as a rational being, I could never accept.

Sometimes I felt harassed. Mother would not leave me in peace. I had my little cubicle in the western wing of the house across the hall. At the other end used to be my father's room. He would sit there all day, as I thought, poring over books, of philosophy, one would suspect, considering the array of volumes on the shelves around him along the wall, in Sanskrit, Tamil and English; the *Upanishads*, with commentaries and interpretations by Shankara, Ramanuja and all the "world teachers." There were books on Christianity and Plato and Socrates in gilt-edged volumes. I had no means of verifying how much use he made of them. His room was out of bounds to me. He always sat cross-legged on the floor, before a sloping teakwood desk, turning over the leaves of an enormous tome; in my state of ignorance, I imagined that the treasury of philosophy at his elbow was being exploited. But it was only later in life that I learnt that the mighty tomes on his desk were ledgers and all his hours were spent in adding, subtracting and multiplying figures. He had multifarious accounts to keep—payments to men from the village cultivating our paddy fields; loans to others on promissory notes; trust funds of some temple or a minor. All kinds of persons sat patiently on the *pyol* of the house, and entered his room when summoned; there would follow much talking, signing of papers and counting of cash taken out of the squat wrought-iron safe with imposing handles and a tricky locking system. It stood there three-foot high, and seemed to have become a part of my father's personality. Out of it flowed cash and into it went documents. It was only after my father's death that I managed to open the safe, after a good deal of trial and error. While examining the papers I discovered that the library of philosophy had been hypothecated to him by some poor academic soul who could never redeem it. But Father had never disturbed the loaded shelves, except for dusting the books, since he wanted them to be in good condition when redeemed by their hapless owner. However, it was a godsend for me. I always sneaked into his room to look at their titles when he was away at the well for his bath, which kept him off long enough for me to examine the books. For a long time he would not let me handle them. "You wouldn't know what they say," he said. At a later stage he relented, and allowed me to take one book at a time, with warnings and admonitions. "Don't fold the covers back, but only half-open them, so that their backs are not creased—the books have to be returned in good condition, remember."

I selected, as he ordered, one book at a time. I loved the weight, feel and scent of every volume—some of them in a uniform series called the "Library of World Thought." I sat up in my room leaning on a roll of bedding and pored over each volume. I cannot pretend that I understood everything I read. I had had no academic training or discipline, not having gone beyond Matriculation, which I never passed, even after three attempts. After Father's death, I gave up, realizing suddenly it was silly to want to pass an examination. Who were they to test and declare me fit or unfit—for what? When this thought dawned, I stopped in my tracks in my fourth effort. I bundled and threw up into the loft all my class notes and examination books.

The loft was in the central hall, a wide wooden panel below the ceiling. From a proper distance, aimed correctly, you could fling anything into it, to oblivion. One had to go up a ladder to reach it, and then move around hunchback fashion to pick up something or for spring-cleaning. But for years no one had been up in the loft, even though it continued to get filled from time to time. In those days, my mother could always find some sturdy-limbed helper ready to go up to sweep and dust or pick up a vessel (all the utensils of brass and bronze she had brought in as a young bride decades ago were stored in the loft). Besides these, there were ledgers, disused lamps, broken furniture pieces, clothes in a trunk, mats, mattresses, blankets and what not. I dreaded her cleaning-up moods, as she always expected my participation. For some time I cooperated with her, but gradually began to avoid the task. She would often complain within my hearing, "When *he* was alive, how much service he could command within the twinkling of an eye. . . . I had to breathe ever so lightly what I needed and he would accomplish it." When she stood there thus, with her arms akimbo and lecturing, I generally retreated. I shut the door of my room and held my breath until I could hear her footsteps die away. She was too restless to stay in one place, but moved about, peeping into various corners of the house. She would suddenly suspect that the servant girl might have fallen asleep somewhere in that vast acreage and go on a hunt for her. She was in a state of anxiety over one thing or another; if it was not the servant, it would be about the well in the back yard; she must run up to it and see if the rope over the pulley was properly drawn away and secured to the post, or whether it had slipped into the well through the girl's carelessness. "If the rope falls into the well . . ." and she would go into a detailed account of the consequences; how there was no one around, as they had had in the old days, who would run up and get a new rope or fetch the diver with his hooks and harpoons to retrieve the rope.

It was a sore trial for me each day. I could not stand her. Her voice got on my nerves while she harangued, reprimanded or bawled at the servant girl. I shut and bolted the door of my room. I wanted peace of mind to go through the book in hand, *Life of Ramakrishna*, passages from Max Müller, Plato's *Republic*—it was a privilege to be able to be a participant in their thoughts. I felt thrilled to be battling with their statements and wresting a meaning out of them. Whatever they might have meant, they all seemed to hold forth the glory of the soul, which made me survey myself top to toe and say, "Sambu, who are you? You are not the creature with a prickly stubble on the chin, scar on the knee-cap, with toenail splitting and turning blue . . . you are actually made of finer stuff." I imagined myself able to steer my way through the traffic of constellations in the firmament, in the interstellar spaces, and along the Milky Way; it enabled me to overlook the drab walls around me and the uninspiring spectacles outside the window opening on Kabir Street. Into this, shattering my vision, would come hard knocks on my door. Mother would be standing there crying, "Why do you have to close this door? Who is there in this house to disturb you or anyone? Not like those days . . . Whom are you trying to shut out?" I could only look on passively. I was aware that she was ready for a battle, but I had not based my life on a war-footing yet. She looked terrifying with her grey unkempt hair standing like a halo around her head, her eyes spitting fire. I felt nervous, the slightest wrong move could spark off a conflagration.

I don't know what came over her six months after her husband's death. At the first shock of bereavement she remained subdued. For months and months she spoke little, spent much of her time in the *puja* room, meditating and chanting holy verse in an undertone. She went about the business of running the house without any fuss, never noticing anything too closely. She left me very much alone, though hinting from time to time that I should study and pass my B.A. In those days, some of the flotsam and jetsam who had been thriving indefinitely on my father's hospitality were still occupying various portions of my house. As long as they were all there, Mother kept herself in the background and behaved like a gentle person. Probably she had a code as to how she should behave in the presence of hangers-on. When I got the last of them out—that was the mad engineer, who had sought shelter from his brothers scheming to poison him and who finally had to be bundled off with the help of neighbours and the driver of the ambulance van—she began to breathe freely and probably felt that the stage had been cleared for her benefit. Following it, her first hostile act was to shut my father's room and put a lock on the door. I was aghast when I realized that access to the books was cut off. As she spent most of her time in the middle block of the house, I had to be running after her, begging for the key if I wished to see a book. At first, she would not yield. "Read your school books first and pass your examination," she said. "Time enough for you to read those big books, after you get your degree. Anyway, you won't understand them. Do you know what your father used to say? He said that he could not make them out himself! What do you say to that?"

"I don't doubt it. Did he at any time try? He always sat with his back to them." She grew angry at this remark. "Don't laugh at your elders, who have nurtured you," she would say and move off dramatically to end the conversation. I had to follow her, begging, "The key, please, Mother. . . ." I was young enough in those days not to feel discouraged. Finally she would say, "Don't mess up the books. You are so persistent—if you could have shown half this persistence in your studies!" I hated her at such moments. Why should she attach importance to examinations and degrees? Traditional and habitual manner of thought. Her sister's sons at Madras were all graduates, and she felt humiliated in family circles when they compared my performance. Before I finally gave up studies, whenever the Matriculation results were announced she would scream, "You have failed again! You fool! You are a disgrace. . . ."

I would shout back, "What can I do? You think marks are to be bought in the market?"

After some more exchanges of the same kind, she would break down and have a quiet cry in a corner, abandoning for the day her normal activities, not even lighting the lamp in the *puja* room in the evening. A deadly gloom would descend on the house, everything still and silent, no life stirring even slightly. We would become petrified figures in that vast house. I would feel upset and oppressed in this atmosphere and leave without a word, to seek some bright spots such as the town library, the marketplace, the college sports ground, and, more than any other place, the Boardless Hotel, to pass the time in agreeable company.

Instead of the dark house to which I usually sneaked back, today when I returned from the Boardless I found the light in the hall burning. I was puzzled. I went up a few steps in the direction of my room and stopped. I heard voices in the hall and a lot of conversation. My mother's voice was the loudest, sounded as spirited as in her younger days. She was saying. "He is not a bad boy, but likes to sound so. If we talk to him seriously, he'll certainly obey me." The other one was gruff-voiced and saying, "You should not have let him go his way at all; after all, young persons do not know what is good for them, it is for the elders to give them the necessary guidance." I was hesitating, wondering how to reach the door to my room, unlock it without being noticed. If they heard the click of the key, they were bound to turn their attention on me. My door was at the end of the veranda, and I could not possibly go past the window without being seen. I felt hunted. I could not go back to the Boardless. I quietly sat down on the *pyol* of the house, leaning against the pillar supporting the tiled roof, stretched my legs and resigned myself to staying there all night, since from the tenor of the dialogue going on there was no indication it would ever cease. The gruff voice was saying, "What keeps him out so late?" My mother was saying, "Oh, this and that. He spends a lot of time at the library, reads so much!" I appreciated my mother for saying this. I never suspected that she had such a good opinion of me. What secret admiration she must be having—never showing any sign of it outside. It was a revelation to me. I almost felt like popping up and shouting, "Oh, Mother, how nice of you to think so well of me! Why could you not say so to me?" But I held myself back.

He asked, "What does he plan to do?"

"Oh!" she said, "he has some big plans, which he won't talk about now. He is very deep and sensitive. His ambition is to be a man of learning. He spends much time with learned persons. . . ."

"My daughter, you know, is also very learned. She reads books all the time. . . ."

"Sambu has read through practically all the volumes that his father left for him in that room. Sometimes I just have to snatch the books from him and lock them away so that he may bathe and eat! I don't think even an M.A. has read so much!"

"I really do not worry what he will do in life, though holding some position or an office is the distinguishing mark of a man." He recited a Sanskrit line in support of this. "Let him not strain in any manner except to be a good husband. My daughter's share of the property . . ." Here he lowered his voice and they continued to talk in whispers.

At dawn my mother caught me asleep on the *pyol* when she came out to sweep the front steps and wash the threshold as others before her had been doing for one thousand years. She was aghast at seeing me stretched out there. At some part of the night I must have fallen asleep. I think they were passing on to some sort of reminiscences far into the night, and they were both convulsed with laughter at the memory of some ancient absurdity. I had never heard my mother laughing so much. She seemed to have preserved a hidden personality especially for the edification of her old relatives or associates, while she presented to me a grim, serious, director-general aspect. It was foolish and thoughtless of me to have lain there and get caught so easily. Luckily her guest had gone to the back yard for a bath and had not seen me. Otherwise he'd have suspected that I had come home drunk, and been abandoned by undesirable companions at our door. Ah, how I wish he had seen me in this condition, which would have been a corrective to all the bragging my mother had been indulging in about me. She hurriedly woke me up. "Sleeping in the street! What'll people think! Why didn't you go into your room? Did you return so late? What were you doing all the time?" There was panic in her tone, packed with suspicion that I must have been drinking and debauching—the talk of the town was the opening of a nightclub called Kismet somewhere in the New Extension, where the youth of the city were being lured. Someone must have gossiped about it within her hearing. I was only half-awake when she shook me and whispered, "Get into your room first—"

"Why?" I asked, sitting up.

"I do not want you to be seen here. . . ."

"I found you talking to someone and so I . . ." I had no rational conclusion to my sentence.

She gripped my arm and pulled me up, probably convinced that I needed assistance. I made a dash for my door, shut myself in and immediately resumed my sleep, a part of my mind wondering whether I should not have said, "I was at Kismet. . . ." I got up later than usual. There was no trace of the visitor of the night, which made me wonder if I had been having nightmares. "He left early to catch the bus," explained Mother when I was ready for coffee. I accepted her explanation in silence, refraining from asking further questions. I felt a premonition that some difficult time was ahead. We met at the middle courtyard as usual, where I accepted my coffee after a wash at the well. Normally we would exchange no words at this point; she would present a tumbler of coffee when I was seen at the kitchen door. There our contact would stop on most days, unless she had some special grievance to express, such as a demand for house-tax or failure on the part of the grocer or the milk-supplier. I'd generally listen passively, silently finish the coffee and pass on, bolt myself in, dress and make my exit by the veranda as unobtrusively as possible. But today, after coffee, she remarked, "The servant girl hasn't come yet. Of late she is getting notions about herself." I repressed my remarks, as my sympathies were all on the side of that cheerful little girl, who had to bear a lot of harsh treatment from her mistress. After this information Mother said, "Don't disappear, stay in. . . ." and she allowed herself a mild smile; she seemed unusually affable; this combined with all the good things she had been saying last night bewildered me. Some transformation seemed to be taking place in her; it didn't suit her at all to wear a smile; it looked artificial and waxwork-like and toothy. I wished I could fathom her mind; the grimness and frown and growl were more appropriate for her face. I said, "I have some work to do and must go early."

"What work?" she asked with a mischievous twinkle in her eyes. I felt scared. There were a dozen excuses I could give; should I tell her about Varma's treasure-hunt (on Mondays he brought a sheaf of planchette messages purporting to give directions for a buried trea-sure in the mountains and sought my interpretation of them), or the little note I had promised a college student on Jaina philosophy, or apt quotations for a municipal councillor's speech for some occasion. I was afraid my mother would pooh-pooh them, and so I just said, "I have many things to do—you wouldn't understand." Normally she would burst out, "Understand! How do you know? Have you tried? Your father never kept anything from me." But today she just said, "Very well, I don't want to bother you to tell me," with a mock-sadness in her voice. It was clear that she was continuing the good-will she had exhibited last night before the stranger. I felt uneasy. She was playacting, for what purpose I could not guess.

Presently she followed me into my room and said, "You may go after listening to me. Your business can wait for a while." She sat down on my mat and invited me to sit beside her to listen atten-tively. I felt nervous. This was not her sitting hour; she'd be all over the place, sweeping, washing, cleaning and driving the girl about.

But today what could be the important item of business, suspending all else?

It was not long in coming. "Do you know who has come?" I knew I was being pushed to the wall. Sitting so close to her made me uneasy. I felt embarrassed, especially when I noticed a strand of white beard on her chin. Was she aware of its existence? Ridiculous if she was going about, behaving as if it weren't there. "Grey-beard loon . . ." A phrase emerged now out of the miasma of assorted reading of hypothecated property. I recollected her boasts before the visitor about my studious habits. After waiting for me to say something (luckily I was brooding over Shakespeare's line—or was it Coleridge's?—otherwise I would have promptly said, "Some dark, hook-nosed fellow with a tuft—I couldn't care less who," every word of which would have irritated her), she explained, "The richest man in our village: a hundred acres of paddy, coconut garden—from the coconut garden alone his income would be a lakh of rupees, and from cattle . . . They are distantly related to us. . . ." She went into genealogical details explaining the family alliances of several generations and dropping scores of names. She was thorough. I was amazed at the amount of information stored in her mind; she knew also where every character lived, scattered though they were between the Himalayas in the North and the tip of Cape Comorin in the South. I was fascinated by the way she was piling up facts in order to establish the identity of the man with the tuft. I felt like the Wedding-Guest in "The Ancient Mariner." I could not break away. Here was another line floating up from the literary scrap acquired from my hypothecated property: "Hold off!" the Wedding-Guest wailed, "unhand me," but the Ancient Mariner gripped his wrist and said with a far-away look, "With my cross-bow I shot the Albatross." While my head buzzed with these irrelevant odds and ends, my mother was concluding a sentence: "The girl has studied up to B.A. and is to be married in June—he is keen that it should be gone through without any delay. She is his last issue and he is anxious to settle her future . . . and the settlement he has proposed is very liberal. . . ." I remained silent. I could now understand the drift of her conversation. She mentioned, "The horoscopes match very well. He came here only after the astrologers had approved."

"Where did he get my horoscope?" I asked.

"They took it from your father many, many years ago; they were such good friends and neighbours in our village." She added again, "They were such good friends that they vowed on the day the girl was born to continue the friendship with this alliance. On the very day she was born, you were betrothed," she said calmly, as if it were the normal thing.

"What are you saying? Do you mean to say you betrothed to me a child only a few hours old?"

"Yes," she said calmly.

"Why? why?" I asked, unable to comprehend her logic. "Don't you see how absurd it is?"

"No," she said. "They are a good family, known and attached to us for generations."

"It's idiotic," I cried. "How can you involve me in this manner? What was my age then?"

"What does it matter?" she said. "When I was married I was nine and your father thirteen, and didn't we lead a happy life?"

"That's irrelevant, what you have done with your lives. How old was I?"

"Old enough, about five or six, what does it matter?"

"Betrothed? How? By what process?"

"Don't question like that. You are not a lawyer in a court," she said, dropping her mask of friendliness.

"I may not be a lawyer, but remember that I am not a convict either," I said, secretly wondering if it was a relevant thing to say.

"You think I am a prisoner?" she asked, matching my irrelevancy.

I remained silent for a while and pleaded, "Mother, listen to me. How can any marriage take place in this fashion? How can two living entities possessing intelligence and judgement ever be tied together for a lifetime?"

"How else?" she said, and picking up my last word, "What lifetime? Of course, every marriage is for a lifetime. No one marries anew every month."

I felt desperate and cried, "Idiotic! Don't be absurd, try to understand what I am saying. . . ."

She began to wail loudly at this. "Second time you are hurling an insulting word. Was it for this I have survived your father? How I wish I had mounted the funeral pyre as our ancients decreed for a widow; they knew what a widow would have to face in life, to stand abusive language from her own offspring." She beat her forehead with such violence that I feared she might crack her skull. Face flushed and tears streaming down her cheeks, she glared at me; I quailed at her look and wished that I could get up and escape. At close quarters, unaccustomed as I was, it was most disturbing. While she went on in the same strain, my mind was planning how best to get away, but she had practically cornered me and was hissing and swaying as she spoke. I began to wonder if I had thoughtlessly used some bad word and was going over our conversation in a reverse order. My last word was "idiotic," nothing foul and provocative in such a word. Most common usage. "Idiot" would have been more offensive than "idiotic." "Idiotic" could be exchanged between the best of friends under any circumstance of life and no one need flare up. Before this word she had said, "No one marries anew every month." I never said that they did. What a civilization, "A Wounded Civilization," a writer had called it. I could not help laughing slightly at the thought of the absurdity of it all. It provoked her again. Wiping her eyes and face with the tip of her sari, she said, "You are laughing at me! Yes, I've made a laughingstock of myself bringing you up, tending you, nursing you and feeding you, and keeping the house for you. You feel so superior and learned because of the books your father has collected laboriously in the other room. . . ."

"But they weren't his . . . only someone's property mortgaged for a loan. . . ." I said, unable to suppress my remark.

And she said, "With all that reading you couldn't even get a B.A.! While every slip of a girl is a graduate today." Her voice sounded thick and hoarse due to the shouting she had indulged in.

I abruptly left, snatching my *kurta* and the upper cloth which were within reach, though I generally avoided this dress as it made one look like a political leader. I preferred always the blue bush-shirt and dhoti or pants, but they were hanging by a hook on the wall where Mother was leaning. As I dashed out I heard her conclude: ". . . any date we mention, that man will come and take us to see the girl and approve. . . ." So, she was imagining herself packing up, climbing a bus for the village with me in tow, to be received at that end as honoured visitors and the girl to be paraded before us bedecked in gold and silk, waiting for a nod of approval from me. "Idiotic," I muttered again, walking down our street.

Going down Market Road, I noticed Dr. Kishen arrive on a scooter at M.M.C., already opened by his general assistant named Ramu, who fancied himself half a doctor and examined tongue and pulse and dispensed medicine when the doctor's back was turned. The doctor did not mind it, as Ramu was honest and rendered proper account of his own transactions. The doctor on noticing me said, "Come in, come in." A few early patients were waiting with their bottles. He was one who did not believe in tablets, but always wrote out a prescription for every patient, and Ramu concocted the mixture and filled the bottles. The doctor always said, "Every prescription must be a special composition to suit the individual. How can mass-produced tablets help?" He wrote several lines on a sheet of paper and then turned the sheet of paper and wrote along the margin, too; he challenged anyone to prove that his prescriptions were not the longest: "I'll give free medicine to anyone who can produce a longer prescription anywhere in this country!" And his patients, mostly from the surrounding villages, sniggered and murmured approval. When he hailed me I just slowed down my pace but did not stop. "Good morning, Doctor. I'm all right. . . ." He cut me short with, "I know, I know, you are a healthy animal of no worth to the medical profession, still I want to speak to you. . . . Come in, take that chair, that's for friends who are in good health; sick people sit there." He flourished his arm in the direction of a teakwood bench along a wall and a couple of iron folding chairs. He went behind a curtain for a moment and came out donning his white apron and turned the hands of a sign on the wall which said DOCTOR IS IN, PLEASE BE SEATED. He briefly glanced through a pile of blotters and folders advertising new infallible drugs and swept them away to a corner of his desk. "Of value only to the manufacturers, all those big companies and multinationals, not to the ailing population of our country. I never give these smart canvassing agents in shirt-sleeves and tie more than five minutes to have their say, and one minute to pick up their samples and literature and leave. While there are other M.D.s in town who eat out of their hands and have built up a vast practise with physician samples alone!" Ramu went round collecting the bottles from those occupying the bench. "Why don't you give me a cheque?" asked the doctor.

I thought he was joking and said, "Yes, of course, why not?" to match what I supposed was his mood, and added, "How much? Ten thousand?"

"Not so much," he said, "Less than that. . . ." He took out a small notebook from the drawer and kept turning its leaves. At this moment an old man made his entry, coughing stentoriously. The doctor looked up briefly and flourished his hand towards the bench. The old man didn't obey the direction but stood in the middle of the hall and began, "All night . . ." The doctor said, "All right, all right . . . sit down and wait. I'll come and help you to sleep well tonight." The man subsided on the bench, a sentence he had begun trailing away into a coughing fit.

The doctor said, "Two hundred and forty-five rupees up to last week . . . none this week." I now realized that this was more than a joke. I was aghast at this demand. He thrust his notebook before me and said, "Twenty visits at ten rupees a visit. I have charged nothing for secondary visits, and the balance for medicine. . . ." The cough-stricken patient began to gurgle, cleared his throat and tried to have his say. The doctor silenced him with a gesture. A woman held up a bawling kid and said, "Sir, he brings up every drop of milk. . . ." The doctor glared at her and said, "Don't you see I'm busy? Am I the four-headed Brahma? One by one. You must wait."

"He brings up . . ."

"Wait, don't tell me anything now." After this interlude he said to me, "I don't generally charge for secondary visits—I mean a second call, which I can respond to on my way home. I charge only for visits which are urgent. In your case I've not noted the number of secondary visits."

I was mystified and said, "You have yourself called me a healthy brute, so what's it all about?"

"Don't you know? Has your mother never spoken to you?"

"No, never, I never thought . . . Yes, she spoke about my marrying some girl, worried me no end about it," I said, and added, "Doctor, if you can think of some elixir which'll reduce her fervour about my marriage . . ."

"Yes, yes, I'm coming to it. It's a thing that is weighing on her mind very much. She feels strongly that there must be a successor to her when she leaves." The doctor seemed to be talking in conundrums. The day seemed to have started strangely. "Has she not discussed her condition with you?" Before I could answer him or grasp what he was saying, the man with the cough made his presence felt with a deafening series, attracting the doctor's attention, and as the doctor rose, the woman lifted the child and began, "He doesn't retain even a drop. . . ." The doctor said to me, "Don't go away. I'll dispose of these two first." He took the squealing baby and the cougher, one by one, behind the curtain, and came back to his table and wrote a voluminous prescription for each, and passed them on to Ramu through a little window. Presently he resumed his speech to me, but was interrupted by his patients, who wanted to know whether the mixture was to be drunk before or after a meal and what diet was to be taken. He gave some routine answer and muttered to me, "It's the same question again and again, again and again—whether they could have buttermilk or *rasam* and rice or bread and coffee, and whether before or after—what does it matter? But they want an answer and I have to give it, because the medical profession has built up such rituals! Ha! ha!"

At this moment two others approached his desk, having waited on the bench passively all along. He gestured them to return to their seats, and rose saying, "Follow me, we will have no peace here. . . ." I followed him into his examination room, a small cabin with a high table, screened off and with a lot of calendar pictures plastered on the wall. He asked me to hoist myself on the examining table as if I were a patient, and said, "This is the only place where I can talk without being interrupted." I had been in suspense since his half-finished statements about my mother. He said, "Your mother is in a leave-taking mood. . . ." I was stunned to hear this. I could never imagine my mother in such a mood. No one seemed to have her feet more firmly planted on the earth, with her ceaseless activities around the house, and her strident voice ringing through the halls. The doctor had said "leave-taking." How could she ever leave her universe? It was inconceivable. My throat went dry and my heart raced when I tried to elicit further clarification from him. I said weakly, "What sort of leave-taking? Thinking of retiring to Benares?"

"No, farther than that," said the doctor, indicating heaven, after lighting a cigarette. The little cabin became misty and choking. I gently coughed out the smoke that had entered my lungs without my striking a match. The smoke stung my eyes and brought tears, observing which the doctor said sympathetically, "Don't cry. Learn to take these situations calmly; you must think of the next step to take, practically and calmly." He preached to me the philosophy of detachment, puffing away at his cigarette, and not minding in the least the coughing, groaning and squealing emanating from the bench in the hall. I felt bad to be holding up the doctor in this manner. But I had to know what he was trying to say about my mother through his jerky half-statements. He asked suddenly, "Why hasn't she been talking to you?" I had to explain to him that I came home late and left early, and we met briefly each day. He made a deprecatory sound with his tongue and remarked, "You are an undutiful fellow. Where do you hide yourself all day?"

"Oh, this and that," I said, feeling irritated. "I have to see people and do things. One has to live one's own life, you know!"

"What people and what life?" pursued the doctor relentlessly. I couldn't explain to him really how I spent the day. He'd have brushed aside anything I said. So I thought it best to avoid his question and turn his thoughts to my mother. Here he had created a hopeless suspense and tension in me, and was wandering in his talk, puffing out smoke and tipping the ash on the cement floor. What an untidy doctor—the litter and dust and ash alone was enough to breed disease and sickness—he was the most reckless doctor I'd ever come across. As more patients came into the other room, Ramu parted the curtain and peeped in to say, "They are waiting." This placed some urgency into the whole situation and the doctor hastily threw down the cigarette, crushed it under his shoe and said, "For four months I have been visiting your home off and on, some days several times— that little girl would come running and panting to say, 'Come, Doctor, at once, Amma is very ill, at once.' When such a call is received I never ignore it. I drop whatever I may have on hand and run to the patient. Giving relief to the suffering is my first job. . . . Sometimes the girl would come a second time, too."

"What was it?" I asked, becoming impatient.

"Well, that's what one has to find out; I'm continuously watching and observing. It's not in my nature to treat any complaint casually and take anything for granted. . . ." He was misleading himself, according to what I could observe of his handling of his patients. After a lot of rambling, he came to the point: "She is subject to some kind of fainting, which comes on suddenly. However, she is responding to treatment; I think it must be some kind of cardiac catch, if I may call it so, due to normal degenerative process. We can keep her going with medicines, but how long one cannot say. . . ."

"Does she know?" I asked tremblingly.

"Yes, I had to talk to her about it in a way, and she has understood perfectly. She has a lot of philosophy, you know. Perhaps you don't spend any time with her. . . ." I remained dumb. The doctor's observations troubled my conscience. I had not paid any attention to my mother, to her needs or her wants or her condition, and had taken her to be made of some indestructible stuff. "The only thing that bothers her now is that you will be left alone; she told me that if only you could be induced to marry . . ."

So that was it! I understood it now. She must have been busy all afternoon sending the little girl to the post-office to buy postcards, and then writing to her relations in the village to find a bride for me, and she had finally succeeded in reviving old relationships and promises and getting the tufted man down with his proposals. What a strain it must have been to organize so much in her state of cardiac degeneration, performing her daily duties without the slightest slackening. In fact, she seemed to have been putting on an exaggerated show of vitality when I was at home, probably suffering acutely her spells of whatever it was while I sat listening or lecturing at the Boardless till midnight! I felt guilty and loathed myself and my self-centered existence. Before I left, the doctor uttered this formula: "Well, such is my finding. Take a second opinion if you like. I'd not at all mind it. Can you let me have your cheque tomorrow?"

When I emerged from the anteroom, the waiting patients looked relieved. Outside in the street I hesitated for a moment and turned my feet homeward instead of, as was my invariable custom, to the Boardless.

When I opened the door of my room and appeared before my mother, she was taken aback, having never seen me home at this hour. I was happy to find her as active as ever, impossible to connect it with the picture conjured by the doctor's report, although I seemed to note some weak points in her carriage and under her eyes. I kept staring at her. She was puzzled. I wanted to burst out, "How do you feel this morning? All right? Possibility of falling into a faint?" I swallowed my words. Why should I mention a point which she had kept from me? That might upset her, better not show cognizance of it. She wanted to ask, perhaps, "Why are you at home now?" But she didn't. I felt grateful to her for her consideration. We looked at each other for some time, each suppressing the question uppermost in our minds. Only the little servant girl opened her eyes wide and cried, "You never come at this time! Are you going to eat? Amma has not prepared any food as yet. . . ." "Hey, you keep quiet," Mother ordered her; she turned to me. "I'm about to light the oven. This girl arrived so late today! Is there anything you'd like?" What a change was coming over us all of a sudden. I could hardly believe my ears or eyes—remembering the tenor of our morning conversation. I went back to my room, wondering what I should do if she had her attack while I was here. She seemed to be all right; still, I'd a feeling of anxiety about leaving her there and going away to my room. Somehow I had an irrational anxiety that if I lost her from view for a moment anything might happen. I settled down in my room, leaving the door ajar, and tried to read; while my eyes scanned the lines, my thoughts were elsewhere. Suppose she had a seizure and suddenly passed away, without ever knowing that I was desperate to please her by agreeing to this frightful marriage. I hated it, but I had to do a thing I hated to please a dying mother. It was pathetic, her attempt single-handed to find me a bride in her condition. One had to do unpleasant things for another person's sake. Did not Rama agree to exile himself for fourteen years to please Dasaratha? My own hardship would be nothing compared to what Rama underwent, living like a nomad in the forests for fourteen years. In my case, at worst I'd have to suffer being wedded to a girl I didn't care for, which was nothing if one got used to it, and it'd help an old woman die in peace.

She had cooked some special items for me as if I were a rare guest. The lunch was splendid. She had put out a banana leaf for me in the corridor and arranged a sitting plank for me beside the rosewood pillar in the half-covered open court. She explained, "It's too stuffy with smoke in the kitchen. Your father did everything perfectly, but neglected the kitchen—never provided a chimney or window . . . if the firewood is not dry the smoke irritates my eyes till I think I'll go blind. One'd almost lose one's sight in the stinging smoke, but I've got used to it; even if I lose my sight it will not matter. But whoever comes after me . . ." This was the nearest hint of both her health and the successor to the kitchen. I absorbed the hint but had no idea what I should say; I felt confused and embarrassed. "We shall have to do something about it," I said, gratefully eating the rare curry with five vegetables she had prepared for me. I was amazed at her efficiency. I was an unexpected guest, but within a couple of hours she had managed to get the food ready. She must have been driving the little girl with a whip to run up and buy all the needed stuff for this lunch, all done quietly without giving a clue to the guest of honour lounging in his room with a book in hand. She must have been several times on the point of asking why I was back home at this hour, and I was on the point of asking for details of her symptoms; but both of us talked of other things. After lunch I retired to my room. I couldn't shut the door and rest. I frequently emerged from my shelter and paced the length of the house, up and down from the front door to the back yard, areas which I had not visited for months and months. I noticed without obviously watching how my mother was faring. She had eaten her lunch, and was chewing her betel nut and clove as had been her practise for years and years. That the shop was closed for the day was indicated by the faint aroma of cloves that hung about her presence, as I had noticed even as a child, when I trailed behind her at all hours, while my father sat counting cash in his room. She used to look like a goddess in her bright silk sari and straight figure, with diamonds sparkling in her ears.

She had unrolled a mat and was lying with her head resting on a plank in the corridor, which was her favourite spot. When she saw me pass, she sat up and asked, "Want anything?"

"No, no, don't disturb yourself. Just a glass of water, that's all." I went into the kitchen and poured a tumbler of water out of the mud jug, took a draught of unwanted cold water and went back to my room. This was an unaccustomed hour at home and I could not overcome the feeling of strangeness. She seemed all right and I felt relieved. She produced a tumbler of coffee when I reappeared in her zone, after an afternoon nap. I began to feel bored and wanted to go out to my accustomed haunts, the public library, the town-hall, the riverside at Nallappa's Grove and finally the Boardless. Normally I'd start the day at the Boardless, finish my rounds and end up there again.

When I was satisfied she was normal, I had a wash at the well, dressed, and started out. I went to the back portion, where she was scrubbing the floor, to tell her I was going out, casually asking, "Where is that girl? Why are you doing it yourself?"

"That girl wanted the day off. The floor is so slippery. Nothing like doing things yourself if your limbs are strong enough. . . ." she said.

I said very calmly and casually, "If you like, you may tell that man to come for a talk and arrange our visit to the village. You may write to him to come anytime," and without further talk, I briskly left.

All evening my mind was preoccupied. I was not the sort to explain my personal problems to anyone, and so when I sat beside Varma at the Boardless and he asked me, "Anything wrong? You have come so late," I gave some excuse and passed on to other subjects. The six o'clock group arrived—the journalist whom we called the universal correspondent, since he couldn't name any paper as his, an accountant in some bank, a schoolmaster and a couple of others whose profession and background were vague—and assembled in its corner. The talk was all about Delhi politics as usual—for and against Indira Gandhi—with considerable heat but in hushed tones, because Varma threw a hint that walls have ears. I'd normally participate in this to the extent of contradicting everyone and quoting Plato or Toynbee. But today I just listened passively, and the journalist said, "Where is your sparkle gone?" I said I had a sore throat and a cold coming.

After an hour I slipped out. I crossed Ellaman Street and plodded through the sands of Sarayu and walked down the bank listening o the rustling of leaves overhead and the sound of running water. I was deeply moved by the hour and its quality in spite of my worries. People sat here and there alone or in groups, children were gambolling on the sands. I said to myself, "Oh, the lovely things continue, in spite of the burdens on one's soul. How I wish I could throw off the load and enjoy this hour absolutely. Most people here are happy, chatting and laughing because they are not bothered about a marriage or a mother. . . . God! I wish I could see a way out." I sat on the river parapet and brooded hard and long. Marriage seemed to me most unnecessary, just to please a mother. Supposing the M.M.C. doctor had not spotted me in the morning, I'd have gone my way, leaving marriage and mother to take their own course, that tufted man to go to the devil. I could welcome neither marriage nor my mother's death. They spoke of the horns of dilemma; I understood now what it meant. I felt hemmed in, with all exits blocked—like a rat cornered who must either walk into the trap or get bashed. I was getting more and more confused. No one told me that I should marry or otherwise I'd lose my mother. Mother's health was not dependent on me: the degenerative process must have started very early. I had decided to marry only because it'd make her die peacefully, a purely voluntary decision—no dilemma in any sense of the term. After this elaborate analysis I felt a little lighter in mind. I abandoned myself to the sound of the river and leaves, of the birds chirping and crowing in the dark while settling on their perches for the night.

Two men sitting nearby got up, patting away the sand from their seats. They were engaged in a deep discussion, and as they passed me one was saying, "I'd not rely on any single opinion so fully and get nose-led; one must always get a second opinion before deciding the issue." They were old men, probably pensioners reminiscing on family affairs or official matters. The expression "second opinion" was a godsend and suddenly opened a door for me. My doctor himself constantly recommended a "second opinion." I'd not rely only on the M.M.C. I'd get my mother examined by Dr. Natwar, who was a cardiologist and neurosurgeon, as he called himself, who had his establishment at New Extension. Everyone turned to that doctor at desperate moments. He had acquired many degrees from different continents, and sick persons converged there from all over the country. I was going to ask him point-blank if my mother was to live for some more years or not, and on his judgement was going to depend my marriage. I only prayed, as I trudged back home oblivious of the surroundings, that my mother had taken no action on my impulsive acceptance of the morning. I was confident that she couldn't have reached postal facilities so quickly.

I got up early next morning and met the M.M.C. doctor at his home. He hadn't yet shaved or bathed; with his hair ruffled and standing up he looked more like a loader of rice bags in the market than a physician. "To think one hangs on this loader's verdict on matters of life and death!" I reflected, while he led me in and offered me a cup of coffee. His tone was full of sympathy as he presumed that something had gone wrong with my mother; he was saying, "Oh, don't be anxious, I'll come, she'll be all right, must be another passing fit. . . ." I had to wake up from my reverie as he concluded, "I won't take more than forty minutes to get ready, and the first call will be at your house, although a case of bronchitis at the Temple Street is in a critical stage." Never having practised the art of listening to others, he went on elaborating details of the bronchitis case. When he paused for breath, I butted in hastily to ask, "May I seek a second opinion in my mother's case?"

"Why not? Just the right thing to do. I'm after all as human as yourself—not a Brahma. No one could be a Brahma. . . . Just wait. . . ." He gave me the morning paper and disappeared for forty minutes and reappeared completely transformed into the usual picture of the presiding deity of the M.M.C. He handed me a letter for Dr. Natwar, saying, "He is a good chap, though you may find him rather brusque. Take this letter and get an appointment for your mother and then see me."

I had to spend the whole morning at Dr. Natwar's consulting room in New Extension. A servant took my letter in, and after I had glanced through all the old illustrated magazines heaped on a central table again and again, I sat back resigned to my fate. A half-door kept opening and shutting as sick persons with their escorts passed in and out. After nearly two hours the servant brought back my letter, marked, "Tuesday, 11 a.m." Tuesday was still five days away. Suppose the tufted man came before that? I asked the servant, "Can't I see the doctor and ask for an earlier date?" He shook his head and left. This unseen healer was like God, not to be seen or heard except when he willed it. The demigods were equally difficult to reach.

In her present mood it was not difficult to persuade my mother to submit herself to a second opinion, although I still had to pretend that I knew nothing of the test performed by Dr. Kishen. I had to explain that one had to make sure, at her age, of being in sound condition and what a privilege it would be to be looked over by Dr. Natwar. I didn't tell her that it cost me a hundred rupees for this consultation. Gaffur's taxi was available for fifteen rupees (the old Gaffur as well as the Chevrolet were no more, but his son now sat on the dry fountain, looking like him as I remembered him years ago, with an Ambassador car parked in the road) to take her over to Dr. Natwar's clinic.

Dr. Natwar's electronic and other medical equipment was fitted up in different rooms. I caught a glimpse of my mother as she was being wheeled about from section to section. She looked pleased to be the centre of so much attention and to be put through so many gadgets. She looked gratefully at me every time she passed the hall, as if to say that she had never suspected that I was such a devoted son. The demigod who had taken my letter on the first day appeared and beckoned me to follow him. All the rest had vanished—the trol-ley, the attendants, as well as my mother—had vanished completely, as if they had been images on the screen of a magic-lantern show. I followed him, marvelling at the smooth manoeuvring of the puppets in this institution. On the doctor's word depended my future free-dom. I was ushered into the presence of Dr. Natwar, who seemed quite young for his reputation, a man of slight build and a serious face and small, tight lips which were hardly ever opened except to utter precise directions. His communication with his staff was man-aged with a minimum of speech—with a jerk of his head or the wave of a finger.

"Mr. Sambu, nothing wrong with your mother." He pushed towards me a sheaf of documents and photographs and paper scrolls in a folder. "Keep these for reference: absolutely nothing to warrant this check-up. Blood contents, urine and blood pressure, heart and lungs are normal. Fainting symptoms might have been due to fatigue and starvation over long periods. No medication indicated. She must eat at more frequent intervals, that's all." Getting up, I muttered thanks, but hesitated. He was ready to press the bell for the next case. I shuffled my feet as if to move, but turned round to ask, "How long will she live?" A wry smile came over his face as he rang the bell and said, "Who can answer that question? . . ." As the next visitor was ushered in, he said simply, "I'd not be surprised if she outlived you and me."

If she was going to outlive me and the doctor, I reflected on the way home, why could I not tell her straightaway that the time had come for us to dismiss her tufted cousin and his daughter from our thoughts. But I found her in such a happy mood as we travelled homeward, I didn't have the heart to spoil it. She had already begun to talk of the wedding preparations. "The only thing that bothered me all along was that I might not have the strength to go through it all. Now I can; oh, so many things to do!" I looked away, pretending to watch the passing scenes, cattle grazing in the fields, bullock-cart caravans passing and so forth. What a monomania, this desire to see me wedded! She was saying, "I must write to my brother and his wife to come ahead and help us: invitation letters to be printed and distributed, clothes and silver vessels . . . oh, so much to do. . . . I don't know, but my brother is a practical man. . . ." She went on chattering all the way. I was indifferent. Time enough to throw the bomb-shell. The drive and the air blowing on her face seemed to have stimulated her. With her health assured, she was planning to plunge into matrimonial activities with zest. I couldn't understand what pleasure she derived from destroying my independence and emasculating me into a householder running up to buy vegetables at the bidding of the wife or changing baby's napkin. I shuddered at the prospect.

The moment we got out of the taxi, the little girl came running, holding aloft a postcard. "The postman brought this letter."

"Oh, the letter has come," mother cried, thrilled, and read it standing on the house-steps and declared, "He is coming by the bus at one o'clock—never thought he'd come so soon. . . ."

"Who, the tuft?" I asked.

She looked surprised at my levity. "No, you must not be disrespectful. What if someone has a tuft? In those days everyone was tufted," she said, suppressing her annoyance. She went up the steps into the house, while I paid off the taxi. When she heard the car move off, she came to the street and cried, "Why have you sent the car away? I thought you should meet him at the bus-stand and bring him home, that would have been graceful. Anyhow, hurry up to the bus-stop; you must not keep him waiting, better if you are there earlier and wait for the bus—they are such big people, you have no notion how wealthy and influential they are, nothing that they cannot command; if you went there, they could command big cars for your use, you have no idea. They grow everything in their fields, from rice to mustard, all grains and vegetables, don't have to buy anything from a shop except kerosene. Before you go, cut some banana leaves, large ones from the back-yard garden." I cut the banana leaves as she ordered, went up to the corner shop and bought the groceries she wanted for the feast. I put down the packages while she busied herself in the kitchen and was harrying the servant girl. She was in high spirits, very happy and active. I hated myself for dampening her spirits with what I was about to say. I stood at the kitchen door watching her, wondering how to soften the blow I was about to deliver. She turned from the oven to say, "Now go, go, don't delay. If the bus happens to come before time, it'll be awkward to keep him waiting."

"Can't he find his way, as he did that night? No one went out to receive him then."

"Now this is a different occasion; he is in a different class now. . . ."

"No, I don't agree with you. He is no more than a country cousin of yours, and nothing more as far as I am concerned."

She dropped the vessel she had been holding in her hand, and came up, noticing the change in my tone. "What has come over you?"

"That tufted man is welcome to find his way here, eat the feast you provide and depart. He will not see me at the bus-stand or here."

"He is coming to invite you to meet his daughter. . . ."

"That doesn't concern me. I'm going out on my own business. Feed him well and send him back to the village well-fed, whenever you like; I'm off. . . ."

I went into my room to change and leave by the other door for the Boardless, haunted by the memory of pain on her face. I felt sorry for her and hated myself for what I was. As I crossed the *pyol* of the house and was about to reach the street, she opened the front door and dashed out to block my way, imploring tearfully, "You need not marry the girl or look at her, only I beg you to go up and receive that man. After all, he is coming on my invitation, we owe him that as a family friend, otherwise it'll be an insult and they'll talk of it in our village for a hundred years. I'd sooner be dead than have them say that a wretched widow could not even receive a guest after inviting him. Don't ruin our family reputation."

"Well, he came by himself the other evening."

"Today we've asked him." It was a strain for her to say all this in a soft voice, out of earshot of our neighbours. She looked desperate and kept wiping the tears with her sari and I suddenly felt the pathos of the whole situation and hated myself for it. After all, I had been responsible for the invitation. I wondered what I should do now. She begged, "Meet him, bring him home, eat with him, talk to him and then leave if you like. I'll see that he doesn't mention his daughter, you don't have to bother about the marriage. Do what you like, become a *sanyasi* or a sinner, I won't interfere. This is the last time. I'll not try to advise you as long as I breathe; this is a vow, though let me confess my dream of seeing grandchildren in this house is—" She broke down before completing the sentence. I felt moved by her desperation and secret dreams, pushed her gently back into the house and said, "Get in, get in before anyone sees us. I'll go to the bus-stand and bring him here. I couldn't see him clearly the other day, but I'm sure to recognize him by the tuft."

CAT WITHIN

A passage led to the back yard, where a well and a lavatory under a large tamarind tree served the needs of the motley tenants of the ancient house in Vinayak Mudali Street; the owner of the property, by partitioning and fragmenting all the available space, had managed to create an illusion of shelter and privacy for his hapless tenants and squeezed the maximum rent out of everyone, himself occupying a narrow ledge abutting the street, where he had a shop selling, among other things, sweets, pencils and ribbons to children swarming from the municipal school across the street. When he locked up for the night, he slept across the doorway so that no intruder should pass without first stumbling on him; he also piled up cunningly four empty kerosene tins inside the dark shop so that at the slightest contact they should topple down with a clatter: for him a satisfactory burglar alarm.

Once at midnight a cat stalking a mouse amidst the grain bags in the shop noticed a brass jug in its way and thrust its head in out of curiosity. The mouth of the jug was not narrow enough to choke the cat or wide enough to allow it to withdraw its head. Suddenly feeling the weight of a crown and a blinker over its eyes at the same time, the cat was at first puzzled and then became desperate. It began to jump and run around, hitting its head with a clang on every wall. The shopkeeper, who had been asleep at his usual place, was awakened by the noise in the shop. He peered through a chink into the dark interior, quickly withdrew his head and cried into the night, "Thief! Thief! Help!" He also seized a bamboo staff and started tapping it challengingly on the ground. Every time the staff came down, the jar-crowned cat jumped high and about and banged its hooded head against every possible object, losing its sanity completely. The shopman's cry woke up his tenants and brought them crowding around him. They peered through the chink in the door and shuddered whenever they heard the metallic noise inside. They looked in again and again, trying vainly to make out in the darkness the shape of the phantom, and came to the conclusion, "Oh, some devilish creature, impossible to describe it." Someone ventured to suggest, "Wake up the exorcist." Among the motley crowd boxed in that tenement was also a professional exorcist. Now he was fast asleep, his living portion being at the farthest end.

He earned fifty rupees a day without leaving his cubicle; a circle of clients always waited at his door. His clients were said to come from even distant Pondicherry and Ceylon and Singapore. Some days they would be all over the place, and in order not to frighten the other tenants, he was asked to meet his clients in the back yard, where you would find assembled any day a dozen hysterical women and demented men, with their relatives holding them down. The exorcist never emerged from his habitation without the appropriate makeup for his role—his hair matted and coiled up high, his untrimmed beard combed down to flutter in the wind, his forehead splashed with sacred ash, vermilion and sandal paste, and a rosary of rare, plum-sized beads from the Himalayan slopes around his throat. He possessed an ancient palm-leaf book in which everyone's life was supposed to be etched in mysterious couplets. After due ceremonials, he would sit on the ground in front of the clients with the book and open a particular page appropriate to each particular individual and read out in a singsong manner. No one except the exorcist could make out the meaning of the verse composed in antiquated Tamil of a thousand years ago. Presently he would explain: "In your last life you did certain acts which are recoiling on you now. How could it be otherwise? It is *karma*. This seizure will leave you on the twenty-seventh day and tenth hour after the next full moon, this *karma* will

end. . . . Were you at any time . . . ?" He elicited much information
from the parties themselves. "Was there an old woman in your life
who was not well-disposed to you? Be frank." "True, true," some
would say after thinking over it, and they would discuss it among
themselves and say, "Yes, yes, must be that woman Kamu. . . ." The
exorcist would then prescribe the course of action: "She has cast a
spell. Dig under the big tree in your village and bring any bone you
may find there, and I'll throw it into the river. Then you will be safe
for a while." Then he would thrash the victim with a margosa twig,
crying, "Be gone at once, you evil spirit."

On this night the shopman in his desperation pushed his door,
calling, "Come out, I want your help. . . . Strange things are going
on; come on."

The exorcist hurriedly slipped on his rosary and, picking up his
bag, came out. Arriving at the trouble-spot he asked, "Now, tell me
what is happening!"

"A jug seems to have come to life and bobs up and down, hitting
everything around it bang-bang."

"Oh, it's the jug-spirit, is it! It always enters and animates an
empty jug. That's why our ancients have decreed that no empty
vessel should be kept with its mouth open to the sky but always only
upside down. These spirits try to panic you with frightening sounds.
If you are afraid, it might hit your skull. But I can deal with it."

The shopman wailed, "I have lived a clean and honest life, never
harmed a soul, why should this happen to me?"

"Very common, don't worry about it. It's *karma*, your past
life. . . . In your past life you must have done something."

"What sort of thing?" asked the shopman with concern.

The exorcist was not prepared to elaborate his thesis. He hated his
landlord as all the other tenants did, but needed more time to frame a
charge and go into details. Now he said gently, "This is just a mischievous spirit, nothing more, but weak-minded persons are prone to
get scared and may even vomit blood." All this conversation was
carried on to the accompaniment of the clanging metal inside the
shop. Someone in the crowd cried, "This is why you must have

electricity. Every corner of this town has electric lights. We alone have to suffer in darkness."

"Why don't you bring in a lantern?"

"No kerosene for three days, and we have been eating by starlight."

"Be patient, be patient," said the house-owner, "I have applied for power. We will get it soon."

"If we had electric lights we could at least have switched them on and seen that creature, at least to know what it is."

"All in good time, all in good time, sir, this is no occasion for complaints." He led the exorcist to the shop entrance. Someone flourished a flashlight, but its battery was weak and the bulb glowed like embers, revealing nothing. Meanwhile, the cat, sensing the presence of a crowd, paused, but soon revived its activity with redoubled vigour and went bouncing against every wall and window bar. Every time the clanging sound came the shopman trembled and let out a wail, and the onlookers jumped back nervously. The exorcist was also visibly shaken. He peered into the dark shop at the door and sprang back adroitly every time the metallic noise approached. He whispered, "At least light a candle; what a man to have provided such darkness for yourself and your tenants, while the whole city is blazing with lights. What sort of a man are you!"

Someone in the crowd added, "Only a single well for twenty families, a single lavatory!"

A wag added, "When I lie in bed with my wife, the littlest whisper between us is heard on all sides."

Another retorted, "But you are not married."

"What if? There are others with families."

"None of your business to become a champion for others. They can look after themselves."

Bang! Bang!

"It's his sinfulness that has brought this haunting," someone said, pointing at the shopman.

"Why don't you all clear out if you are so unhappy?" said the shopman. There could be no answer to that, as the town like all towns in the world suffered from a shortage of housing. The exorcist now assumed command. He gestured to others to keep quiet.

"This is no time for complaints or demands. You must all go back to bed. This evil spirit inside has to be driven out. When it emerges there must be no one in its way, otherwise it'll get under your skin."

"Never mind, it won't be worse than our landlord. I'd love to take the devil under my skin if I can kick these walls and bring down this miserable ramshackle on the head of whoever owns it," said the wag. The exorcist said, "No, no, no harsh words, please. . . . I'm also a tenant and suffer like others, but I won't make my demands now. All in proper time. Get me a candle—" He turned to the shopman, "Don't you sell candles? What sort of a shopman are you without candles in your shop!" No one lost his chance to crucify the shopman.

He said, "Candles are in a box on the right-hand side on a shelf as you step in—you can reach it if you just stretch your arm. . . ."

"You want me to go in and try? All right, but I charge a fee for approaching a spirit—otherwise I always work from a distance." The shopman agreed to the special fee and the exorcist cleared his throat, adjusted his coiffure and stood before the door of the shop proclaiming loudly, "Hey, spirit, I'm not afraid, I know your kind too well, you know me well, so . . ." He slid open the shutter, stepped in gingerly; when he had advanced a few steps, the jug hit the ventilator glass and shattered it, which aggravated the cat's panic, and it somersaulted in confusion and caused a variety of metallic pandemonium in the dark chamber; the exorcist's legs faltered, and he did not know for a moment what his next step should be or what he had come in for. In this state he bumped into the piled-up kerosene tins and sent them clattering down, which further aggravated the cat's hysteria. The exorcist rushed out unceremoniously. "Oh, oh, this is no ordinary affair. It seizes me like a tornado . . . it'll tear down the walls soon."

"*Aiyo!*" wailed the shopman.

"I have to have special protection. . . . I can't go in . . . no candle, no light. We'll have to manage in the dark. If I hadn't been quick enough, you would not have seen me again."

"*Aiyo!* What's to happen to my shop and property?"

"We'll see, we'll see, we will do something," assured the other heroically; he himself looking eerie in the beam of light that fell on him from the street. The shopman was afraid to look at him, with his grisly face and rolling eyes, whose corners were touched with white sacred ash. He felt he had been caught between two devils—difficult to decide which one was going to prove more terrible, the one in the shop or the one outside. The exorcist sat upright in front of the closed door as if to emphasize, "I'm not afraid to sit here," and commanded, "Get me a copper pot, a copper tumbler and a copper spoon. It's important."

"Why copper?"

"Don't ask questions. . . . All right, I'll tell you: because copper is a good conductor. Have you noticed electric wires of copper overhead?"

"What is it going to conduct now?"

"Don't ask questions. All right, I'll tell you. I want a medium which will lead my mantras to that horrible thing inside."

Without further questioning, the shopman produced an aluminum pot from somewhere. "I don't have copper, but only aluminum. . . ."

"In our country let him be the poorest man, but he'll own a copper pot. . . . But here you are calling yourself a *sowcar,* you keep nothing; no candle, no light, no copper. . . ." said the exorcist.

"In my village home we have all the copper and silver . . ."

"How does it help you now? It's not your village house that is now being haunted, though I won't guarantee this may not pass on there. . . . Anyway, let me try." He raised the aluminum pot and hit the ground; immediately from inside came the sound of the jug hitting something again and again, "Don't break the vessel," cried the shopman. Ignoring his appeal the exorcist hit the ground again and again with the pot. "That's a good sign. Now the spirits will speak. We have our own code." He tapped the aluminum pot with his knuckles in a sort of Morse code. He said to the landlord, "Don't breathe hard or speak loudly. I'm getting a message: I'm asked to say it's the spirit of someone who is seeking redress. Did you wrong anyone in your life?"

"Oh, no, no," said the shopman in panic. "No, I've always been charitable. . . ."

The exorcist cut him short. "Don't tell me anything, but talk to

yourself and to that spirit inside. Did you at any time handle . . .
wait a minute, I'm getting the message. . . ." He held the pot's
mouth to his ear. "Did you at any time handle someone else's wife
or money?"

The shopman looked horrified, "Oh, no, never."

"Then what is it I hear about your holding a trust for a
widow . . . ?"

He brooded while the cat inside was hitting the ventilator, trying
to get out. The man was in a panic now. "What trust? May I perish
if I have done anything of that kind. God has given me enough to
live on. . . ."

"I've told you not to talk unnecessarily. Did you ever molest any
helpless woman or keep her at your mercy? If you have done a
wrong in your childhood, you could expiate. . . ."

"How?"

"That I'll explain, but first confess. . . ."

"Why?"

"A true repentance on your part will emasculate the evil spirit."
The jug was hitting again, and the shopman became very nervous
and said, "Please stop that somehow, I can't bear it." The exorcist lit
a piece of camphor, his stock-in-trade, and circled the flame in all
directions. "To propitiate the benign spirits around so that they may
come to our aid . . ." The shopman was equally scared of the benign
spirits. He wished, at that pale starlit hour, that there were no spirits
whatever, good or bad. Sitting on the *pyol,* and hearing the faint
shrieking of a night bird flying across the sky and fading, he felt he
had parted from the solid world of men and material and had drifted
on to a world of unseen demons.

The exorcist now said, "Your conscience should be clear like the
Manasaro Lake. So repeat after me whatever I say. If there is any
cheating, your skull will burst. The spirit will not hesitate to dash
your brains out."

"Alas, alas, what shall I do?"

"Repeat after me these words: I have lived a good and honest
life." The shopman had no difficulty in repeating it, in a sort of low
murmur in order that it might not be overheard by his tenants. The
exorcist said, "I have never cheated anyone."

". . . cheated anyone," repeated the shopman.

"Never appropriated anyone's property. . . ."

The shopman began to repeat, but suddenly stopped short to ask, "Which property do you mean?"

"I don't know," said the exorcist, applying the pot to his ear. "I hear of some irregularity."

"Oh, it's not my mistake. . . ." the shopman wailed. "It was not my mistake. The property came into my hands, that's all. . . ."

"Whom did it belong to?"

"Honappa, my friend and neighbour, I was close to his family. We cultivated adjoining fields. He wrote a will and was never seen again in the village."

"In your favour?"

"I didn't ask for it; but he liked me. . . ."

"Was the body found?"

"How should I know?"

"What about the widow?"

"I protected her as long as she lived."

"Under the same roof?"

"Not here, in the village. . . ."

"You were intimate?"

The shopman remained silent. "Well, she had to be pro-tected. . . ."

"How did she die?"

"I won't speak a word more—I've said everything possible; if you don't get that devil after all this, you'll share the other's fate. . . ." He suddenly sprang on the exorcist, seized him by the throat and commanded, "Get that spirit out after getting so much out of me, otherwise . . ." He dragged the exorcist and pushed him into the dark chamber of the shop. Thus suddenly overwhelmed, he went in howling with fright, his cry drowning the metallic clamour. As he fumbled in the dark with the shopman mounting guard at the door, the jug hit him between his legs and he let out a desperate cry, "Ah! Alas! I'm finished," and the cat, sensing the exit, dashed out with its metal hood on, jumped down onto the street and trotted away. The exorcist and the shopman watched in silence, staring after it. The shopman said, "After all, it's a cat."

"Yes, it may appear to be a cat. How do you know what is inside the cat?"

The shopman brooded and looked concerned. "Will it visit us again?"

"Can't say," said the exorcist. "Call me again if there is trouble," and made for his cubicle, saying, "Don't worry about my *dakshina* now. I can take it in the morning."

THE EDGE

When pressed to state his age, Ranga would generally reply, "Fifty, sixty or eighty." You might change your tactics and inquire, "How long have you been at this job?"

"Which job?"

"Carrying that grinding wheel around and sharpening knives."

"Not only knives, but also scythes, clippers and every kind of peeler and cutter in your kitchen, also bread knives, even butcher's hatchets in those days when I carried the big grindstone; in those days I could even sharpen a maharaja's sword" (a favourite fantasy of his was that if armies employed swords he could become a millionaire). You might interrupt his loquaciousness and repeat your question: "How long have you been a sharpener of knives and other things?" "Ever since a line of moustache began to appear here," he would say, drawing a finger over his lip. You would not get any further by studying his chin now overlaid with patchy tufts of discoloured hair. Apparently he never looked at a calendar, watch, almanac or even a mirror. In such a blissful state, clad in a dhoti, khaki shirt and turban, his was a familiar figure in the streets of Malgudi as he slowly passed in front of homes, offering his service in a high-pitched, sonorous cry, "Knives and scissors sharpened."

He stuck his arm through the frame of a portable grinding apparatus; an uncomplicated contraption operated by an old cycle wheel connected to a foot-pedal. At the Market Road he dodged the traffic and paused in front of tailor's and barber's shops, offering his services. But those were an erratic and unreliable lot, encouraging him by word but always suggesting another time for business. If they were not busy cutting hair or clothes (tailors, particularly, never seemed to have a free moment, always stitching away on overdue orders), they locked up and sneaked away, and Ranga had to be watchful and adopt all kinds of strategies in order to catch them. Getting people to see the importance of keeping their edges sharp was indeed a tiresome mission. People's reluctance and lethargy had, initially, to be overcome. At first sight everyone dismissed him with, "Go away, we have nothing to grind," but if he persisted and dallied, some member of the family was bound to produce a rusty knife, and others would follow, vying with one another, presently, to ferret out long-forgotten junk and clamour for immediate attention. But it generally involved much canvassing, coaxing and even aggressiveness on Ranga's part; occasionally he would warn, "If you do not sharpen your articles now, you may not have another chance, since I am going away on a pilgrimage."

"Makes no difference, we will call in the other fellow," someone would say, referring to a competitor, a miserable fellow who operated a hand grinder, collected his cash and disappeared, never giving a second look to his handiwork. He was a fellow without a social standing, and no one knew his name, no spark ever came out of his wheel, while Ranga created a regular pyrotechnic display and passing children stood transfixed by the spectacle. "All right," Ranga would retort, "I do not grudge the poor fellow his luck, but he will impart to your knife the sharpness of an egg; after that I won't be able to do anything for you. You must not think that anyone and everyone could handle steel. Most of these fellows don't know the difference between a knife blade and a hammerhead."

Ranga's customers loved his banter and appreciated his work, which he always guaranteed for sixty days. "If it gets dull before then, you may call me son of a. . . . Oh, forgive my letting slip such words. . . ." If he were to be assailed for defective execution, he could always turn round and retort that so much depended upon the quality of metal, and the action of sun and rain, and above all the care in handling, but he never argued with his customers; he just resharpened the knives free of cost on his next round. Customers always liked to feel that they had won a point, and Ranga would say to himself, "After all, it costs nothing, only a few more turns of the wheel and a couple of sparks off the stone to please the eye." On such occasions he invariably asked for compensation in kind: a little rice and buttermilk or some snack—anything that could be found in the pantry (especially if they had children in the house)—not exactly to fill one's belly but just to mitigate the hunger of the moment and keep one on the move. Hunger was, after all, a passing phase which you got over if you ignored it. He saw no need to be preoccupied with food. The utmost that he was prepared to spend on food was perhaps one rupee a day. For a rupee he could get a heap of rice in an aluminum bowl, with unexpected delicacies thrown in, such as bits of cabbage or potato, pieces of chicken, meat, lime-pickle, or even sweet *rasagulla* if he was lucky. A man of his acquaintance had some arrangement with the nearby restaurants to collect remnants and leftovers in a bucket; he came over at about ten in the night, installed himself on a culvert and imperiously ladled out his hotchpotch—two liberal scoops for a rupee. Unless one looked sharp, one would miss it, for he was mobbed when the evening show ended at Pearl Cinema across the street. Ranga, however, was always ahead of others in the line. He swallowed his share, washed it down at the street tap and retired to his corner at Krishna Hall, an abandoned building (with no tangible owner) which had been tied up in civil litigations for over three generations, with no end in sight. Ranga discovered this hospitable retreat through sheer luck on the very first day he had arrived from his village in search of shelter. He occupied a cozy corner of the hall through the goodwill of the old man, its caretaker from time immemorial, who allotted living space to those whom he favoured.

Ranga physically dwelt in the town no doubt, but his thoughts were always centred round his home in the village where his daughter was growing up under the care of his rather difficult wife. He managed to send home some money every month for their maintenance, particularly to meet the expenses of his daughter's schooling. He was proud that his daughter went to a school, the very first member of his family to take a step in that direction. His wife, however, did not favour the idea, being convinced that a girl was meant to make herself useful at home, marry and bear children. But Ranga rejected this philosophy outright, especially after the village schoolmaster, who gathered and taught the children on the *pyol* of his house, had told him once. "Your child is very intelligent. You must see that she studies well, and send her later to the Mission School at Paamban" (a nearby town reached by bus).

Originally Ranga had set up his grinding wheel as an adjunct to the village blacksmith under the big tamarind tree, where congregated at all hours of the day peasants from the surrounding country, bringing in their tools and implements for mending. One or the other in the crowd would get an idea to hone his scythe, shears or weeding blade when he noticed Ranga and his grinding wheel. But the blacksmith was avaricious, claimed twenty paise in every rupee Ranga earned, kept watch on the number of customers Ranga got each day, invariably quarrelled when the time came to settle accounts and frequently also demanded a drink at the tavern across the road; which meant that Ranga would have to drink, too, and face his wife's tantrums when he went home. She would shout, rave and refuse to serve him food. Ranga could never understand why she should behave so wildly—after all, a swill of toddy did no one any harm; on the contrary, it mitigated the weariness of the body at the end of a day's labour, but how could one educate a wife and improve her understanding? Once, on an inspiration, he took home a bottle for her and coaxed her to taste the drink, but she retched at the smell of it and knocked the bottle out of his hand, spilling its precious contents on the mud floor. Normally he would have accepted her action without any visible protest, but that day, having had company and drunk more than normal, he felt spirited enough to strike her, whereupon she brought out the broom from its corner and lashed him with it. She then pushed him out and shut the door on him. Even in that inebriate state he felt relieved that their child, fast asleep on her mat, was not watching. He picked himself up at dawn from the lawn and sat ruminating. His wife came over and asked, "Have you come to your senses?" standing over him menacingly.

After this crisis Ranga decided to avoid the blacksmith and try his luck as a peripatetic sharpener. Carrying his grinding gear, he left home early morning after swallowing a ball of *ragi* with a bite of raw onion and chillies. After he gave up his association with the blacksmith, he noticed an improvement in his wife's temper. She got up at dawn and set the *ragi* on the boil over their mud oven and stirred the gruel tirelessly till it hardened and could be rolled into a ball, and had it ready by the time Ranga had had his wash at the well. He started on his rounds, avoiding the blacksmith under the tamarind tree, crisscrossed the dozen streets of his village, pausing at every door to announce, "Knives and cutters sharpened." When he returned home at night and emptied his day's collection on his wife's lap, she would cry greedily, "Only two rupees! Did you not visit the weekly market at . . . ?"

"Yes, I did, but there were ten others before me!"

His income proved inadequate, although eked out with the wages earned by his wife for performing odd jobs at the Big House of the village. Now she began to wear a perpetual look of anxiety. He sounded her once if he should not cultivate the blacksmith's company again, since those who had anything to do with iron gathered there. She snarled back, "You are longing for that tipsy company again, I suppose!" She accused him of lack of push. "I suppose you don't cry loud enough, you perhaps just saunter along the streets mumbling to yourself your greatness as a grinder!" At this Ranga felt upset and let out such a deafening yell that she jumped and cried, "Are you crazy? What has come over you?" He explained, "Just to demonstrate how I call out to my patrons when I go on my rounds, a fellow told me that he could hear me beyond the slaughteryard. . . ."

"Then I suppose people scamper away and hide their knives on hearing your voice!" And they both laughed at the grim joke.

The daughter was now old enough to be sent to the Mission School at Paamban. Ranga had to find the money for her books, uniform, school fee and, above all, the daily busfare. His wife insisted that the girl's schooling be stopped, since she was old enough to work; the rich landlords needed hands at their farms, and it was time to train the girl to make herself useful all round. Ranga rejected her philosophy outright. However meek and obedient he might have proved in other matters, over the question of his daughter's education he stood firm. He was convinced that she should have a different life from theirs. What a rebel he was turning out to be, his wife thought, and remained speechless with amazement. To assuage her fears he asked, "You only want more money, don't you?"

"Yes, let me see what black magic you will perform to produce more money."

"You leave the girl alone, and I will find a way. . . ."

"Between you two . . . well, you are bent upon making her a worthless flirt wearing ribbons in her hair, imitating the rich folk.

. . . If she develops into a termagant, don't blame me, please. She is already self-willed and talks back."

Presently he undertook an exploratory trip to Malgudi, only twenty-five miles away. He came back to report: "Oh, what a place, it is like the world of God Indra that our pundits describe. You find everything there. Thousands and thousands of people live in thousands of homes, and so many buses and motorcars in the streets, and so many barbers and tailors flourishing hundreds of scissors and razors night and day; in addition, countless numbers of peeling and slicing knives and other instruments in every home, enough work there for two hundred grinders like me; and the wages are liberal, they are noble and generous who live there, unlike the petty ones we have around us here."

"Ah, already you feel so superior and talk as if they have adopted you."

He ignored her cynicism and continued his dream. "As soon as our schoolmaster finds me an auspicious date, I will leave for the town to try my luck; if it turns out well, I will find a home for us so that we may all move there; they have many schools and our child will easily find a place." His wife cut short his plans with, "You may go where you like, but we don't move out of here. I won't agree to lock up this house, which is our own; also, I won't allow a growing girl to pick up the style and fashions of the city. We are not coming. Do what you like with yourself, but don't try to drag us along." Ranga was crestfallen and remained brooding for a little while, but realized: "After all, it is a good thing that's happening to me. God is kind, and wants me to be free and independent in the town. . . . If she wants to be left behind, so much the better."

"What are you muttering to yourself?" she asked pugnaciously. "Say it aloud."

"There is wisdom in what you say; you think ahead," he replied, and she felt pleased at the compliment.

In the course of time a system evolved whereby he came home to visit his family every other month for three or four days. Leaving his grinding apparatus carefully wrapped up in a piece of jute cloth at Krishna Hall, he would take the bus at the Market Gate. He always anticipated his homecoming with joy, although during his stay he would have to bear the barbed comments of his wife or assuage her fears and anxieties—she had a habit of hopping from one anxiety to another; if it was not money, it was health, hers or the daughter's, or some hostile acts of a neighbour, or the late hours his daughter kept at school. After three days, when she came to the point of remarking, "How are we to face next month if you sit and enjoy life here?" he would leave, happy to go back to his independent life, but heavy at heart at parting from his daughter. For three days he would have derived the utmost enjoyment out of watching his daughter while she bustled about getting ready for school every morning in her uniform—green skirt and yellow jacket—and in the evening when she returned home full of reports of her doings at school. He would follow her about while she went to wash her uniform at the well and put it out to dry; she had two sets of school dress and took good care of them, so that she could leave for school each day spick-and-span, which annoyed her mother, who commented that the girl was self-centred, always fussing about her clothes or books. It saddened Ranga to hear such comments, but he felt reassured that the girl seemed capable of defending herself and putting her mother in her place.

At the end of one of his visits to the family he stood, clutching his little bundle of clothes, on the highway beyond the coconut grove. If he watched and gesticulated, any lorry or bus would stop and carry him towards the city. He waited patiently under a tree. It might be hours but he did not mind, never having known the habit of counting time. A couple of lorries fully laden passed and then a bus driven so rashly that his attempt to stop it passed unnoticed.

"Glad I didn't get into it. God has saved me, that bus will lift off the ground and fly to the moon before long," he reflected as it churned up a cloud of sunlit dust and vanished beyond it. Some days, if the time was propitious, he would be picked up and deposited right at the door of Krishna Hall; some days he had to wait indefinitely. His daughter, he reflected with admiration, somehow caught a bus every day. "Very clever for her age." He prayed that his wife would leave her alone. "But that girl is too smart," he said to himself with a chuckle, "and can put her mother in her place." He brooded for a moment on this pleasant picture of the girl brushing off her mother, rudely sometimes, gently sometimes, but always with success, so that

sometimes her mother herself admired the girl's independent spirit.
That was the way to handle that woman. He wished he had learnt
the technique, he had let her go on her own way too long. But God
was kind and took him away to the retreat of Krishna Hall; but for
the daughter he would not be visiting his home even once in three
years. The girl must study and become a doctor—a lady doctor was
like an empress, as he remembered the occasions when he had to
visit a hospital for his wife's sake and wait in the corridor, and noticed how voices were hushed when the "lady" strode down that
way.

He noticed a coming vehicle at the bend of the road. It was
painted yellow, a peculiar-looking one, probably belonging to some
big persons, and he did not dare to stop it. As it flashed past, he
noticed that the car also had some picture painted on its side. But it
stopped at a distance and went into reverse. He noticed now that the
picture on the car was of a man and a woman and two ugly children
with some message. Though he could not read, he knew that the
message on it was TWO WILL DO, a propaganda for birth control. His
friend the butcher at the Market Road read a newspaper every day
and kept him well-informed. The man in the car, who was wearing a
blue bush-shirt, put his head out to ask. "Where are you going?"

"Town," Ranga said.

The man opened the door and said, "Get in, we will drop you
there." Seated, Ranga took out one rupee from his pocket, but the
man said, "Keep it." They drove on. Ranga felt happy to be seated
in the front; he always had to stand holding on to the rail or squat on
the floor in the back row of a bus. Now he occupied a cushioned
seat, and wished that his wife could see and realize how people
respected him. He enjoyed the cool breeze blowing on his face as the
car sped through an avenue of coconut trees and came to a halt at
some kind of a camp consisting of little shacks built of bamboo and
coconut thatch. It seemed to be far away from his route, on the
outskirts of a cluster of hamlets. He asked his benefactor, "Where
are we?"

The man replied breezily, "You don't have to worry, you will be
taken care of. Let us have coffee." He got off and hailed someone
inside a hut. Some appetizing eatable on a banana leaf and coffee in a

little brass cup were brought out and served. Ranga felt revived, having had nothing to eat since his morning *ragi*. He inquired, "Why all this, sir?"

The man said benignly, "Go on, you must be hungry, enjoy."

Ranga had never known such kindness from anyone. This man was conducting himself like a benign god. Ranga expected that after the repast they would resume their journey. But the benign god suddenly got up and said, "Come with me." He took him aside and said in a whisper, "Do not worry about anything. We will take care of you. Do you want to earn thirty rupees?"

"Thirty rupees!" Ranga cried, "What should I do for it? I have not brought my machine."

"You know me well enough now, trust me, do as I say. Don't question and you will get thirty rupees if you obey our instruction; we will give you any quantity of food, and I'll take you to the town . . . only you must stay here tonight. You can sleep here comfortably. I'll take you to the town tomorrow morning. Don't talk to others, or tell them anything. They will be jealous and spoil your chance of getting thiry rupees. . . . You will also get a transistor radio. Do you like to have one?"

"Oh, I don't know how to operate it. I'm not educated."

"It is simple, you just push a key and you will hear music."

He then took Ranga to a secluded part of the camp, spoke to him at length (though much of what he said was obscure) and went away. Ranga stretched himself on the ground under a tree, feeling comfortable, contented and well-fed. The prospect of getting thirty rupees was pleasant enough, though he felt slightly suspicious and confused. But he had to trust that man in the blue shirt. He seemed godlike. Thirty rupees! Wages for ten days' hard work. He could give the money to his daughter to keep or spend as she liked, without any interference from her mother. He could also give her the radio. She was educated and would know how to operate it. He wondered how to get the money through to her without her mother's knowledge. Perhaps send it to her school—the writer of petitions and addresses at the post office in the city would write down the money-order for him and charge only twenty-five paise for the labour. He was a good friend, who also wrote a postcard for him free of charge whenever he had to order a new grinding wheel from Bangalore. Ranga became wary when he saw people passing; he shut his eyes and fell into a drowse.

The blue bush-shirt woke him up and took him along to another part of the camp, where inside a large tent a man was seated at a desk. "He is our chief," he whispered. "Don't speak until he speaks to you. Answer when he questions. Be respectful. He is our officer." After saying this, he edged away and was not to be seen again.

Ranga felt overawed in the presence of the officer. That man had a sheet of paper in front of him and demanded. "Your name?" He wrote it down. "Your age?"

Ranga took time to comprehend, and when he did he began to ramble in his usual manner, "Must be fifty or seventy, because I . . ." He mentioned inevitably how a thin line of moustache began to appear when he first sharpened a knife as a professional. The officer cut him short. "I don't want all that! Shall I say you are fifty-five?" "By all means, sir. You are learned and you know best."

Then the officer asked, "Are you married?"

Ranga attempted to explain his domestic complications: the temper of his present wife, who was actually his second one; how he had to marry this woman under pressure from his relatives. He explained, "My uncle and other elders used to say, 'Who will be there to bring you a sip of gruel or hot water when you are on your death bed?' It's all God's wish, sir. How can one know what He wills?" The officer was annoyed but tried to cover it up by going on to the next question: "How many children?"

"My first wife would have borne ten if God had given her long life, but she fell ill and the lady doctor said . . ." He went into details of her sickness and death. He then went on to some more personal tragedies and suddenly asked. "Why do you want to know about all this sorrowful business, sir?" The officer waved away his query with a frown. Ranga recollected that he had been advised not to be talkative, not to ask, but only to answer questions. Probably all this formality was a prelude to their parting with cash and a radio. The officer repeated. "How many children?"

"Six died before they were a year old. Do you want their names? So long ago, I don't remember, but I can try if you want. Before the seventh I vowed to the Goddess on the hill to shave my head and roll bare-bodied around the temple corridor, and the seventh survived by the Goddess's grace and is the only one left, but my wife does not understand how precious this daughter is, does not like her to study but wants her to become a drudge like herself. But the girl is wonderful. She goes to a school every day and wants to be a lady doctor. She is a match for her mother."

The officer noted down against the number of children "Seven" and then said commandingly, "You must have no more children. Is that understood?" Ranga looked abashed and grinned. The officer began a lecture on population, food production and so forth, and how the government had decreed that no one should have more than two children. He then thrust forward the sheet of paper and ordered, "Sign here." Ranga was nonplussed. "Oh! if I had learnt to read and write . . . !"

The officer said curtly, "Hold up your left thumb" and smeared it on an inking pad and pressed it on the sheet of paper. After these exertions, Ranga continued to stand there, hoping that the stage had arrived to collect his reward and depart. He could cross the field, go up to the highway and pay for a bus ride, he would have money for it. But the officer merely handed him a slip of paper and cried, "Next." An orderly entered, pushing before him a middle-aged peasant, while another orderly propelled Ranga out of the presence of the officer to another part of the camp, snatched the slip of paper from his hand and went away, ignoring the several questions that Ranga had put to him. Presently Ranga found himself seized by the arm and led into a room where a doctor and his assistants were waiting at a table. On the table Ranga noticed a white tray with shining knives neatly arrayed. His professional eye noted how perfectly the instruments had been honed. The doctor asked, "How many more?" Someone answered, "Only four, sir." Ranga felt scared when they said, "Come here and lie down," indicating a raised bed. They gently pushed him onto it. One man held his head down and two others held his feet. At some stage they had taken off his clothes and wrapped him in a white sheet. He felt ashamed to be stripped thus, but bore it as perhaps an inevitable stage in his progress towards affluence. The blue bush-shirt had advised him to be submissive. As he was lying on his back with the hospital staff standing guard over him, his understanding improved and his earlier suspicions began to crystallize. He recollected his butcher friend reading from a newspaper how the government was opening camps all over the country where men and women were gathered and operated upon so that they could have no children. So this was it! He was seized with panic at the prospect of being sliced up. "Don't shake, be calm," someone whispered softly, and he felt better, hoping that they would let him off at the last minute after looking him over thoroughly. The blue-shirt had assured him that they would never hurt or harm an old man like him. While these thoughts were flitting across his mind, he noticed a hand reaching for him with a swab of cotton. When the wrap around him was parted and fingers probed his genitals, he lost his head and screamed, "Hands off! Leave me alone!" He shook himself free when they tried to hold him down, butted with his head the man nearest to him, rolled over, toppling the white tray with its knives. Drawing the hospital wrap around, he stormed out, driven by a desperate energy. He ran across the fields screaming, "No, I won't be cut up. . . ." which echoed far and wide, issuing from vocal cords cultivated over a lifetime to overwhelm other noises in a city street with the cry, "Knives sharpened!"

GOD AND THE COBBLER

Nothing seemed to belong to him. He sat on a strip of no-man's-land
between the outer wall of the temple and the street. The branch of a
margosa tree peeping over the wall provided shade and shook down
on his head tiny whitish-yellow flowers all day. "Only the gods in
heaven can enjoy the good fortune of a rain of flowers," thought the
hippie, observing him from the temple steps, where he had stationed
himself since the previous evening. No need to explain who the
hippie was, the whole basis of hippieness being the shedding of identity and all geographical associations. He might be from Berkeley or
Outer Mongolia or anywhere. If you developed an intractable hir-
suteness, you acquired a successful mask; if you lived in the open,
roasted by the sun all day, you attained a universal shade transcend-
ing classification or racial stamps and affording you unquestioned
movement across all frontiers. In addition, if you draped yourself in a
knee-length cotton dhoti and vest, and sat down with ease in the dust
anywhere, your clothes acquired a spontaneous ochre tint worthy of
a *sanyasi*. When you have acquired this degree of universality, it is
not relevant to question who or what you are. You have to be taken
as you are—a breathing entity, that's all. That was how the wayside
cobbler viewed the hippie when he stepped up before him to get the
straps of his sandals fixed.

He glanced up and reflected, "With those matted locks falling on
his nape, looks like God Shiva, only the cobra coiling around his
neck missing." In order to be on the safe side of one who looked so
holy, he made a deep obeisance. He thought, "This man is tramping
down from the Himalayas, the abode of Shiva, as his tough leather
sandals, thick with patches, indicate." The cobbler pulled them off
the other's feet and scrutinized them. He spread out a sheet of paper,

a portion of a poster torn off the wall behind him, and said, "Please step on this, the ground is rather muddy." He had a plentiful supply of posters. The wall behind him was a prominent one, being at a crossing of Ramnagar and Kalidess, leading off to the highway on the east. Continuous traffic passed this corner and poster-stickers raced to cover this space with their notices. They came at night, applied thick glue to a portion of the wall and stuck on posters announcing a new movie, a lecture at the park or a candidate for an election, with his portrait included. Rival claimants to the space on the wall, arriving late at night, pasted their messages over the earlier ones. Whatever the message, it was impartially disposed of by a donkey that stood by and from time to time went over, peeled off the notice with its teeth and chewed it, possibly relishing the tang of glue. The cobbler, arriving for work in the morning, tore off a couple of posters before settling down for the day, finding various uses for them. He used the paper for wrapping food when he got something from the corner food shop under the thatched roof; he spread it like a red carpet for his patrons while they waited to get a shoe repaired and he also slept on it when he felt the sun too hot. The hippie, having watched him, felt an admiration. "He asks for nothing, but everything is available to him." The hippie wished he could be composed and self-contained like the cobbler.

The previous day he had sat with the mendicants holding out their hands for alms on the temple steps. Some of them able-bodied like himself, some maimed, blind or half-witted, but all of them, though looking hungry, had a nonchalant air which he envied. At the evening time, worshippers passing the portals of the temple flung coins into the alms bowls, and it was a matter of luck in whose bowl a particular coin fell. There was a general understanding among the mendicants to leave one another alone to face their respective luck, but to pick a coin up for the blind man if it fell off his bowl. The hippie, having perfected the art of merging with his surroundings, was unnoticed among them. The priest, being in a good mood on this particular evening, had distributed to the mendicants rice sweetened with *jaggery*, remnants of offerings to the gods. It was quite filling, and after a drink of water from the street tap, the hippie had slept at the portal of the temple.

At dawn, he saw the cobbler arrive with a gunny sack over his shoulder and settle down under the branch of the margosa; he was struck by the composition of the green margosa bathed in sunlight looming over the grey temple wall. The hippie enjoyed the sense of peace pervading this spot. No one seemed to mind anything—the dust, the noise and the perils of chaotic traffic as cycles and pedestrians bumped and weaved their way through Moroccans, lorries and scooters, which madly careered along, churning up dust, wheels crunching and horns honking and screaming as if antediluvian monsters were in pursuit of one another. Occasionally a passer-by gurgled and spat out into the air or urinated onto a wall without anyone's noticing or protesting. The hippie was struck by the total acceptance here of life as it came.

With his head bowed, the cobbler went on slicing off leather with an awl or stabbed his bodkin through and drew up a waxed thread, while stitches appeared at the joints as if by a miracle, pale strands flashing into view like miniature lightning. The cobbler had a tiny tin bowl of water in which he soaked any unruly piece of leather to soften it, and then hit it savagely with a cast-iron pestle to make it limp. When at rest, he sat back, watching the passing feet in the street, taking in at a glance the condition of every strap, thong and buckle on the footwear parading before his eyes. His fingers seemed to itch when they did not ply his tools, which he constantly honed on the curbstone. Observing his self-absorption while his hands were busy, the hippie concluded that, apart from the income, the man derived a mystic joy in the very process of handling leather and attacking it with sharpened end. For him, even food seemed to be a secondary business. Beyond beckoning a young urchin at the corner food shop to fetch him a cup of tea or a bun, he never bothered about food. Sometimes, when he had no business for a long stretch, he sat back, looking at the treetop ahead, his mind and attention switched off. He was quite content to accept that situation, too—there was neither longing nor regret in that face. He seldom solicited work vociferously or rejected it when it came. He never haggled when footwear was thrust up to him, but examined it, spread out the poster under the man's feet, attended to the loose strap or the worn-out heel and waited for his wages. He had to be patient; they always took time to open the purse and search for a coin. If the customer was too niggardly, the cobbler just looked up without closing his

fingers on the coin, which sometimes induced the other to add a
minute tip, or made him just turn and walk off without a word.

While the cobbler was stitching his sandals, the hippie sat down
on the sheet of paper provided for him. He was amused to notice that
he had lowered himself onto the head of a colorful film star. Not that
he needed a paper to sit upon, but that seemed to be the proper thing
to do here; otherwise, the cobbler was likely to feel hurt. The hippie
was quite used to the bare ground; perhaps in due course he might
qualify himself to sit on even a plank of nails with beatitude in his
face. It was quite possible that his search for a guru might culminate
in that and nothing more. In his wanderings he had seen in Benares
yogis sitting on nails in deep meditation. He had seen at Gaya a
penitent who had a long needle thrust through his cheeks—only it
interfered with his tongue, which he didn't mind, since he was under
a vow of silence. The hippie had watched at Allahabad during
Kumbha Mela millions praying and dipping at the confluence of the
rivers Jumna and Ganges. In their midst was a *sadhu* who had a full-
grown tiger for company, claiming it to be his long-lost brother in a
previous birth; men handled deadly cobras as if they were ropes.
There were fire-eaters, swallowers of swords and chewers of glass
and cactus. Or the yogis who sat in cremation grounds in a cataleptic
state, night and day, without food or movement, unmindful of the
corpses burning on the pyres around them. In Nepal, a person produced a silver figure out of thin air with a flourish of his hand and
gave it to the hippie; he treasured it in his bag—a little image of a
four-armed goddess. In every case, at first he was filled with wonder
and he wanted to learn their secret, found the wonder-workers willing to impart their knowledge to him for no higher exchange than a
pellet of opium; but eventually he began to ask himself, "What am I
to gain by this achievement? It seems to me no more than a moon
walk. Only less expensive." He found no answer that satisfied his
enquiry. He noticed on the highway, in villages and rice fields, men
and women going about their business with complete absorption—
faces drawn and serious but never agitated. He felt that they might
have a philosophy worth investigating. He travelled by train, trekked
on foot, hitchhiked in lorries and bullock carts. Why? He himself
could not be very clear about it.

He wished to talk to the cobbler. He took out a *beedi*, the leaf-

wrapped tobacco favoured by the masses. (The cigarette was a so-
phistication and created a distance, while a *beedi*, four for a paisa,
established rapport with the masses.) The cobbler hesitated to accept
it, but the hippie said, "Go on, you will like it, it's good, the Parrot
brand. . . ." The hippie fished matches from his bag. Now they
smoked for a while in silence, the leafy-smelling smoke curling up in
the air. Auto-rickshaws and cycles swerved around the corner. An
ice-cream-seller had pushed his barrow along and was squeaking his
little rubber horn to attract customers, the children who would burst
out of the school gate presently. By way of opening a conversation,
the hippie said, "Flowers rain on you," pointing to the little whitish-
yellow flowers whirling down from the tree above. The cobbler
looked and flicked them off his coat and then patted them off his
turban, which, though faded, protected him from the sun and rain
and added a majesty to his person. The hippie repeated, "You must
be blessed to have a rain of flowers all day."

The other looked up and retorted, "Can I eat that flower? Can I
take it home and give it to the woman to be put into the cooking pot?
If the flowers fall on a well-fed stomach, it's different—gods in
heaven can afford to have flowers on them, not one like me."

"Do you believe in God?" asked the hippie, a question that surprised the cobbler. How could a question of that nature ever arise?
Probably he was being tested by this mysterious customer. Better be
careful in answering him. The cobbler gestured towards the temple
in front and threw up his arm in puzzlement. "He just does not
notice us sometimes. How could He? Must have so much to look
after." He brooded for a few minutes at a picture of God, whose
attention was distracted hither and thither by a thousand clamouring
petitioners praying in all directions. He added, "Take the case of our
big officer, our collector—can he be seen by everyone or will he be
able to listen to everyone and answer their prayers? When a human
officer is so difficult to reach, how much more a god? He has so
much to think of. . . ." He lifted his arms and swept them across the
dome of heaven from horizon to horizon. It filled the hippie with a
sense of immensity of God's program and purpose, and the man
added, "And He can't sleep, either. Our pundit in this temple said in
his lecture that gods do not wink their eyelids or sleep. How can
they? In the winking of an eyelid, so many bad things might happen.

The planets might leave their courses and bump into one another, the sky might pour down fire and brimstone or all the demons might be let loose and devour humanity. Oh, the cataclysm!" The hippie shuddered at the vision of disaster that'd overtake us within one eye-winking of God. The cobbler added, "I ask God every day and keep asking every hour. But when He is a little free, He will hear me; till then, I have to bear it."

"What, bear what?" asked the hippie, unable to contain his curiosity.

"This existence. I beg Him to take me away. But the time must come. It'll come."

"Why, aren't you happy to be alive?" asked the hippie.

"I don't understand you," the cobbler said, and at that moment, noticing a passing foot, he cried, "Hi! That buckle is off. Come, come, stop," to a young student. The feet halted for a second, paused but passed on. The cobbler made a gesture of contempt. "See what is coming over these young fellows! They don't care. Wasteful habits, I tell you. That buckle will come off before he reaches his door; he will just kick the sandals off and buy new ones." He added with a sigh, "Strange are their ways nowadays. For five paise he could have worn it another year." He pointed to a few pairs of sandals arrayed on his gunnysack and said, "All these I picked up here and there, thrown away by youngsters like him. Some days the roadside is full of them near that school; the children have no patience to carry them home, or some of them feel it is a shame to be seen carrying a sandal in hand! Not all these here are of a pair or of the same color, but I cut them and shape them and color them into pairs." He seemed very proud of his ability to match odd shoes. "If I keep them long enough, God always sends me a customer, someone who will appreciate a bargain. Whatever price I can get is good enough."

"Who buys them?"

"Oh, anybody, mostly if a building is going up; those who have to stand on cement and work prefer protection for their feet. Somehow I have to earn at least five rupees every day, enough to buy some corn or rice before going home. Two mouths waiting to be fed at home. What the days are coming to! Not enough for two meals. Even betel leaves are two for a paisa; they used to be twenty, and my wife must chew even if she has no food to eat. God punishes us in this life. In my last birth I must have been a moneylender squeezing the life out of the poor, or a shopkeeper cornering all the rice for profits—till I render all these accounts, God'll keep me here. I have only to be patient."

"What do you want to be in your next birth?"

The cobbler got a sudden feeling again that he might be talking to a god or his agent. He brooded over the question for some time. "I don't want birth in this world. Who knows, they may decide to send me to hell, but I don't want to go to hell." He explained his vision of another world where a mighty accountant sat studying the debits and credits and drawing up a monumental balance sheet appropriate for each individual.

"What have you done?" asked the hippie.

A suspicion again in the cobbler's mind that he might be talking to a god. "When you drink, you may not remember all that you do," he said. "Now my limbs are weak, but in one's younger years, one might even set fire to an enemy's hut at night while his children are asleep. A quarrel could lead to such things. That man took away my money, threatened to molest my wife, and she lost an eye in the scuffle when I beat her up on suspicion. We had more money, and a rupee could buy three bottles of toddy in those days. I had a son, but after his death, I changed. It's his child that we have at home now."

"I don't want to ask questions," said the hippie, "but I, too, set fire to villages and, flying over them, blasted people whom I didn't know or see."

The cobbler looked up in surprise. "When, where, where?"

The hippie said, "In another incarnation; in another birth. Can you guess what may be in store for me next?"

The cobbler said, "If you can wait till the priest of the temple comes . . . A wise man, he'll tell us."

The hippie said, "You were at least angry with the man whose hut you burned. I didn't even know whose huts I was destroying. I didn't even see them."

"Why, why, then?" Seeing that the other was unwilling to speak, the cobbler said, "If it had been those days, we could have drunk and eaten together."

"Next time," said the hippie, and rose to go. He slipped his feet into the sandals. "I'll come again," he said, though he was not certain where he was going or stopping next. He gave the cobbler twenty-five paise, as agreed. He then took the silver figure from his bag and held it out to the cobbler. "Here is something for you. . . ."

The cobbler examined it and cried, "Oh, this is Durga the goddess; she will protect you. Did you steal it?"

The hippie appreciated the question as indicating perfectly how he had ceased to look respectable. He replied, "Perhaps the man who gave it to me stole it."

"Keep it, it'll protect you," said the cobbler, returning the silver figure. He reflected, after the hippie was gone, "Even a god steals when he has a chance."

HUNGRY CHILD

With thatched sheds constructed in rows, blindingly floodlit, an old football ground beyond the level-crossing had been transformed into Expo '77–78 by an enterprising municipal committee. At the Expo, as they claimed, you could get anything from a pin to an automobile, although the only automobile in sight was a 1930 Ford displayed under a festoon of coloured bulbs and offered as a prize to anyone with a certain lucky number on his ticket. Special buses leaving the Market Road disgorged masses of humanity at the Expo archway all day. Loudspeakers mounted on poles every few yards saturated the air with an amalgam of commercial messages and film-songs, against the unceasing din of the crowd. The organizers had succeeded in creating an incredible world of noise, glare, dust and litter.

Raman found the crowd tiresome and the assaults on his eardrums painful. He wished that nature had provided the human ear with a flap to shut off noise. "Oh, then how blissfully I could move about, untouched by that incessant ranting about Tiger-brand underwear or that obscene film-song conveying the heartache of some damn fool. . . ." He further reflected, "I came here to escape boredom, but this is hell, a bedlam. . . ." He regretted the trip he had undertaken from Ellaman Street, but he could not make up his mind to leave; the bustle and pandemonium seemed to take him out of himself, which relief he needed these days. He drifted along with the crowd, occasionally pausing to take a professional and critical look at a signboard or poster. The one that arrested his attention at the moment was a huge placard outside a stall, depicting a woman who had the body of a fish from the waist down. He speculated how he would have dealt with this fish-woman if he had had a chance to design this and other signboards. He would have imparted a touch of refinement to the

Expo and also minted money if only he had cared to seek their patronage. But he was in the grip of a deadly apathy. He saw no point in any sort of activity. For months he had not gone near his workshed, which proved a blessing to his rival Jayaraj of the Market Gate. "Let him prosper," Raman reflected, "although he has the artistic sense of a chimpanzee." He stared at the picture of the fish-woman with a mixture of disgust and fascination, while the promoter of this show stood on a platform and appealed through a tin mega-phone, "Don't miss the chance to see this divine damsel, a celestial beauty living half-sunk in water; rare opportunity, talk to her, ask her questions and she will answer. . . ."

"What questions?" Raman asked himself. Could he ask how she managed not to catch a cold or what fabric was best suited to clothe her scaly body? While he was hesitating whether to go in or not, he heard over the babble the announcement "Boy of five, calls himself Gopu, cries for his parents, come at once to the Central Office and take him. . . ." For the fourth time this message was coming through the loudspeakers. He pulled himself out of the spell cast by the fish-woman, determined to go up and take a look at the lost child. "Must know what sort of a child gets lost. What sort of parents are those that prove so careless, or have they wilfully abandoned the child? Perhaps a bastard or a delinquent to be got rid of. . . ." He moved towards the Central Office, cleaving his way through a long queue of people outside a medical exhibition displaying human kidney, heart, lungs and foetus, in glass jars, along with an X-ray of a live person.

On the way he noticed pink, gossamer-like candy spinning out of a rotating trough on wheels and bought one—it was very light but huge, and covered his face when he tried to bite it. "Rather absurd to be nibbling this in public," he thought. He held it away as if bearing it for someone else, and discreetly bit off mouthfuls now and then with relish. "Sweetest stuff on earth," he reflected. Holding it like a bouquet in one hand, only a few wisps around his mouth to betray his weakness for it, he stepped into the Central Office, which was at the southern gateway of the Expo. A busy place with typists at work and a variety of persons rushing in and out. In their midst he noticed a boy sitting on a bench, vigorously swinging his legs and amusing himself by twisting and bending and noisily rocking the bench on its ricketty, uneven legs, much to the annoyance of a clerk at a table who kept saying, "Quiet, quiet, don't make all that noise," at which the boy, who had rotund cheeks and a bulbous nose, grimaced with satisfaction, displaying a row of white teeth minus the two front ones. "Must be seven, not five," Raman thought on noticing it. Raman held up to him the half-eaten candy, at which the boy shot forward as if from a catapult, snatched it and buried his face in its pink mass. Raman appreciated his gusto and patted his head. The grumpy office clerk looked up to ask, "Are you taking him away?"

"Yes," said Raman on a sudden impulse. The other thrust a register at him and said, "Sign here." Raman signed illegibly as "Loch Ness Monster."

"Why don't you people keep an eye on your children? Don't lose him again. . . . It's a bother to keep such a boy here . . . can't attend to any routine work. Now I'll have to stay here till midnight to clear my papers," said the clerk.

"You announced that he was crying?"

"He is not the sort, but one has to say so, otherwise parents will never turn up until they are ready to go home, leaving it to us to keep watch over the little devils. It's a trick. Where is his mother?"

"Over there, waiting outside," said Raman, and extended a hand, which the boy readily clutched. They marched off and were soon lost in the crowd. While piloting the boy through, Raman kept turning over in his mind the word "mother." It was tantalizing. How he wished he had a wife waiting outside. The grumpy clerk had somehow assumed that he had one. "Naturally," Raman reflected, "I look quite wife-worthy. Nothing wrong with me—an outstanding, original signboard painter with a satisfactory bank-balance, and an owner of property extending on the sands of Sarayu, with a workshed. . . ." Apart from this adopted child, there was bound to be another, his own, inside Daisy. Who could say? Even at this moment, she might be wanting to send a desperate appeal, "You have made me pregnant!" and that would serve her right for being such a bigoted birth-controller and busybody, as she fancied, always intruding into the privacy of every home in town or village, remonstrating with couples not to produce children. She had arrogated to herself too much, and what a fool he was to have trailed behind her! Not his fault, really! She had seduced him by asking him to blazon on every wall in the countryside her silly message NO MORE CHILDREN, and forced him to travel and live with her in all sorts of lonely places; and how could the vows of virginity ever survive under such conditions? It'd be the funniest irony of the century if, for all her precautions and theories, she became desperately, helplessly pregnant and sought his help! He felt tickled at the prospect and laughed to himself. The boy, clutching at his finger, now looked up and also grinned. Raman looked at his merry face and asked, "Why do you laugh?" "I do not know," said the boy, and grinned again.

It was difficult to progress through the crowd, especially with the boy's feet faltering and lagging at every eating-stall in his route. Expo '77 had provided snacks and drinks at every stop. Mounds of green chillies, cucumber and tomato, vegetable *bajjis*, wafer-like *appalam* sizzling in oil and expanding like the full moon before your eyes or fresh golden *jilebis* out of the frying pan, not to mention scores of other delicacies, enticing passers-by both by sight and smell.

Raman felt a surge of compassion for the child, who had taken to him so spontaneously. "Do you like to eat?" he asked.

"Yes," said the boy promptly, and pointed at a cotton-candy trolley. Raman was afraid to let go of the boy's finger for fear he might get lost again, and left him to use the other hand for gesticulating or eating. Soon the boy buried his face in the crimson floral mass and lost interest in the other sights of the exhibition. When it was finished Raman asked, "Ice-cream?" The boy nodded appreciatively and Raman bought two cones of chocolate ice-cream and kept the boy company. Raman forgot for the moment his own travail, the gloom and boredom which had seized him, making existence a dreary cycle of morning, noon and night. He asked himself as he watched the boy, "Why am I happy to find him happy? Who is he? Perhaps my child in our last incarnation." He wondered in what other way he could make the child happy. "Do you want to ride on that wheel?" he asked, pointing at the Giant Wheel, which groaned and whined and carried one sky-high. Of course, the boy welcomed the idea. Raman pushed the boy along towards the wheel, and took his seat in the cradle, holding the boy at his side. "Good way to keep him from eating," Raman thought. He was getting concerned with the boy's health. Should he complain of stomach ache, he would never forgive himself for overfeeding him. As he sat waiting to be whirled up on the Giant Wheel, he had enough time to reflect on the situation which was developing. This child didn't seem to bother about his parents. Perhaps an orphan who had strayed into the exhibition grounds? But how nice to think he was not going to be an orphan anymore. He would train him to address him as "Daddy" or "Appa." As the Giant Wheel went up gradually, his thoughts too soared. The boy clutched his arms tightly. Raman murmured, "Don't be afraid, I'm here, enjoy yourself." If people questioned him, "Who is this child?" he would reply, "My son . . . you remember Daisy? She had brought him up in a convent, one of her funny notions, but I took him away; you know a child must be raised in the atmosphere of a home."

"Where is his mother?" they might ask.

"I don't know, she ran away with somebody," he would say as a revenge for the anguish Daisy had caused him by letting him down, at the last moment, on the eve of their wedding, after having slept with him day after day. He suddenly glanced to his side and asked, "What is your age?" The boy blinked and shook his head. Raman pronounced, "You are not less than seven years," and to the question as to how Daisy could have a seven-year-old son, since she had come down to this town only two or three years before, he replied aloud, "I'll have to invent an answer, that's all." At this the boy looked up bewildered and asked, "When will this go up fast?" Raman felt he would be quite content to stay there and not go up higher, as he feared it might make him uncomfortable. But the boy was evidently becoming impatient. In order to divert his attention, he engaged him in conversation. "Will you come with me to my house?"

"I feel hungry," said the boy. "I want something to eat."

Marvelling at his appetite, Raman said, "If you come to my house, you will have all the eating things."

The boy sat up attentively. "Chocolates or ice-cream or bubble-gum?"

"Yes, everything, and also plenty of *jilebi*. . . ."

"I like *jilebi*—surely . . ." the boy said, happy at the thought, and enquired, "Can I help myself or should I ask you each time?"

"It will all be yours; you may take and eat as much as you like," Raman said.

The boy's mouth watered at this vision. "My father says I'll be sick if I eat!"

"Where is he?" The boy shook his head. "Is he somewhere in this exhibition?"

The boy somehow did not wish to pursue the subject. Evidently he was afraid that he might be handed over and thus lose access to all that store of chocolate and bubble-gum. Raman said, "Of course, you must not eat too much, you will have tummy-ache."

"No, I won't," said the boy confidently. "When my uncle came, you know how much I ate?" He spread out his arms to indicate a vast quantity. Raman felt happy to note the health of the boy; otherwise if he was sickly he might have to take him to Malgudi Medical Centre to be treated by Dr. Krishna. Oh, he could not stand the anxiety if the child became sick, with no one to look after him at home. Of course, he'd have to give him a room. The room he had cleaned for Daisy in the hope she was going to occupy it next day was still there, but she had deserted him. The boy could make it his own room, keep his clothes, books and toys, and have his bed there. He hoped that he would sleep alone and not cry out at night. He must train the boy to sleep alone and look after his books and clothes; he could send him to Kala Primary School, not too good, but he knew the headmistress, having given her a signboard free for her school. Actually a two-by-six plank, and he had used plastic emulsion with a sprinkling of silver powder. The school was across the road near the temple, and the boy should be trained to go up and return home by himself. Unfortunately, he would have to come to an empty house after school.

A pang shot through his heart, but for Daisy messing up his life his aunt would still be there, as she had been since his childhood. She would have lived there to her last hour. She had felt that she must clear the way for Daisy by banishing herself to distant Benares. Ah! when she managed the home, he did not have to bother about food—food and snacks she provided at all hours, always stayed at home and opened the door for him at any hour, day or night. Nowadays he mostly starved, too weary even to make coffee or go up to the Boardless Hotel, where the company bored him lately. He could not stand the repetitive talk and smugness. Could be that the mistake lay in him. He must have changed after Daisy's treacherous act, soured perhaps. Day after day of emptiness, nothing to plan, nothing to look forward to, life of frustration and boredom, opening his eyes every morning to a blank day, feeling on awakening, "Another damned day," in a house totally deserted and empty, no life of any sort—even the house sparrows seemed to have fled, while there used to be hordes of them chirping and flitting about the storeroom filled with rice and grains; now there was nothing, only emptiness. Raman felt sometimes that he was witnessing a historical process, how a structure decayed and became an archaeological specimen. Now things will change with a child in the house, who would brighten up the surroundings. He must fix brighter lamps in all the rooms, most of the bulbs had fused out and not been replaced. He was going to throw himself zestfully into the role of a father and bring up the child so that he would grow into a worthy citizen, cultured and urbane. He had neglected his profession after Daisy's exit, he must set out and revisit the clients every morning and write signboards again, he would need all the money to bring up the boy, later to put him in Lovedale Boarding at Ooty. He said to the boy, "You'll go to school, a nice place, where you'll get many friends. . . ." The boy's face fell on hearing it and he said emphatically, "I won't go to school. Don't like it. . . ."

"Why?"

"Why! Because they'll beat me." Raman tried to argue him out of his fear, but the boy was adamant and was in tears as he repeated, "No school, no school. . . ."

"All right, you don't have to go to school, come with me and eat chocolates," Raman said soothingly, making a mental note to stop by Chettiar Stores and buy sweets. "It'll take time, I must not rush him," he told himself. "By easy stages, I'll persuade him. I remember how I hated school myself. . . ."

After the Giant Wheel, the boy wanted a ride in a toy-train circling the grounds. When it stopped after one round, the boy refused to leave his seat but demanded another round and another. He had had four excursions but would not get off the train. Raman, too, enjoyed the thrill of the ride and could forget Daisy for the time being. After the train ride and more eating, Raman realized, thanks to the boy, he'd also been gorging himself, though he had had nothing to eat since the morning. Now he felt cheerful. "The boy's company has been a tonic to me, revived me," he reflected. How much more it was going to mean when he came to live with him! Except for his working hours, Raman would devote all his time to keeping the boy company. He must buy some storybooks and read them to him regularly; tell him the story of Ramayana. When the boy halted his steps at a stand where some gigantic *bondas* were being lifted out of a deep frying pan, Raman said resolutely, "No, my boy. . . ." fearing that the boy might start vomiting if he sent anything more down his throat—he himself was beginning to feel an uncomfortable rumbling inside. Instead of buying *bondas*, he took him to watch some shows: a parrot performing miniature circus feats, a dog picking out playing cards, a motorcyclist's daredevil ride within a dome—the boy shrieked in excitement.

The boy exhibited, when he had a chance, signs of mischief: he toppled flower pots, tore off posters, performed an occasional somersault wherever he found a little free space, splashed water from fountains, particularly on passing children; he also wrenched himself free and dashed forward to trip up any other boy of his age or tug at the pigtail of a girl; he picked up pebbles and aimed them at lightbulbs. Raman held him in check no doubt, but secretly enjoyed his antics. Raman felt nervous while standing in a queue with the boy since no one could foresee what he would do at the back of a person ahead. Raman admired the little fellow's devilry and versatility, but held him in check, more to prevent his being thrashed by others. He told himself, "Normal high spirits, it'll be canalized when he is put in school. In our country we don't know how to handle children without impairing their development."

They were now near a merry-go-round. "I want to ride that horse," the boy declared as he noticed other children seated on caparisoned horses. Raman was wondering how safe it'd be to send him flying alone, since he did not wish to go on a ride. He said, "You have been on that Giant Wheel, it is the same thing. . . ."

"No," said the boy, stamping his foot, "I want to ride that horse. . . ." Raman did not know how to handle the situation. He tried to divert his attention by suggesting something to eat or drink, although he knew it would not be safe. The boy merely said, "Yes, after the horse-ride."

"Ah, they are showing a movie there, let us see it," Raman cried with sudden enthusiasm. The boy briefly turned in the direction indicated, seeing only a thick wall of backs hiding his view, and shook his head. Raman said, "I'll lift you so high . . . you'll be able to see better than others. . . ."

The boy persisted, "I want to go on that horse." Without a word Raman hoisted him on his shoulder and moved towards the screen, saying, "Yes, yes, later, now a lot of tigers and monkeys in that movie. See them first or they'll be gone soon. . . ." The boy was heavy and his muddy unshod feet were soiling Raman's clothes, and he was also kicking in protest, but Raman was determined to take him away from the merry-go-round and moved to a vantage position in the crowd watching the movie. He panted with the effort to move with that load on his shoulder. He himself could hardly see the screen except in patches between the shoulders in front. He couldn't guess what the movie was, but hoped there would be a tiger and monkey in it as promised by him. The child should not lose trust in him and think he was a liar. "What do you see?" he asked the boy. From his eminence, he replied, "No monkey, a man is kicking a ball— Get me a ball?"

"Yes, I'll buy you one," said Raman. "We will buy it when we leave." He had seen a shop choked with plastic goods and rubber balls, though he could not recollect exactly where. He would investigate and buy a couple of balls, one to be kept in reserve in case the other was lost. His whole frame vibrated as the boy, spotting someone from his height, suddenly let out a thundering shout: "Amma!" He wriggled, freed himself and slid down from Raman's shoulder, shot along through the crowd and reached a group resting on a patch of grass beside the Life Insurance stall, the only quiet spot in the exhibition. Raman followed him. In the centre of the group was a man, tall and hefty, perhaps a peasant from a village, a middle-aged woman in a brown sari and two girls; packages and shopping-bags lying about on the ground indicated that they were on an excursion and would return to their village by bus at night. The boy flew like an arrow into their midst! They got up and surrounded him and fired questions at him over the general hubbub of the exhibition. Raman could hear the hefty man's voice booming, "Where have you been, you rascal? We have missed the bus on account of you," and then he saw him twist the boy's ear and slap him. "Oh!" groaned

Raman, unable to stand the sight of it. "Oh, don't," he cried. Before the man could repeat the dose, the boy's mother, with shrill protests, drew him away and warded off the second blow the man was aiming. Raman realized that this was the end of a dream, sought the exit and the road back to his home on the sands of Sarayu.

EMDEN

When he came to be named the oldest man in town, Rao's age was estimated anywhere between ninety and one hundred and five. He had, however, lost count of time long ago and abominated birthdays; especially after his eightieth, when his kinsmen from everywhere came down in a swarm and involved him in elaborate rituals, and with blaring pipes and drums made a public show of his attaining eighty. The religious part of it was so strenuous that he was laid up for fifteen days thereafter with fever. During the ceremony they poured pots of cold water, supposedly fetched from sacred rivers, over his head, and forced him to undergo a fast, while they themselves feasted gluttonously. He was so fatigued at the end of the day that he could hardly pose for the group photo, but flopped down in his chair, much to the annoyance of the photographer, who constantly withdrew his head from under the black hood to plead, "Steady, please." Finally, he threatened to pack up and leave unless they propped up the old gentleman. There were seventy-five heads to be counted in the group—all Rao's descendants one way or another. The photographer insisted upon splitting the group, as otherwise the individuals would be microscopic and indistinguishable on a single plate. That meant that after a little rest Rao had to be propped up a second time in the honoured seat. When he protested against this entire ceremony, they explained, "It's a propitiatory ceremony to give you health and longevity."

"Seems to me rather a device to pack off an old man quickly," he said, at which his first daughter, herself past sixty, admonished him not to utter inauspicious remarks, when everyone was doing so much to help.

By the time he recovered from his birthday celebrations and the group photo in two parts could be hung on the wall, the house had become quiet and returned to its normal strength, which was about twenty in all—three of his sons and their families, an assortment of their children, nephews and nieces. He had his room in the right wing of the house, which he had designed and built in the last century as it looked. He had been the very first to buy a piece of land beyond Vinayak Street; it was considered an act of great daring in those days, being a deserted stretch of land from which thieves could easily slip away into the woods beyond, even in daylight; the place, however, developed into a residential colony and was named Ratnapuri, which meant City of Gems.

Rao's earlier years were spent in Kabir Street. When he came into his own and decided to live in style, he sold off their old house and moved to Ratnapuri. That was after his second wife had borne him four daughters, and the last of them was married off. He had moved along with his first wife's progeny, which numbered eight of varying ages. He seemed to be peculiarly ill-fated in matrimony—his uncle, who cast and read the stars for the whole family, used to say that Rao had Mars in the seventh house, with no other planet to checkmate its fury, and hence was bound to lose every wife. After the third marriage and more children, he was convinced of the malevolence of Mars. He didn't keep a record of the population at home—that was not his concern—his sons were capable of running the family and managing the crowd at home. He detached himself from all transactions and withdrew so completely that a couple of years past the grand ceremony of the eightieth birthday he could not remember the names of most of the children at home or who was who, or how many were living under his roof.

The eightieth birthday had proved a definite landmark in his domestic career. Aided by the dimming of his faculties, he could isolate himself with no effort whatever. He was philosophical enough to accept nature's readjustments: "If I see less or hear less, so much the better. Nothing lost. My legs are still strong enough to take me about, and I can bathe and wash without help. . . . I enjoy my food and digest it." Although they had a dining table, he refused to change his ancient habit of sitting on a rosewood plank on the floor and eating off a banana leaf in a corner of the dining hall. Everything for him went on automatically, and he didn't have to ask for anything, since his needs were anticipated; a daughter-in-law or niece or granddaughter or a great-grand someone or other was always there to attend him unasked. He did not comment or question, particularly not question, as he feared they would bawl in his left ear and strain their vocal cords, though if they approached his right ear he could guess what they might be saying. But he didn't care either way. His retirement was complete. He had worked hard all his life to establish himself, and provide for his family, each figure in the two-part group photograph owing its existence to him directly or indirectly. Some of the grandchildren had been his favourites at one time or another, but they had all grown out of recognition, and their names—oh, names! they were the greatest impediments to speech—every name remains on the tip of one's tongue but is gone when you want to utter it. This trick of nature reduces one to a state of babbling and stammering without ever completing a sentence. Even such a situation was acceptable, as it seemed to be ordained by nature to keep the mind uncluttered in old age.

He reflected and introspected with clarity in the afternoons—the best part of the day for him, when he had had his siesta; got up and had his large tumbler of coffee (brought to his room exactly at three by one of the ministering angels, and left on a little *teapoy* beside the door). After his coffee he felt revived, reclined in his easy-chair placed to catch the light at the northern window, and unfolded the morning paper, which, after everyone had read it, was brought and placed beside his afternoon coffee. Holding it close enough, he could read, if he wiped his glasses from time to time with a silk rag tied to the arm of his chair; thus comfortably settled, he half-read and half-ruminated. The words and acts of politicians or warmongers sounded stale—they spoke and acted in the same manner since the beginning of time; his eyes travelled down the columns—sometimes an advertisement caught his eye (nothing but an invitation to people to squander their money on all kinds of fanciful things), or reports of deaths (not one recognizable name among the dead). On the last page of the paper, however, half a column invariably gripped his attention—that was a daily report of a religious or philosophical discourse at some meeting at Madras; brief reports, but adequate for him to brush up his thoughts on God, on His incarnations and on definitions of Good and Evil. At this point, he would brood for a

while and then fold and put away the paper exactly where he had
found it, to be taken away later.

When he heard the hall clock chime four, he stirred himself to go
out on a walk. This part of the day's routine was anticipated by him
with a great thrill. He washed and put on a long shirt which came
down to his knees, changed to a white dhoti, wrapped around his
shoulder an embroidered cotton shawl, seized his staff and an umbrella and sallied out. When he crossed the hall, someone or other
always cautioned him by bellowing, "Be careful. Have you got the
torch? Usual round? Come back soon." He would just nod and pass
on. Once outside, he moved with caution, taking each step only after
divining the nature of the ground with the tip of his staff. His whole
aim in life was to avoid a fall. One false step and that would be the
end. Longevity was guaranteed as long as he maintained his equilib-
rium and verticality. This restriction forced him to move at snail's
pace, and along a well-defined orbit every evening.

Leaving his gate, he kept himself to the extreme left of the street,
along Vinayak Street, down Kabir Lane and into Market Road. He
loved the bustle, traffic and crowds of Market Road—paused to gaze
into shops and marvel at the crowd passing in and out perpetually.
He shopped but rarely—the last thing he remembered buying was a
crayon set and a drawing book for some child at home. For himself
he needed to buy only a particular brand of toothpowder (most of his
teeth were still intact), for which he occasionally stopped at Chettiar's at the far end of Market Road, where it branched off to Ellaman Street. When he passed in front of the shop, the shopman
would always greet him from his seat, "How are you, sir? Want
something to take home today?" Rao would shake his head and cross
over to the other side of the road—this was the spot where his orbit
curved back, and took him homeward, the whole expedition taking
him about two hours. Before 6:30, he would be back at his gate,
never having to use his torch, which he carried in his shirt pocket
only as a precaution against any sudden eclipse of the sun or an
unexpected nightfall.

The passage both ways would always be smooth and uneventful,
although he would feel nervous while crossing the Market Gate,
where Jayaraj the photo-framer always hailed him from his little
shop, "Grand Master, shall I help you across?" Rao would spurn that

offer silently and pass on; one had to concentrate on one's steps to avoid bumping into the crowd at the Market Gate, and had no time for people like Jayaraj. After he had passed, Jayaraj, who enjoyed gossiping, would comment to his clients seated on a bench, "At his age! Moves through the crowd as if he were in the prime of youth. Must be at least a hundred and ten! See his recklessness. It's not good to let him out like this. His people are indifferent. Not safe these days. With all these lorries, bicycles and auto-rickshaws, he'll come to grief someday, I'm sure. . . ."

"Who's he?" someone might ask, perhaps a newcomer to the town, waiting for his picture to be framed.

"We used to call him Emden.* We were terrified of him when we were boys. He lived somewhere in Kabir Street. Huge, tall and imposing when he went down the road on his bicycle in his khaki uniform and a red turban and all kinds of badges. We took him to be a police inspector from his dress—not knowing that he wore the uniform of the Excise Department. He also behaved like the police—if he noticed anyone doing something he did not like, he'd go thundering at him, chase him down the street and lay the cane on his back. When we were boys, we used to loiter about the market in gangs, and if he saw us he'd scatter us and order us home. Once he caught us urinating against the school wall at Adam's Street, as we always did. He came down on us with a roar, seized four of us and shook us till our bones rattled, pushed us up before the headmaster and demanded, 'What are you doing, Headmaster? Is this the way you train them? Or do you want them to turn out to be guttersnipes? Why don't you keep an eye on them and provide a latrine in your school?' The headmaster rose in his seat, trembling and afraid to come too close to this terrible personality flourishing a cane. Oh, how many such things in his heyday! People were afraid of him. He might well have been a policeman for all his high-and-mighty style, but his business was only to check the taverns selling drinks— And you know how much he collected at the end of the day? Not less than five hundred rupees, that is, fifteen thousand a month, not even a governor could earn so much. No wonder he could build a fancy

* A German warship that shelled Madras in 1916; ever since, the term indicates anyone who is formidable and ruthless.

house at Ratnapuri and bring up his progeny in style. Oh, the airs that family give themselves! He narrowly escaped being prosecuted—if a national award were given for bribe-taking, it would go to him: when he was dismissed from service, he gave out that he had voluntarily retired! None the worse for it, has enough wealth to last ten generations. Emden! Indeed! He married several wives, seems to have worn them out one after another; that was in addition to countless sideshows, ha! ha! When we were boys, he was the talk of the town: some of us stealthily followed and spied on his movements in the dark lanes at night, and that provided us a lot of fun. He had great appetite for the unattached female tribe, such as nurses and schoolmistresses, and went after them like a bull! Emden, really! . . ." Jayaraj's tongue wagged while his hands were cutting, sawing and nailing a picture frame, and ceased the moment the work was finished, and he would end his narrations with: "That'll be five rupees—special rate for you because you have brought the picture of Krishna, who is my family god. I've not charged for the extra rings for hanging. . . ."

Rao kept his important papers stacked in an *almirah*, which he kept locked, and the key hidden under a lining paper in another cupboard where he kept his clothes and a few odds and ends, and the key of this second cupboard also was hidden somewhere, so that no one could have access to the two cupboards, which contained virtually all the clues to his life. Occasionally on an afternoon, at his hour of clarity and energy, he'd leave his easy-chair, bolt the door and open the first cupboard, take out the key under the paper lining, and then open the other cupboard containing his documents—title-deeds, diaries, papers and a will.

Today he finished reading the newspaper in ten minutes, and had reached his favourite column on the last page—the report of a discourse on reincarnations, to explain why one was born what he was and the working of the law of *karma*. Rao found it boring also: he was familiar with that kind of moralizing and philosophy. It was not four yet; the reading was over too soon. He found an unfilled half-hour between the newspaper reading and his usual time for the evening outing. He rose from the chair, neatly folded the newspaper and put it away on the little stool outside his door, and gently shut and bolted the door—noiselessly, because if they heard him shut the door, they would come up and caution him, "Don't bolt," out of fear that if he fell dead they might have to break the door open. Others were obsessed with the idea of *his* death as if they were all immortals!

He unlocked the cupboard and stood for a moment gazing at the papers tied into neat bundles—all the records of his official career from the start to his "voluntary retirement" were there on the top shelf, in dusty and yellowing paper: he had shut the cupboard doors tight, yet somehow fine dust seeped in and settled on everything. He dared not touch anything for fear of soiling his fingers and catching a cold. He must get someone to destroy them, best to put them in a fire; but whom could be trust? He hated the idea of anyone reading those memos from the government in the latter days of his service— he'd prefer people not to know the official mess and those threats of enquiries before he quit the service. The Secretary to the Government was a demon out to get his blood—inspired by anonymous letters and backbiters. Only one man had stood by him—his first assistant, wished he could remember his name or whereabouts—good fellow; if he were available he'd set him to clean and arrange his *almirah* and burn the papers: he'd be dependable, and would produce the ash if asked. But who was he? He patted his forehead as if to jerk the memory-machine into action. . . . And then his eyes roved down to the next shelf; he ran his fingers over then lovingly—all documents relating to his property and their disposal after his death. No one in the house could have any idea of it or dare come near them. He must get the lawyer-man (what was his name again?) and closet himself with him someday. He was probably also dead. Not a soul seemed to be left in town. . . . Anyway, must try to send someone to fetch him if he was alive, it was to be done secretly. How? Somehow.

His eyes travelled to a shelf with an assortment of packets containing receipts, bills and several diaries. He had kept a diary regularly for several years, recording a bit of daily observation or event on each page. He always bought the same brand of diary, called "Matchless"—of convenient size, ruled pages, with a flap that could be buttoned so that no one could casually open its pages and read its contents. The Matchless Stationery Mart off the main market manufactured it. On the last day of every December he would stop by

for a copy costing four rupees—rather expensive but worth the price
. . . more often than not the man would not take money for it, as
he'd seek some official favour worth much more. Rao was not the
sort to mind dispensing his official favours if it helped some poor
soul. There was a stack of thirty old diaries in there (at some point in
his life, he had abandoned the practise), which contained the gist of
all his day-to-day life and thought: that again was something, an
offering for the God of Fire before his death. He stood ruminating at
the sight of the diaries. He pulled out one from the stack at random,
wiped the thin layer of dust with a towel, went back to his chair and
turned over the leaves casually. The diary was fifty-one years old.
After glancing through some pages, he found it difficult to read his
own close calligraphy in black ink and decided to put it back, as it
was time to prepare for his walk. However, he said to himself, "Just
a minute. Let me see what I did on this date, on the same day, so
long ago. . . ." He looked at the calendar on the wall. The date was
the twentieth of March. He opened the diary and leafed through the
earlier pages, marvelling at the picture they presented of his early
life: what a lot of activities morning till night, connected with the
family, office and personal pursuits! His eyes smarted; he skipped
longer passages and concentrated on the briefer ones. On the same
day fifty-one years ago—the page contained only four lines, which
read: "Too lenient with S. She deserves to be taught a lesson. . . ."
This triggered a memory, and he could almost hear the echo of his
own shouting at somebody, and the next few lines indicated the
course of action: "Thrashed her soundly for her own good and left.
Will not see her again. . . . How can I accept the responsibility? She
must have had an affair—after all a D.G.* Wish I had locked her in
before leaving." He studied this entry dispassionately. He wondered
who it was. The initial was not helpful. He had known no one with a
name beginning with S. Among the ladies he had favoured in his
days, it could be anyone . . . but names were elusive anyway.

With great effort, he kept concentrating on this problem. His
forehead throbbed with the strain of concentration. Of course, the
name eluded him, but the geography was coming back to him in
fragments. From Chettiar Stores . . . yes, he remembered going up

---

* Dancing Girl, a term denoting a public woman in those days.

Market Road . . . and noted the light burning at the shop facing him even at a late hour when returning home; that meant he had gone in that narrow street branching off from Market Road at that point, and that led to a parallel street . . . from there one went on and on and twisted and turned in a maze of by-lanes and reached that house—a few steps up before tapping gently on the rosewood door studded with brass stars, which would open at once as if she was waiting on the other side; he'd slip in and shut the door immediately, lest the neighbours be watching, and retrace his steps at midnight. But he went there only two days in the week, when he had free time. . . . Her name, no, could not get it, but he could recollect her outline rather hazily—fair, plump and loving and jasmine-smelling; he was definite that the note referred to this woman, and not to another one, also plump and jasmine-smelling somewhere not so far away . . . he remembered slapping a face and flouncing out in a rage. The young fellow was impetuous and hot-blooded . . . must have been someone else, not himself in any sense. He could not remember the house, but there used to be a coconut palm and a well in the street in front of the house . . . it suddenly flashed across his mind that the name of the street was Gokulam.

He rose and locked away the diary and secreted the key as usual, washed and dressed, and picked up his staff and umbrella and put on his sandals, with a quiet thrill. He had decided to venture beyond his orbit today, to go up and look for the ancient rosewood, brass-knobbed door, beside the coconut tree in that maze. From Chettiar Stores, his steps were bound to lead him on in the right direction, and if S. was there and happened to stand at the street door, he'd greet her . . . he might not be able to climb the four steps, but he'd offer her a small gift and greeting from the street. She could come down and take it. He should not have slapped her face . . . he had been impetuous and cruel. He should not have acted on jealousy . . . he was filled with remorse. After all, she must have shown him a great deal of kindness and given him pleasure ungrudgingly—otherwise, why would one stay until midnight?

While he tap-tapped his way out of his house now, someone in the hall enquired as usual, "Got your torch? Rather late today. Take care of yourself." He was excited. The shopman on the way, who habitually watched and commented, noted that the old man was moving rather jauntily today. "Oh, Respected One, good day to you, sir," said Mani from his cycle shop. "In such a hurry today? Walk slowly, sir, road is dug up everywhere." Rao looked up and permitted himself a gentle nod of recognition. He did not hear the message, but he could guess what Mani might be saying. He was fond of him—a great-grandson of that fellow who had studied with him at Albert Mission School. Name? As usual Mani's great-grandfather's name kept slipping away . . . he was some Ram or Shankar or something like that. Oh, what a teaser! He gave up and passed on. He kept himself to the edge as usual, slowed down his pace after Mani's advice; after all, his movement should not be noticeable, and it was not good to push oneself in that manner and pant with the effort.

At Jagan's Sweets, he halted. Some unknown fellow at the street counter. Children were crowding in front of the stall holding forth money and asking for this and that. They were blocking the way. He waited impatiently and tapped his staff noisily on the ground till the man at the counter looked up and asked, "Anything, master?" Rao waved away the children with a flourish of his stick and approached the counter and feasted his eyes on the heaped-up sweets in different colours and shapes, and wished for a moment he could eat recklessly as he used to. But perhaps that'd cost him his life today—the secret of his survival being the spartan life he led, rigourously suppressing the cravings of the palate. He asked, "What's fresh today?" The man at the counter said, "We prepare everything fresh every day. Nothing is yesterday's. . . ." Rao could only partly guess what he was saying but, without betraying himself, said, "Pack up *jilebi* for three rupees. . . ." He counted out the cash carefully, received the packet of *jilebi*, held it near his nostrils (the smell of food would not hurt, and there was no medical advice against it), for a moment relishing its rose-scented flavour; and was on his way again. Arriving at the point of Chettiar Stores, he paused and looked up at his right—yes, that street was still there as he had known it. . . .

Noticing him hesitating there, the shopman hailed from his shop, "Oh, grand master, you want anything?" He felt annoyed. Why couldn't they leave him alone? And then a young shop assistant came out to take his order. Rao looked down at him and asked, pointing at the cross street, "Where does it lead?"

"To the next street," the boy said, and that somehow satisfied him. The boy asked, "What can I get you?"

"Oh, will no one leave me alone?" Rao thought with irritation. They seemed to assume that he needed something all the time. He hugged the packet of sweets close to his chest, along with the umbrella slung on the crook of his arm. The boy seemed to be bent on selling him something. And so he said, "Have you sandalwood soap?" He remembered that S., or whoever it was, used to be fond of it. The boy got it for him with alacrity. Its fragrance brought back some old memories. He had thought there was a scent of jasmine about S., but he realized now that it must hve been that of sandalwood. He smelt it nostalgically before thrusting it into his pocket. "Anything else, sir?" asked the boy. "No, you may go," and he crossed Market Road over to the other side.

Trusting his instinct to guide him, he proceeded along the cross street ahead of Chettiar Stores. It led to another street running parallel, where he took a turn to his left on an impulse, and then again to his right into a lane, and then left, and then about-turn—but there was no trace of Gokulam Street. As he tap-tapped along, he noticed a cobbler on the roadside, cleared his throat, struck his staff on the ground to attract attention and asked, "Here, which way to Gokulam Street?" At first, the cobbler shook his head, then, to get rid of the enquirer, pointed vaguely in some direction and resumed his stitching. "Is there a coconut tree in this street?" The other once again pointed along the road. Rao felt indignant. "Haughty beggar," he muttered. "In those days I'd have . . ." He moved on, hoping he'd come across the landmark. He stopped a couple of others to ask the same question, and that did not help. No coconut tree anywhere. He was sure that it was somewhere here that he used to come, but everything was changed. All the generations of men and women who could have known Gokulam Street and the coconut tree were dead—new generations around here, totally oblivious of the past. He was a lone survivor.

He moved cautiously now, as the sun was going down. He became rather nervous and jabbed his staff down at each step, afraid of stumbling into a hole. It was a strain moving in this fashion, so slow and careful, and he began to despair that he'd ever reach the Market

Road again. He began to feel anxious, regretted this expedition. The family would blame him if he should have a mishap. Somehow he felt more disturbed at the thought of their resentment than of his own possible suffering. But he kept hobbling along steadily. Some passers-by paused to stare at him and comment on his perambulation. At some point, his staff seemed to stab through a soft surface; at the same moment a brown mongrel, which had lain curled up in dust, in perfect camouflage, sprang up with a piercing howl; Rao instinctively jumped, as he had not done for decades, luckily without falling down, but the packet of *jilebi* flew from his grip and landed in front of the mongrel, who picked it up and trotted away, wagging his tail in gratitude. Rao looked after the dog helplessly and resumed his journey homeward. Brooding over it, he commented to himself, "Who knows, S. is perhaps in this incarnation now. . . ."

GLOSSARY

almirah: cupboard
appalam: fried delicacy made of rice and other grains
bajji: a sort of cutlet made with sliced vegetables
beedi: leaf-wrapped tobacco
bhairavi raga: a melodic classification
Bhajan: a collective prayer, song
bhang: narcotic made from hemp
bonda: fried eatable made with flour
brinjal: eggplant
bund: elevated border of tank or river
chappati: wheat-flour pancake
choultry: rest-house for travellers
circar: government
dakshina: fee
darshan: grace conferred on the beholder of a godly person
dhall: lentil
dhobi: laundry boy or washerman
dhoti: sarong-like men's garment, tucked and knotted at the waist
dosai: fried cake made of rice paste
idli: steamed rice cake
jaggery: product similar to brown sugar, made by boiling sugarcane
    juice
Javali: a musical composition
jilebi: a sweet
jutka: two-wheeled, horse-drawn carriage
karma: Hindu theological idea meaning destiny, desert; the doctrine
    that one's present actions continue to have effects in another
    incarnation

kurta: flowing shirt
lakh: a hundred thousand
lathi: heavy stick, often bamboo, bound with iron
Muhurtam: auspicious moment
namaste: greeting—"I bow before thee"
Om: a mystical syllable
paisa (pl. paise): the smallest coin; one hundred make one rupee
Pallavi: special item in a musical concert
pandal: special shed put up for an assembly
payasam: sweet soup
pie: the smallest coin in the old currency
Pongal: harvest festival
puja: worship, offering
punnaga varali: a particular melody
pyol: platform built along the house wall that faces the street
ragi: millet
rasagulla: sweet made from condensed milk
rasam: lentil soup
sadhu: hermit or recluse
Sandhi: devotions at morning, noon, and evening
sanyasi: an ascetic who has renounced the world
shikari: professional hunter
sowcar: businessman or financier
Swarga Loka: heaven
teapoy: small table
thali: sacred marriage badge, symbol of wifehood
thambura: stringed instrument used for accompaniment